To The Ahil's
saw this book
and thought of
you guys.
we love you
Love The Kahler

DESPERATE
MEASURES

A NOVEL

DESPERATE MEASURES

KRISTEN MCKENDRY

Covenant Communications, Inc.

Printed in the United States of America
First Printing: November 2013

19 18 17 16 15 14 13   10 9 8 7 6 5 4 3 2 1

ISBN 978-1-62108-571-3

To Kaylene, Richard, Brad, Carrie, Alisse, Will, Brian, and Carol
I'm glad we're family!

Acknowledgments

THERE ARE MANY PEOPLE INVOLVED in bringing a book to life. I am grateful to all of those at Covenant who have worked to get this book off the ground, especially my patient editor, Samantha, and Kelly Peterson, who came up with the beautiful cover. My covers are always perfect.

Writing involves a good bit of research, even for fiction. I stumbled across Port Dover, Ontario, while real-estate hunting and immediately knew I wanted to use it as a jumping-off point for the setting of parts of this story. I have fictionalized many things but not the beauty, energy, and happy feel of the place.

I have spent many years lugging a bagpipe case and eight yards of wool around Highland Games on two sides of the continent, so I couldn't resist throwing bagpipes into the story. Thank you to Mark Lass, who got me started, to Ian and Craig MacDonald, and to my husband for their excellent, patient teaching. Any deficiencies in my piping are my fault, not theirs. Thank you to the friends I've made at St Andrews Pipes and Drums—you're what keeps me coming back.

Thank you to my sons for letting me use bits of them in this story and for teaching me to look for the humor in everything. And thank you to my husband for making me slow down and take that second look.

Chapter One

"I PITY THE MAN WHO marries you. He'll have his hands full."

So said Newton Fisher three months before he proposed to me.

Well, let me correct that. He never actually proposed—not properly, that is. We were driving home from band practice with two twelve-year-old band members carpooling in the backseat, and Newton was going on at some length about his opinion of the music the pipe major had selected. Suddenly, he interrupted himself, turned toward me with a somewhat fierce expression, and said, "When's the university semester over?"

"Christmas break starts December 15," I said.

"Then we'll get married at Christmas," Newton said.

He gave me a challenging look, and I replied, startled, "All right."

"I still think he could have chosen a half-decent hornpipe," Newton said, going back to his complaining without a pause.

Larry and Liam, the two boys in the backseat, stared at the back of his head in bemused silence. Two days later, on the way to another band practice, Newton tossed a little velvet box into my lap. I opened it to find a slim gold band with a solitary diamond. I put it on my finger, put the box in the glove compartment, and nothing more was said about the subject until he phoned me at home a week later to inform me he had booked a hall for the reception.

At this point in the narrative, Newton always interrupts me and says that isn't the way it happened at all. But I remember vividly every detail because I have kept a meticulous journal since I was seven years old, and every fact about each day's events was faithfully recorded immediately upon my arrival home every night. Whenever Newton disagrees with me about the way a certain event transpired, I have only to pull out the appropriate volume and show him in black and white the facts of the matter. Because Newton has not kept a similar journal, he cannot argue with mine.

I have had frequent occasion to employ my journal for this purpose throughout the twenty-three years of our marriage.

* * *

I should, perhaps, point out that I had known Newton Fisher for approximately four years when I accepted his unorthodox proposal. It wasn't an impulsive gesture on his part—I found out later that he had in fact been planning to marry me from the first moment he saw me. He didn't inform me of the fact at the time, however, because I was seventeen, just starting as a student at the University of Toronto, when we first met. He waited until I was a sedate, mature twenty-one before marrying me. I, on the other hand, had not considered the idea of marrying him until it was actually put to me, and I was as astonished to hear myself agree to it as were Larry and Liam (who, incidentally, played the bagpipes for our reception three months later).

The reason for my astonishment was that I had started out not liking Newton very much. There was a friendly animosity between us right from the start, when he appeared out of the blue at one of our band practices and proceeded to take over. My feelings never bloomed into outright irritation but settled somewhere in the region of determined tolerance. When or how this changed into affection, I cannot guess. On this topic, my usually loquacious journal for once lapses into silence. However it came about, the day Newton tossed the ring into my lap, I realized I cared for him a great deal, and I did not stop to analyze it. It seemed only natural to agree, and I have not regretted it for a moment since.

Well, I suppose I am straying slightly from the truth. There were eight times in my life when I regretted marrying Newton Fisher. Those were the eight times I found myself being turned inside out in the delivery room. At those moments, I could have found it in me to wish I had never heard of Newton Fisher. But, of course, such extreme emotion can be forgiven under the circumstances, and I trust I have returned to my usual amiable self immediately afterward each time.

The results of these eight deliveries were my eight children. I suppose most people would consider eight a rather large number, but I come from Utah, where many families amount to that number, if not more. I myself was the third of nine, so eight was not a staggering number for me. I had assumed since childhood that that was just the way things would go.

Newton, however, was born and bred in Toronto, Canada, where the average family has one or two, maybe three at a stretch. He was the eldest of two children himself, and judging from his mother, it was wise that she stopped when she did. A week before we were married, Newton and I sat down with our clipboards and had a lengthy discussion about several pertinent matters, including the size of family we intended to have. He was floored by my nonchalant mention of numbers.

"Annie, you can't possibly have that many," he protested. "We can't afford that many."

"You are a psychiatrist. We can afford a dozen."

"I will lose my mind."

"Your partner can give you free therapy."

"You will lose your figure."

"I will when I'm forty anyway," I reasoned peacefully, charmed at this indirect compliment.

As I predicted, Newton quickly discovered he enjoyed fatherhood after all. When child number eight arrived, he hardly gave the ink on the birth certificate time to dry before burbling on about what to name "the next one." I informed him politely but firmly that there would be no next one, at least not immediately, and so far—as the youngest nears three—there hasn't been.

* * *

In a household of eight children, six of them boys, one learns to appreciate the quiet times. One Saturday afternoon, while the older boys were at rugby practice, Newton and I hired the Burke girl down the street (whose name was something like Candy or Brandy or Mandy; I never could keep it straight) to babysit and spent a couple of hours at the central library together. Most couples would not consider this a romantic sort of date, but I would beg to differ. Nothing is more soothing and stimulating at the same time than sitting side by side in a silent room, reading and soaking in the silence while holding hands with one's spouse.

On this occasion, I looked up from my magazine to find Newton scowling at me. As this was his usual expression, I was not alarmed. I merely waited for him to express his thoughts.

"This is a ridiculous article," he said in a stage whisper. "The writer of it should be forever barred from publication."

I craned to see what journal he held, expecting *Psychology Today* or something similar. He was holding *Canadian Woman's Weekly*.

"There is an entire three-page article about how to find fulfillment through self-indulgence."

"Surely not."

"'Give in to impulse. Your subconscious is sending you a message,'" he quoted, then sighed. "Which would be fine, except this writer's subconscious appears to be narcissistic."

I laid down my own *National Geographic* and pulled his magazine closer. "'I decided not to deny myself anything. It was time to stop being a caregiver and start caring for myself,'" I read.

"It's this focus on the self that I object to," Newton said, forgetting to whisper as he gained momentum.

"How did she give up being a caregiver without being swallowed by an avalanche of laundry?" I asked, peering closer.

"It's a total disregard for the welfare of the family and society as a whole," Newton went on. "I am of the opinion that, from a sound psychological point of view—"

I will spare the reader Newton's professional views. Suffice it to say that he went on at some length. After a few polite coughs from the librarian, I smoothly interrupted the monologue. "My subconscious is sending me a message," I announced.

"—which neatly ties together the arguments of both Jung and Zhuang Zi," Newton continued.

"It's saying there's just enough time to go get ice cream before we have to go home and rescue BrandyMandyCandy."

"Though Taoist philosophy admittedly oversimplifies the—"

"Or would Baskin Robbins be too self-indulgent?" I added.

"Exactly as I was saying to Angus the other day," Newton finished with a nod.

I blinked. "Angus?" I hadn't heard him come into the monologue.

"Surely you remember Angus," Newton said. "Long shaggy hair. Six foot four. We've known him for years."

"I know who Angus Puddicombe is," I said through slightly gritted teeth. "But I didn't know he was in town."

"Not that I mind his hair," Newton added. "I would wear mine long myself if I had the opportunity."

"Don't be silly, Newton, you would look like an aging flower child. Angus only gets away with it because he's so tall and thin. We should have him over for dinner."

"I invited him for tomorrow night," Newton said, turning the page of his magazine. "Didn't I tell you?"

"That's marvelous. When did he get back from Washington?"

"Just last week. He dropped by the office on Friday, all excited about some research he's been doing on something or other. I confess I was thinking about one of my passive-aggressive patients and didn't pay much attention."

"I'll do up something Canadian for him," I said, setting aside my *National Geographic* again. "I could make maple-glazed ham."

"He's been away from Canada for two months," Newton said. "I'm sure he hasn't gone through maple-syrup withdrawal in that short a time." He paused. "Did you say something about ice cream?"

* * *

When Angus arrived at the house the next evening, he wore a battered tweed jacket and carried a fistful of grocery-store flowers, which he thrust at me before swooping down to kiss my cheek.

I caught a whiff of the cigarettes he smoked and wished for the hundredth time that I could cure him of the habit. It was the only thing about him that I could find fault with. I held the flowers in one arm and gave him a hug with the other. "They're beautiful," I told him. "I'll use them for the centerpiece at dinner."

"Angus!" Six-year-old Maisie launched herself at him from the stairs, and he caught her midair and swung her around, endangering the umbrella stand. The other children gathered around eagerly. Angus was always good for entertainment and, more often than not, kept Jolly Ranchers in his pockets. He dug out a handful now, and the kids passed them around, ignoring the bits of lint stuck to the wrappers.

We met Angus Puddicombe when Newton was an adjunct professor at the University of Toronto. Though they were in different fields—Newton in psychiatry and Angus in history—they bumped into each other at a faculty event and hit it off immediately. Newton admittedly has poor social skills and a penchant for making long speeches. Angus expected none of the former and possessed amazing patience for the latter. He reminded me a bit of an abandoned puppy, unkempt and scrawny, with an air about him of never having had enough food or sleep. I admit I often thought of him more as one of the children than as one of the adults in the group. We'd moved from Toronto to our current home in Port Dover, in southern Ontario on the shore of Lake Erie, when Maisie (child number seven) was born, and Angus had followed us five years later. He'd bought a rundown but once-beautiful Victorian house, already furnished, and now taught Canadian History at a local high school.

"Come in and sit down. Dinner's just about ready," I said. I left them to it and carried the flowers into the kitchen. I couldn't find a vase, so I stuffed them into a mason jar and set them in the middle of the table. We always ate in the kitchen. We had a dining room, but it served as an office and homework spot, and I hadn't seen the top of the table in years.

"Would you believe I saw someone putting up his Christmas lights already on my way over here?" Angus remarked, following me. "It's not even Labor Day yet."

"Maybe he wants to get a head start before the temperature drops," I said. It could get down to thirty-five or forty below in the winter.

"What's he planning to do, use orange lights and turn them on for Halloween?" Newton asked.

I think Newton was secretly defeated by Christmas lights. Our neighbors all up and down the street were heavily into decorating, throwing nets of white lights over low bushes, attaching beautiful lights along the eaves of their houses, following every roofline, surrounding every window frame. Some used the dangly kind that looked like glittering stalactites the colors of candy canes. One neighbor had fanciful lit-up statues of deer and polar bears on his lawn, which moved their heads in slow and graceful bows. Some put fake candelabra in the windows. Newton invariably plunked three spotlights in the ground and angled them toward our house to give it a demonic red glow, and that was all. Personally, I think he was reluctant to admit to acrophobia, but that was all right with me. I would prefer he avoid ladders and tromping all over the roof anyway.

During dinner, the kids wanted to hear all about Angus's adventures in Washington State, which, being on the other side of the border and continent, might as well be on the other side of the planet, since they hadn't ever been there.

"You'd like it," Angus assured them with his mouth full. "Beautiful trees, beautiful ocean, beautiful museums—"

"Bleh," Enoch said.

"Beautiful rocky beaches with beautiful girls on them—"

"Bleh," Enoch said again.

His older brother Isaac poked him with his elbow and said, "Speak for yourself."

"And I saw a really beautiful cougar skeleton on the side of the road once."

"That's more like it."

"Something had eaten it completely clean. I don't know what would eat a cougar; do you? Maybe vultures."

"Cool!"

My dinner was starting to taste a little off, and I changed the topic.

"Remind us what you were researching there," I prompted brightly.

Angus leaned forward, oblivious to his shirt front dragging in his gravy. "In 1905, there was a train robbery just outside of Tacoma. The railroad payroll was stolen and never recovered, and the villains were never found."

"Yes, I remember you wrote a book about it, laying out the various hypotheses, didn't you?"

Angus nodded eagerly. "Well, I think now I may know what really happened," he said. "I came across some very interesting information in Seattle. In fact, they're publishing a new edition of the book with my findings added in a new chapter. It comes out in the spring. I'll make sure you get a copy."

"That is wonderful," I told him. I was glad to hear about his publishing successes. I'd always felt a little guilty about his leaving his tenured position at the university to follow us to Port Dover. At the high school, he certainly couldn't be earning what he'd earned as a professor, but if he was able to augment his finances with his books, it made me feel better.

"Put me down for two copies," I told him. "I'll buy one for Newton's mother for her birthday."

"My mother?" Newton blinked at me. "The only book she's ever read is the *TV Guide*."

"So what's the answer to the mystery?" Isaac asked. "Who stole the money?"

"Ah, you'll have to read the new edition to find out," Angus said, grinning and wiggling his eyebrows.

The boys groaned.

"Who wants dessert?" I asked, gathering plates. "I picked up some key lime pie at Sally's Bakery yesterday."

Jane recoiled, her eyes wide. "Where's Chairman Meow?"

"Why? What's the matter?"

Scott dug her in the ribs and laughed. "She said 'key lime pie' not 'feline pie.'"

There was general laughter, more so when the cat in question poked an inquisitive head out of Angus's capacious tennis shoe by the door.

Chairman Meow was an indeterminate breed, a stray that had fastened himself to our family when we moved in. He was one of us now, and we all took turns caring for him, but ten-year-old Jane was his special favorite. Jane, who tended to be a bit shier around people than her siblings, felt the same toward him.

After three servings of dessert all around, Angus let the older boys haul him out to the driveway for a game of basketball. They didn't often get a chance to play against someone of Angus's height. Judging by the pounding and shouting that followed, Angus was enjoying it as much as the children. I distinctly heard him call, "Twelve to two! Neener neener neener!"

Newton helped me carry the empty bowls to the sink, and I ran hot water over them.

"Do you think Angus really has solved a hundred-year-old mystery?" I asked.

"Doesn't matter. What matters is convincing the editors that he has," Newton said philosophically.

"But it's terribly exciting," I said, reaching for the plastic scrubby. "Why won't he tell us what he found out? What evidence could possibly still be around after all this time to confirm one theory over another?"

Newton cornered Andrew, our youngest, and lifted him onto the counter. Andrew sat drumming his heels on the cupboard while Newton expertly ran a rag over our son's pie-smeared face. He pulled the rag away and gave a mock astonished gasp. "Look! It's an Andrew! And what's that you have all over your face? It's a smile! Is that a smile? Wipe that off immediately!" He rubbed Andrew's face again with the rag and pulled it away. "Oh no! It's still there! Mom, what are we going to do? Andrew has a smile smeared all over his face!"

"Try again," I said.

Again, he applied the rag. Andrew gave a muffled giggle. Newton peeked beneath the washcloth.

"Nope, still there. It won't come off. I guess there's nothing for it. He'll have to go out with a smile all over him."

He lifted Andrew down, and the little boy toddled off, laughing. Newton tossed the rag onto the counter. I scooped it up and dropped it in the dish on the edge of the sink.

"No water on the counter. The Formica is peeling badly enough as it is."

"It is pretty bad, isn't it?" Newton bent over to examine the warped counter and the shard of white Formica hanging loose on the edge. "Maybe it's time for a new countertop."

My heart quickened. "Really? That would be lovely. This one is so scarred and damaged I can hardly tell if it's clean."

Newton rubbed a hand over his jaw, musing. "Of course, it means lifting the sink. Might as well get a new one put in while we're at it—this one is all rust-stained and chipped."

"As long as we're doing that, we could repaint the cupboards, and the kitchen would look like new," I said.

"You were always talking about wanting a longer counter and more cupboard space," Newton said. "If we're ever going to extend the counter, now's the logical time to do it. It could wrap around to make a U-shaped kitchen, and you'd have 50 percent more storage space."

"It would mean having to replace the linoleum."

"We could install tile instead."

"We might have room for one of those big double fridges." I was really getting into this. "Imagine, room for everyone's water bottles!"

"I think we'd have to rewire the kitchen. I don't know if our current wiring would support a big fridge like that."

"What does that entail? Knocking out the drywall?"

"Yes. You have always said the paint color in here reminds you of bile anyway."

I frowned. "We'd have to paint the hall too, then, because it runs right into the kitchen. It would look funny being a different color."

"I wouldn't paint the hall until I extended that powder room like we've talked about," Newton said. We had talked several times about adding a shower to the two-piece, main-floor bathroom. That would give us three—a real luxury when you have eight kids.

"We can't extend the bathroom until we move the front closet," I reminded him. "If we make the closet smaller, the shower will fit just fine. But where do we put all the stuff in the closet? We'd miss the storage space."

"We've talked about building a storage shed in the backyard," Newton said. "There's no reason all the basketballs and roller blades and tennis racquets have to be in the front closet. That could all go in a shed."

"You'd never get a truck in there to pour a cement pad for a shed," I said.

"We'd have to take out a portion of the fence," Newton agreed. "After the truck is finished, we could put in a side gate. Easy access to the boulevard."

"So if the neighbors ask why we're tearing down the fence in the backyard, I can tell them it's because my Formica is peeling!"

"And we're gutting the rest of the house besides." Newton started to laugh.

"Who's gutting the house?" Angus had come in behind us and was looking astonished.

"We're just fantasizing," I told him, lifting Chairman Meow off the counter, where he'd been creeping toward the butter dish in the hope that we wouldn't notice him, and setting him on the floor. "We won't really do it."

"I wouldn't recommend it," he agreed glumly. "I'm in the middle of adding an office onto the back of my house. You wouldn't believe the trouble I've had with my contractor. Crooked windows, wiring not up to code, no water barrier on the foundation. Way over budget. The man has the brains of a blueberry."

"Then why did you hire him?" I asked. "You're supposed to interview contractors very carefully upfront before committing to anything. I saw a design show on TV about it."

Angus waved a hand. "I know all that. But the reality is, you phone eighteen contractors, and you end up going with the only one who ever bothers to return your call. You can't pick and choose, you know. And since I've been away, he's been working unsupervised. An unwise move, I admit. I was hoping it would be finished by the time I got home, but no joy."

"Why do you need to add on an office, anyway?" Newton asked him. "You have five bedrooms in that drafty old house. Couldn't you have used one of those?"

"They're all upstairs. I wanted an office on the ground floor. That way when I'm too old someday to climb the stairs, it can serve as my bedroom and workspace."

It saddened me, suddenly, to think of energetic, enthusiastic Angus growing slowly into a stooped old man with arthritic hips. And if he kept smoking, he'd end up with emphysema, hauling one of those canisters around on a pushcart. I toyed with the idea of finding him a wife so he wasn't alone in that big, old house. A good woman would have a positive influence on him. I said nothing about it, though. Newton wouldn't have stood for my interfering, and Angus would have been humiliated. But I made myself a mental note to keep my eyes open.

"Thank you for dinner, but I'd better head home now." Angus sighed.

"Can't you stay longer?" I swatted Chairman Meow away again as he made another foray for the butter.

"You know, you could just do this," Newton murmured and put the cover on the dish.

"A lot of things get out of hand when you're gone for two months," Angus said. "I only have one more week before school starts again and lots to do between now and then."

"Don't remind me." I had heard other mothers express relief and delight at the thought of school resuming, but secretly, I hated it. I liked having my kids around me and the lazy freedom of summer. I thought of the back-to-school shopping yet to do, the return to the grueling routine of alarm clocks, homework, piano lessons, and—worst of all—having to pack school lunches again. Last spring, I calculated I'd made roughly 7,345 sack lunches in my time, and I had 25,503 still to make before Andrew was out of school. It was a depressing thought. How many cheese sandwiches could a person stand before insanity set in?

Angus left amid fond shouts of farewell from the children and much back-pounding from Newton. I extracted a promise from him that he would come again next Friday for dinner. I decided to invite the first counselor in the Primary presidency to dinner that evening too. Sylvia was a sweet woman, thirty years old and unmarried (and admittedly, the only unmarried female I could think of at the moment). I decided not to mention this decision to Newton until the last minute.

At the corner of the street, Angus honked a good-bye and waved his left arm vigorously out the window of his Honda. He turned into the traffic on Bleasdale Road and was lost to sight.

* * *

Sylvia accepted the invitation, albeit unwitting of my ulterior motives; I had neglected to mention the fact that a handsome eligible professor would also be coming. The following Thursday, I phoned to remind Angus of the dinner. Angus's answering machine kicked on, and his bright voice cheerfully said, "This is Angus Puddicombe. Actually, it isn't, it's his machine. Please leave your message at the beep, and if this is Wendell, I'm not paying you another penny until the leak is fixed, so don't bother asking."

Wendell must be the ham-fisted contractor, I decided. I left my reminder and hung up. And didn't mention that Sylvia would be joining us. Well, after all, he would find that out eventually anyway, right?

* * *

Angus didn't come.

Sylvia enjoyed the roast chicken and potatoes, helped clear the table, told funny stories, and answered with a straight face when eight-year-old Ethan asked her (in all seriousness) if she liked the Mormon Pterodactyl Choir. She was a perfectly charming guest. But the whole point of her coming had been—secretly—to meet Angus Puddicombe, and he never showed. He also never called, which wasn't like him. After Sylvia left that evening, still oblivious to my devising, I tried phoning Angus. There was no answer.

"Do you think he's all right?" I asked Newton. "He's never stood us up before."

"Oh, I'm sure he's fine. Probably got to reading or something and lost track of time," Newton said. He wiggled his eyebrows at me. "Or maybe his contractor goofed and walled him up in the new office without a doorway to get out of."

"It's not funny. I'm worried."

Newton glanced at my face, and his lips twitched. "Angus is forty-four years old. He can take care of himself," he said gently.

Chapter Two

THERE WAS NO SENSE PUTTING it off. School was indeed looming closer, and I hadn't begun to prepare. On Saturday morning, I rounded up all eight children and drove them to First Prize Haircutters to get their summer locks shorn. Isaac, at nineteen, protested that he was too old to be driven for a haircut by his mommy, but when I pointed out that I was paying, he acquiesced. The panic-eyed women at the shop saw my van pull up, and two of them promptly went on lunch break, though it was only ten o'clock. I left my brood in the grim hands of the other beauticians and went next door to do some grocery shopping. Seven heads of hair always took at least an hour. They wouldn't even miss me.

Andrew, though two and a half, barely had any hair yet—just a ring of golden curls at the nape of his neck, hardly worth the ten dollars to cut it—so I took him with me. He liked riding around in the grocery cart, swinging his legs, waving at people, and trying to grasp anything and everything with his sticky hands and pull it into the cart.

I knew the aisles like I knew the tracery of my varicose veins. I hardly had to think about it as I flew down the lanes, whooshing oatmeal and toilet paper and carrots into my cart. It took a lot to feed my army, especially since the older boys had hit puberty, and I always felt as if I were stocking up a Cold War bunker rather than buying the week's meals. While other women dawdled and hummed over labels, I whizzed past, recklessly tossing items onto the pile with hardly a glance. After the thousandth time, really, what was the point of looking?

At last the cart was full, and I knew the hairdressers would be just wrapping up. I balanced a bag of frozen peas on the top of the pile and handed Andrew a bag of romaine lettuce to hold like a sheaf of roses. Then I steered toward the front of the store where the checkout counters stood.

The line-up at the cashier was ten carts deep and rapidly getting longer. I swung my groaning cart into line and watched the sole cashier tap slowly on the register with impossibly long red nails. Her fingers looked like chili peppers. I was surprised she could dress herself, her nails were so long. I sighed. The hairdressers were going to hate me.

Andrew was, fortunately, a patient child. He reached behind him into the cart, found a box of Honey Nut Cheerios, and ripped it open. Quietly and neatly, he began to eat handfuls. I waited. The customer at the front of the line pulled out a wad of coupons and began going through them to weed out the applicable ones. I waited some more. A baby farther back in the line began to grizzle. My feet began to hurt.

I started thinking about the article Newton had shown me about the woman who had followed her every impulse down the path to theoretical self-fulfillment. I wondered what my subconscious would say to me if I took the time to listen. Well, why not? I had time to kill. The woman with the coupons was arguing over one that had expired three days earlier, and she looked ready to pitch camp right there at the counter. So I thought about it. Weeded through the distractions and things to do, past the worry about Angus in my head, to see what lay at the core. But the only impulse I could identify was to abandon my cart in the line-up and walk out. I wasn't sure that would lead to fulfillment, and it certainly wouldn't be productive. I looked around for something to distract me.

There was a harried-looking woman behind me. She had a cart full of granola bars; a gift-wrapped, one-serving, microwaveable meatloaf; a bag of lemons; and drain cleaner. I thought she looked like she could use some cheering up. I cleared my throat politely and said, "I challenge you to a purse duel."

She blinked at me. "A what?"

"We see who has the most outlandish stuff in her purse. It passes the time."

She looked down at the black bag slung over her shoulder, then at my smaller canvas bag, and her eyes lit up. "You're on," she said. She rummaged inside and came up with a small Troll doll with pink hair and a bikini.

I reached into my purse and pulled out a Batman action figure. Jane had painted his blue tights to look like tartan trews.

The woman dug in her purse again and presented a miniature game of Travel Boggle. I countered with a deck of cards with Betty Boop imprinted on the back.

Other women in the crowd were beginning to take an interest. The elderly woman behind my opponent peered over her shoulder. "You gotta admit, that's good," she said.

My opponent looked nervous. She next produced a six-inch screwdriver. I matched it with a miniature ratchet set that was missing two of its heads. There were murmurs of appreciation from the audience.

"Take that!" She thrust forward an autographed theater program from a production of *The Sound of Music*, dated 1998.

I hesitated, then pulled out the heavy artillery: a grape Bonnie Bell Lipsmacker from 1981. The murmurs of appreciation turned to gasps of awe.

"Oh yeah? Well, I have you now," the woman cried and slapped down a plastic container of peach cobbler.

I smiled. "I'm afraid not," I said and took out a half-used spray can of whipped cream.

"All right, I call that a tie." She laughed and produced two plastic forks. There was a smattering of applause down the line.

We were halfway through the cobbler and whipped cream by the time we arrived at the cash register.

* * *

I spent much of the day sorting school clothes, figuring out who could use whose hand-me-downs, outlining chore charts, and generally plotting my back-to-school strategy. Outfitting and equipping eight children (well, six, as Andrew was too young for school and Isaac had just graduated the previous spring) took on the characteristics of a military campaign. And there were inevitably difficult-to-find things on the list of needs, like size fourteen gym shoes, industrial-strength canvas backpacks, and super-duper calculators that could do everything but operate a space shuttle. Newton kindly volunteered to help me run some of the errands.

But even while we dodged in and out of parking spots and piled up purchases, the nagging thought in the back of my mind was always of Angus. Everyone needed someone in their lives to worry about them, and I guess I was Angus's.

Sunday came, and we still had had no word from him. I went through the usual preparations for church, feeling like my mind was snagged on worry like a bit of cloth fluttering on a thorn bush. Flapping and distressed but not at all useful.

Church is always a bit, well, exhausting for me. It begins with bullying eight children and Newton into Sunday clothes (Newton will deny it, but

I suspect the real reason he gave up academia was that he hated wearing a tie every day). By the time all hair is combed, teeth are brushed (after arguments about whose toothbrush is what color), shoes are found and tied, scripture cases are retrieved, and everyone is crammed into the van, I am already drained. Inevitably, such things as "I forgot I have to give a ten-minute talk today" or "Ethan is wearing pink socks" emanate from the back seat. There is always the flurry of shoving and whining and debate over who gets a window seat (honestly, it's a van—there are *six* window seats).

Routinely, as we finally pull out of the driveway, I grit my teeth and say, "Okay, everybody, feel spiritual, *now!*" We arrive at the church fifteen minutes away and find it still locked because Newton always insists on being so early we arrive before anyone else.

The good thing about this is that we always manage to get a good seat. We commandeer one whole bench in the middle of the chapel, with me at one end and Newton at the other, like bookends, trapping the children between us. As the rest of the congregation gathers over the next half hour, I try to pretend I don't notice that the benches nearest to ours are the last to fill up.

Church itself is always enjoyable, thankfully. The kids, once subdued and resigned to their state, fall into lethargy and remain fairly quiet throughout the three hours of meetings. Andrew, who is ordinarily a tough, independent little boy, inexplicably becomes a limpet during church and clings to me fiercely, rebuffing all attempts of the nursery teacher to get him to join the other children. I have the feeling I'll still be hauling him to my meetings with me when he is twenty-eight.

The ride home is cheerier, with windows rolled down, ties loosened (and occasionally tossed out a window), and the children babbling in friendly fashion with each other.

Today, as soon as I asked what they'd learned in class, however, the van went deathly silent.

"What, didn't anyone pay attention today?" I asked. "Do you remember a story you heard? A scripture? A picture you saw?"

Silence.

"Did anyone tell a joke? Sing a song? See a friend?"

Silence.

"Did anyone tip back on their chair? Cough? Blink?"

Silence.

I turned to Newton. "Did *you* learn anything in church today?"

He hunched his shoulders defensively. "Don't look at me. Sister Hausfrau cornered me in the foyer to tell me about the vision she had of Samuel the Lamanite in her laundry room, and I missed Sunday School."

Her name was, in fact, Sister Halfrow, and her well-documented eccentricity had kept the bishop—and Newton—on their toes for years. Newton was threatening to write a book about her. So far, she had heard a zucchini recite the Psalms, seen a vacuum cleaner levitate, smelled the grapes in her wallpaper ("they smelled distinctly *purple*"), and witnessed the bottled peaches in her store room dance the hora. Last week, it had been King Noah swinging on her backyard swing set. It seemed to me that her visions were becoming more extravagant with time, but so far, she had remained harmless.

The topic of Sister Halfrow was far more interesting than what the children had learned that day, so the rest of the way home, they debated whether the zucchini had recited in Hebrew or in Latin.

* * *

Monday morning, as I made my way through braiding Maisie's hair, putting lunches in backpacks, and rehearsing school-bus rules of etiquette, my mind continued to puzzle over Angus. It was like having an annoying song in your head to which you've forgotten all the words but one phrase of the chorus, so you're condemned to repeat that one phrase over and over again. I had tried phoning him again before the children awoke, but there had been no answer. It was the first day of school for Angus, too, and he should have been home getting ready.

"Maybe the contractor cut his phone line," Newton suggested, dropping a kiss on Andrew's head and snagging his own lunch bag from the counter.

I have been the recipient of a lot of teasing for packing Newton's lunch for him (his mother told me I had taken feminism back a hundred years), but I like to do it. He does so much for me, and it seems like a simple way to show him my affection. It also keeps him from dropping ten dollars every day on a salt-laden, fast-food meal for lunch.

The house was blissfully quiet with everyone else off to school and Isaac down in the basement glued to the Xbox. I did the breakfast dishes and then settled with Andrew on the living room floor to do our daily reading game. I had written several short, easy words on a piece of poster paper, and now I set a single raisin on top of each word. When

I'd first started this game, we had worked on individual sounds and letters (when we'd gotten to the letter *L*, Andrew had insisted it made the sound "whoo whoo," thinking I had said *owl*), but now we were up to such letter combinations as *dog*, *cold*, and *truck*. When Andrew read the word correctly, he got the raisin. After he learned to read a good-sized vocabulary, I would begin combining the words into simple sentences with interchangeable words. This was the method I'd used to teach all of my children to read by age three—though Enoch, as I recalled, had been a bit stubborn and required mini marshmallows rather than raisins to hold his attention.

Andrew did very well this morning, confidently reaching for the raisin after he read each word, and by the time he'd filled his tummy, he had completed every poster. I settled him in bed for his morning nap, accompanied by the picture books he loved so much, and then tried Angus's number again. No answer. I phoned the high school office and asked if Angus had shown up to work.

"He hasn't," the office attendant said, sounding harassed. "There's been no sign of him. We're scrambling to find a substitute to take his classes."

"This is so unlike him," I said, truly troubled now. "He'd never just not show up for work unless something was really wrong."

"Well, if you hear from him, let us know," the woman said and hung up.

I was up to my elbows in homemade spaghetti sauce when the kids started arriving from school. Everyone wanted to tell me about his or her day at once, so I spent the next hour directing conversations like a traffic cop. There were agendas and permission forms to sign, book fees and activity fees to write checks for, lists of needed school supplies to tack to the bulletin board for the next trip to the store, lunch bags to unload and wash, and a couple of notes to write ("Please allow Enoch to sit close to the blackboard, as he is visually impaired in one eye due to an unfortunate self-inflicted injury at the age of seven involving a slingshot and a pencil and an experiment on the saying 'He who spits into the wind . . .'"; "This is to acknowledge receipt of your message. Ethan is very sorry he wrote on the bus seat with a pen, and he has agreed to wash all of the seats after school tomorrow as penance"). I stuck a yellow sticky note to the fridge to remind myself to ask the doctor for a note saying Caleb and Scott were fit to participate in football. (They both agreed it was a wimpy game that required padding and helmets, but they were enthusiastic about joining the team anyway.) I helped Maisie find a baby picture of herself to take to class the next day as part of her "getting to know you" activity. (Okay, I admit, it was a picture of Jane, but at that age, they looked identical, and I couldn't lay my hands on Maisie's album at the moment. Who was to know? Maisie certainly didn't.) I found a new pencil case for Jane, who had already lost hers. And I dug an old, outgrown pair of Enoch's tennis shoes with nonmarking soles out of the basement for Ethan to take to gym.

"Tomorrow is Crazy Dress Day," Jane announced. "We're supposed to dress zany, put our hair up weird, whatever. Can I borrow your purple sweater and those shorts things you wore in high school?"

"They're called culottes," I said. "And I didn't wear them in high school. I mean, we wore culottes in high school, but not *those* ones. Those are new."

"You mean they still make them?" she asked, wide-eyed.

"Yes."

"And you bought them on *purpose*?"

I scowled. "You can borrow them. You'll need a belt."

"Thanks. I'll put my hair up in a ponytail on one side and leave the other side down," she said, planning aloud as she walked away. "And maybe those fake eye lashes I wore for Halloween." It was a switch for her to make the effort to join in with the group, and I wanted to encourage it, so I made myself a note to go hunt for the culottes.

By the time Newton arrived home, supper was on the table, the kids were more or less washed and waiting, the garlic bread was smelling heavenly, and I was exhausted. I thought again of the article writer who had given up caregiving to indulge her every impulse and wondered—if I held still and *really* thought about it this time—what impulse of my own would rise to the surface. I paused halfway to the table, the tray of garlic bread in my hands, and waited. But the only impulse that came to me was *Garlic bread! Now!* So I set it on the table and sat down, contented. It had been a silly article anyway.

The meal was filled with chatter and moans as the kids related all that had happened to them that day, this time to Newton. Newton beamed, exhorted, and expressed outrage at all of the appropriate moments.

I will say, Newton has always been extremely good at listening to the children, and they respond to it like puppies to biscuits. There may be eight of them, but each secretly harbors the belief that they are Dad's personal favorite. Newton just has that special way about him.

* * *

Family night is always a hit-or-miss affair at our house. Inevitably, someone has a mountain of homework or an urgent project, one of Newton's patients goes into crisis mode, or there's a sudden attack of flu. But this Monday was a success; school hadn't really gotten underway yet, so there was no homework to contend with, Newton's patients mercifully decided to have a quiet night, and everyone was miraculously healthy at the same time. We gathered in the living room and had a brief lesson on personal responsibility (with an eye toward school starting), and sang a few favorite songs accompanied by Scott on his banjo ("The Wise Man and the Foolish Man" for the younger children, "True to the Faith" for the older boys, and Mozart's "Ave Verum Corpus" for Newton). There was a coordinating of calendars—who needed the car when—and then we adjourned to the kitchen for brownies in a mug. At that point, the children scattered to their own devices, and I cleaned up the chaotic cushions in the living room with a feeling of smug satisfaction. Another triumph.

I know some families who rejoice in such small triumphs every week. In the early years of motherhood, I took it for granted that our family would meet every goal and smoothly accomplish every worthy aspiration. Experience has made me wiser, and now I'm just happy if we can get through family night with all egos intact and no blood on the floor.

* * *

Tuesday morning was more or less a repeat of the previous morning. It was easy to slip back into the school routine after so many years of doing it, but it saddened me too. It was difficult to let go of the long, unstructured summer, the picnics on the sundrenched beach, the hikes along the rocky Bruce Trail, the sleeping in with sunlight streaming through the white curtains . . . knowing that winter was around the corner. No one had warned me when I'd left the heat of the Utah desert to go to the University of Toronto at the tender age of seventeen that I would end up marrying a Canadian and staying. And certainly no one—least of all Newton—had warned me about Canadian winters. It wasn't the forty-below temperatures or the three feet of snow or even the freezing rain that wore me down so much as the lack of sunlight for five months of the year. I wondered if I had seasonal affective disorder. Certainly, the prospect of yet another gray winter made me feel uncomfortably homicidal. Or maybe that was just the menopause. Beyond that, of course, I was by now feeling sick with anxiety about Angus. Altogether, it was a rather depressing sort of day.

That afternoon, I was watching TV in the family room when the kids started to arrive home from school. Scott poked his head in to say hi.

"Hi. How was your day?" I wiped at my eyes and reached for the remote to turn the TV off.

Scott noted my tears and the used Kleenex I gripped. "Watching *Pride and Prejudice* again?" he asked knowingly.

"No. Puppy chow commercial." I sniffled.

"What's for snack?" he asked, eyeing my empty bowl on the coffee table.

"Cottage cheese," I said. No way was I going to divulge my stash of Heavenly Hash hidden in the chest freezer under the turkey burger. (Sometimes extreme measures are justified. Mothers of eight don't get many personal indulgences. I mean, are *we* not people too?)

There was a bang and clatter down the hall, and I hurried into the kitchen to find Jane sitting at the table with her head in her arms. Her book bag lay on the floor. As I came in, she raised her face, and I could see she was sobbing.

"Honey, sweetheart, what's the matter?" I asked, hurrying to her. I smoothed her hair away from her face (on the one side; the other side being in a ponytail).

"It was so awful, Mom," she wailed. She clutched the front of her—my—purple sweater and pulled at it. "We got the date wrong! Crazy Dress Day is Friday, not today!" She burst into fresh tears and buried her face once more. "Now everyone in the fifth grade thinks I'm insane," came her muffled voice.

I suppose it didn't help the mother-daughter relationship that I couldn't get up off the floor from laughing.

"It's a good thing Dad's a shrink," Enoch murmured, passing through the kitchen. "She's going to need one."

Jane jumped from the table and flew after him with an angry shout, and I heard the two of them brawling in the living room. I shook my head and went upstairs, leaving them to it. A little fisticuffs would make her feel better.

* * *

By Wednesday morning, I had convinced myself something dreadful had happened to Angus.

"There's still no word from him," I told Newton as he dressed for work. "We've got to do something. I'm calling the police."

"Don't you think that's a bit . . . um . . . well, overreactive?" Newton asked hesitantly.

"I don't think so," I said indignantly. "There's been no word from him for days."

"He's a busy man. Maybe he hasn't had time to call."

"He hasn't been to work."

"True. But there must be a logical reason."

"Name it."

He hesitated, then nodded. "You're right. He wouldn't miss work. Tell you what. On the way home tonight, I'll swing by Angus's house and see what I can find out."

"Would you, please?" I dabbed at my eyes with my wrist. "Thank you."

Newton put a hand on my shoulder and gave it a little squeeze as he passed.

* * *

I tried to keep myself busy all morning. I made a batch of peanut-butter cookies and ate half of them. Not wanting anyone to come home and see I'd eaten half, I then had to eat the other half of the batch to hide the evidence. I took a loaf of pumpkin bread to a neighbor who was ill and then came home and cleaned the bathrooms. And I worked for a while on an article I was writing for a professional journal: "A Comprehensive Analysis of Rules of Heredity among the pre-Columbian Teotihuacano." (When we'd first married, children hadn't come along right away, and I had amused myself obtaining master's degrees in anthropology and linguistics. I still liked to keep my hand in the field occasionally for fun.)

Andrew seemed to sense my distraction and played nicely by himself for most of the morning. I had skipped our reading game today, so he hadn't gotten a midmorning snack. I poked my head into his room and asked him if he'd like some fruit leather.

"ABC?" he asked, looking up from his Legos in confusion.

"Leather. Not letters."

"Oh. Yes, peeze."

I gave him the snack and an additional handful of banana chips as a reward for being so polite and well behaved.

I was hauling a basket of laundry downstairs when the phone rang, and I hurried to snatch up the nearest extension. A blast of static hit my ear.

"Annie? It's An . . ." The voice slipped in and out of hearing as the static swelled like a wave.

"Angus? Is that you?"

"Listen . . . holding me . . . of the note I found."

"We have a bad connection, Angus," I shouted into the phone. "Your voice keeps cutting out. Say that again."

"I found . . . trying to . . ."

"Where are you? I can't hear a word you're saying. I think you're losing the signal."

"Sorry . . . it's hidden . . ."

"What? What's hidden?"

"Hidden in the new edition . . . to help him . . . Don't . . ."

The line went dead.

I stared at the receiver. What on earth had that been about? I quickly dialed Angus's phone, but there was no answer. He must have been on someone's cell phone; he didn't own one himself. He'd always resisted them, saying it would be like constantly babysitting one of those annoying Tamagotchis. (He had a point. I'd been reduced to shutting up Maisie's Tamagotchi in the sound-proof freezer every night and resurrecting it every morning.) I hesitated, then phoned Newton's office. He answered on the third ring.

"I'm in the middle of a session right now," he said briskly. "Can I call you back?"

"Angus just called me," I said.

"There you go! See? I told you—"

"No. There was something weird about it. Something's wrong." Briefly, I told him what I had heard. Newton was quiet for a moment.

"He found a note, he said?"

"I think so. It was so hard to hear him over the static. It sounded like he'd found a note, and something is hidden in the new edition."

"Most likely, it's to do with his train robbery research or something. I wouldn't worry about it, Annie."

"But, Newton, he sounded urgent. You know I've been trying to reach him since Sunday."

"He said 'help him,' not 'help me'?"

"Yes."

"So he's not in any sort of trouble, or he would have said 'help me,' don't you think?"

"I guess so," I said doubtfully.

"Did you dial star-whatever-it-is to call him back?"

"Oh. No. I didn't think of it. It's too late now—I phoned you afterward."

"Look, try him again at home in a while. If you still can't reach him, I'll still plan to drive by his house on the way home to check on him."

"Thank you."

* * *

When Newton arrived home that evening, I immediately knew something was wrong. He was unusually quiet. His face was still, drawn into a small frown, different from his usual scowl. I pulled him into the laundry room— the one room of the house that was usually empty—and turned him to face me.

"What is it, Newton?"

"Angus wasn't home. But the house was unlocked, so I went in and just sort of peered around. I don't think he'd mind."

"Certainly not, when you have his best interests at heart," I assured him.

"It looked to me like he'd left in somewhat of a hurry. I mean, granted, he isn't the most meticulous fellow when it comes to housework, but it just looked very . . . sudden. Dishes still in the sink. A dried-up beef sandwich on a plate in the microwave. It looked like it had been there awhile. Clothes still in the dryer. And there was a pile of mail and newspapers in the mailbox spilling out onto the porch. I gathered them and put them on the table and then locked the house as I left."

He hesitated, and I took hold of his hand. "What else?"

"His car was in the driveway. Locked. The keys were in that dish he keeps inside his front door. Wherever he went, he didn't drive. I asked one of his neighbors, an elderly lady who seemed the type to spend her days with her nose pressed to the window, watching for something to gossip about. She hasn't seen him for several days."

I let out the breath I hadn't realized I'd been holding. "Do you think something has happened to him?"

"I don't know. Possibly. But what?"

"Do you think he's been arrested?"

Newton's eyes widened, and he reared back, away from me.

"What makes you think that?"

"He said 'holding me' when he phoned. I couldn't hear much of what he said, but those two words were clear."

Newton opened his mouth to protest, then stopped, and a funny look came over his face. He closed his mouth again.

"What?"

"Nothing."

"You were about to say he wouldn't have been arrested because he hasn't done anything. And then you stopped, which says to me that you think he *might* have done something. What do you think he's done?"

"I was thinking nothing of the sort," Newton grumbled.

"Yes, you were. I haven't been married to you for twenty-three years for nothing."

Newton scowled. "I was merely going to protest that it does no good to speculate about whether he's been arrested because the information we have would not be furthered by conjecture. Why not simply phone the police station and ask?"

I was going to press further, but I could see from his recalcitrant look that arguing would get me nowhere. I could also see his point, so I went in search of a phone book. Everyone knows 9-1-1 will bring the police, but it's actually quite difficult to find the nonemergency number for them when you want to avoid squad cars and flashing lights. Ten minutes of squinting later, I located the number I wanted.

A switchboard operator who sounded like she was twelve answered the phone.

"I'm sorry to bother you, but could you tell me if an Angus Puddicombe was brought in sometime this week?"

"Brought in?"

"Arrested. Are you holding anyone by that name?"

"Can I ask your name, please?" the teenager squeaked.

"Annie Fisher. I'm a friend of Mr. Puddicombe's, and he has been missing since Friday. Actually, maybe even longer than that." When was the last time I'd actually spoken to Angus? The previous Sunday when he'd come to the house? I sighed. "Actually, he might have been missing almost a week. I don't know."

"I'm afraid I can't give information to the public," the operator said, sounding genuinely sorry. "If you'd like to make a missing persons report . . ."

"Yes, I guess I would. Thank you."

She put me on hold, and I waited. Newton leaned against the door-frame, listening, with his hands in his pockets. After five minutes of canned jazz, a gruff male voice came on the line.

"Constable Donetti."

"My name is Annie Fisher. I want to find out if my friend Angus Puddicombe has been arrested sometime this past week," I said.

"Do you think there's reason he might have been?"

"No. But he is missing, and if he isn't in your cell right now, I don't know where he could be."

There was a pause and the sound of computer keys rattling. Then the gruff voice returned to the phone. "How long has Mr. Puddy—"

"Puddicombe," I supplied helpfully and spelled it for him. More rattling.

"Right. How long has he been missing?"

"Is he, then? He's not in your cell?"

"I can confirm he is not in our custody at this time."

"Was he earlier?"

"I can't answer that," Constable Donetti said firmly.

"Well, if you can't tell me that, maybe you can tell me if I should be making a missing persons report."

"Depends. How long has he been missing, then?"

"I don't know. The last time I saw him was a week ago Sunday, and his neighbor hasn't seen him for several days, but I haven't ascertained whether anyone else has seen him since then." I cocked an eyebrow at Newton.

"The oldest newspaper in the mailbox was Thursday's," Newton said.

If the evening papers had been brought in from earlier in the week, he must have gone missing sometime after that. "Probably late Wednesday night or sometime on Thursday," I told Donetti.

"Then you should make a report. What is his name again?"

"Angus Puddicombe." I spelled it a second time. Newton rolled his eyes and muttered something about the general illiteracy of North American society.

"And what is your relationship to him, please?"

"I told you; I'm his friend."

"How good a friend?"

I didn't like what this might suggest. I frowned at the phone. "My husband and I have known him for years. He and my husband once worked together."

"Ah. Can I get your name, number, and address, please?"

I told him.

"And Mr. Puddicombe's address?"

"I don't know the exact house number, but it's on Rasmussen Road at the corner of Janis, the big, old Victorian with the weeping willow."

"The old Philpott place. I remember it. He hasn't lived there long, then?"

"About a year."

"That long? Boy, time flies," the constable mused. I heard papers rustling. "Have you checked with local hospitals to see if he has been brought in?"

"No," I said. "I didn't think of that."

"Could you name some of his friends or close neighbors, please?"

I thought a moment. "Maybe just some of his colleagues at work. I don't think he has a lot of close friends. And no family that I know of."

"Where does Mr. Puddicombe work?"

"He teaches at Reynolds High. Classes started this week, but he never showed."

"When you saw Mr. Puddicombe that Sunday, would you say he was in a good mood?"

"Of course. Why would you ask?"

Donetti dropped his tone confidentially. "Well, you know, back to school and all that. We get a lot of suicides this time of year."

"Excuse me?" I felt as if I'd been slapped.

"Not usually the teachers though. More the students."

"Angus was in a great mood," I said firmly. "He was looking forward to school resuming. He agreed to come to dinner this past Friday too, but he never came. But listen, I got a strange, staticky phone call from him this afternoon." I told him to the best of my ability every detail of that call. "Because he said someone was holding him, I sort of thought maybe he'd been arrested."

"I'm afraid not," Donetti said, finally yielding the information. "We have no record of bringing in a Mr. Puddicombe all this week."

"Then I don't know who might have been holding him or what he was referring to."

"Do you think he's being held against his will, then? Abducted?"

Of course this possibility had crossed my mind, but I'd shrugged it off as ridiculous. Such things didn't happen to boring, impoverished history teachers.

More rustling papers. "What do you think he might have meant by 'hidden in the new edition,' Mrs. Fisher?"

"He recently updated a book he wrote a few years ago. The publisher is releasing the new edition next spring. I assume that's what he was referring to—something about the new information included in this latest edition."

"What's the book about?"

"A train robbery in Washington State."

"A fiction novel?"

"No, it's a true account."

This seemed to perk him up a bit.

"Do you have a copy of this book?"

"Just the original one," I told him. "The new edition isn't out yet."

"Right. You said. Right." More rustling. "Well, thank you, Mrs. Fisher. We'll look into it. I'll let you know if I need anything else from you."

"Constable Donetti—"

"Something else?"

I didn't know how to explain the urgency I felt, the panicky tone of Angus's voice coming through the static. I had never heard easy-going Angus ever sound that way before, and it had rattled me.

"Please hurry," I finally said.

* * *

I was puttering in the kitchen that evening, sorting through the freezer and figuring out what to leave out for tomorrow's supper, when I heard Maisie in the living room, reading a book to Andrew. It was one of his favorites, nursery rhymes, and he had learned it by heart. She went through "Jack Be Nimble" and "The Old Woman in the Basket," and then she got to the third page.

"Humpty Dumpty sat off a wall," she began in a sing-song voice.

"On a wall," Andrew corrected.

"Off a wall," Maisie repeated.

"You're not reading it right," I heard Ethan pipe up.

"Yes, I am."

"Humpty Dumpty sat *on* the wall."

"He sat *off* it," she insisted. "That's why he broke."

"He had to be on it first before he could be off it," Ethan argued.

I was about to intervene in the fight I knew was sure to come when I heard Newton's voice.

"A correct deduction, Ethan," he said. "But Maisie is also fundamentally correct in her literal interpretation. Here, let me finish it for you."

His voice changed to a lisping squeak as he finished the poem and moved into "Hey Diddle Diddle," only he pronounced it "Hey Piddle Piddle." Ethan challenged him on it.

"Well, it's about a cat, isn't it?" Newton reasoned. "So *piddle* is a totally understandable variation, especially if the cat has not been properly housetrained."

"Read it right!" Andrew said.

"Okay. Hey Fiddle Fiddle . . ."

"No!" the children chorused.

"But it *is* about a fiddle," Newton said. "A cat and a fiddle."

"Da-a-d!" Ethan moaned, giggling.

He went on, switching to a different comical voice for each new rhyme, purposely mispronouncing words, and by the time he'd finished the book, all three children were howling with laughter. I smiled down at the roast I'd taken out of the freezer and wished Newton's former colleagues at the university could have heard this. How had he learned to handle fatherhood and children with such grace? He certainly hadn't learned it from his mother. I couldn't imagine Janet Fisher reading to her children at all, much less putting on squeaky voices. Her idea of grandparenting was to shove the kids in the basement with Popsicles and video games and consider her duty done.

It occurred to me that men in the Church were given a rare thing. They were taught how to be fathers, how to interact with small children. They were given not just lessons but the tools and opportunity to do it, working in Primary or Sunday School or Young Men. And most importantly, they were given permission to emote. Men in general in society were not, I thought, allowed to be squeaky and funny or to act fondly, to be openly loving. They were taught from an early age to be tough, to be go-getters and hard-hitters, to move in the world of finance or business or labor with dignity and confidence. But where were men taught to be sweet and gentle? They could only learn it at home with their own parents, if there. Society didn't encourage it. But at church, they could play with children and laugh and sing and stand up in testimony meeting and cry with impunity. Where else would they get that opportunity?

I felt a sudden surge of gratitude for Newton and for whatever forces had shaped him to be the way he was. Because of him, I had high hopes for my own sons.

* * *

"I think Angus was trying to give us a clue as to his whereabouts," Newton said that night as we were getting ready for bed. "I think that somehow he managed to get hold of a cell phone and make that quick call to you. Assuming he was in a hurry and doing it furtively, behind his abductors' backs, he would only squeeze in the most urgent and important details."

Abductors. I shivered at the word. "But what details? I hardly understood him," I said.

"We won't know what he meant until we see what's in this new edition of his. It's obviously hidden in there somewhere." Newton slung his pants over the back of the armchair at the foot of the bed and slid under the covers beside me. He lay on his back, the blanket tucked tightly across his chest, staring up at the ceiling, looking like Tutankhamen in his coffin. I could imagine his brain clicking around in circles.

"We have to get a copy of his new book," he said.

"It isn't out for months."

"Maybe he had a draft copy in his house."

I rolled over, propped my head up on one hand, and said pointedly, "The house you conscientiously locked up behind you when you left."

"Oh. Yes."

"You don't have a key, do you?"

"No, and before you ask, I am not going to pick his lock, friend or no friend. Maybe the police can get in. Or here's a thought: publishers send out review copies, don't they? You could pose as a book reviewer and get an advance copy."

"Me? Why me?"

"Because I'm too well known," Newton said peacefully. "They'd never fall for it."

I wanted to argue that, but as much as I disliked it, he was probably right. Newton had published widely in his field and had even done a brief and memorable stint as host of a live radio talk show last year. It had ended in a glorious blaze-up when a well-known and politically-connected guest had taken offense to Newton's interpretation of his comments as indicative of severe dysfunction in his spousal relationship. Newton never takes kindly to correction. When the show's producer had called Newton on the carpet for airing his inflammatory opinion, Newton had responded by loudly analyzing the producer's own control issues and "short-man syndrome" . . . but I digress.

The next morning, I dug out my copy of Angus's original book. I had stuck it in a cardboard box in the basement, along with about five thousand other paperbacks I'd promised myself I'd read again but hadn't gotten to and therefore couldn't possibly donate to the library yet. The cover of the book was a Wild-West print showing a steaming nineteenth-century train curving around a cactus-covered hill (someone in the graphics department at the publisher's was sadly mistaken if they thought Saguaro cactus dominated Tacoma). The title was in lurid, red, two-inch letters: *The Great Washington Train Robbery*. (No one at the publisher's had much of a flare for imaginative titles either, apparently.) I jotted down the name of the publisher and went onto the Internet to look up the phone number.

I do not dissemble successfully at the best of times, and in my defense, I will point out that I was somewhat under stress at the time. I cared deeply about Angus, and the thought that he was missing—perhaps abducted— gnawed at me like a gerbil. I will also add in my defense that I have not had much experience in lying. The woman at the publisher refused to send me a review copy or (my next tactic) sell me a copy before the scheduled release date.

"I appreciate that you are anxious to read the book," she said smoothly, "but so are all of our readers. It's great to know Mr. Puddicombe has such a devoted fan. But really, it comes out in April. Surely you can wait that long."

"But Angus's life may depend on our acquiring the new edition right away," I finally said, near tears.

"What are you talking about?"

"It's too long to explain, but I have reason to think Angus Puddicombe has been abducted. I think the clues we need in order to find him are hidden within the new edition of his book."

"You think—um . . . Please hold."

The phone clicked, and I listened irritably to more canned jazz for a full five minutes before the chipper voice came back on the line.

"I'm sorry, but we are not able to give you an advance copy at this time."

My irritation flared into anger. "Oh, come on. I'm not asking you to reveal industrial secrets or anything. I mean, it's not like millions of people are waiting breathlessly for this book to come out. Angus is hardly J. K. Rowling."

"I'm sorry, we can't help you." Her voice had turned distinctly chilly.

"Are you hiding something?"

"I'm not authorized to give you the book, Mrs. Fisher."

"The police will get a warrant and seize a copy, then," I said.

"Thank you for calling," she said and hung up.

"The nerve," I muttered.

I told Newton about the conversation.

"Well, we'll just have to let the police obtain a copy, then," he said reasonably.

"Even if they do, we won't be allowed to see it," I said. "What if whatever references it makes can only be understood by someone who was close to Angus and knew him well? I mean, he did call *me*, not the police."

"True. It does seem that, given the chance, he would have called 9-1-1 if he were being held against his will."

"But he didn't. He called me," I said again. "It's a message meant for me and you, personally."

* * *

In the end, Newton picked Angus's lock. He refused to dress in black and skulk in the dark though. Instead, he parked our car behind Angus's in his driveway for all to see, and we marched up to the door in broad daylight.

"If you act suspicious, you will raise suspicion," he explained, deftly slipping his lock picks back into his pocket and turning the knob. "If you act as if you have every right to do exactly as you're doing, no one ever questions you."

As I followed him into the house, I decided Newton was right. It was all just a matter of confidence—or at least feigning confidence.

And no, I don't know where Newton learned to pick a lock so adeptly. There are shadowy bits of his youth, prior to his joining the Church, that he does not share with me, nor have I asked, not wishing to seem intrusive. If he wanted me to know, he would tell me.

If one has acquired a useful skill and employs it only for good, there is no need, to my way of thinking, to explain or justify said skill. And after all, the police check I'd run on him prior to our marriage had come back clean.

Angus's computer was temporarily housed in one of the bedrooms upstairs, awaiting its move to his still unfinished new office. I found myself tiptoeing upstairs and into the room, even though I knew no one was there. The room was bare other than the ancient desk and chair, a loaded bookcase, and an overflowing wastepaper basket. The computer looked out of place and anachronistic in this room full of Victorian-era furniture. The desk's surface was littered with untidy piles of paper, envelopes, more books, and—I saw with a shudder—pens without their caps. Newton started to sift through the debris about as delicately as if he were panning for gold. I sorted through the books on the shelves, none of which were helpful, being a conglomeration of drab textbooks and dog-eared popular fiction (which rather lowered my opinion of Angus's literary tastes). Disappointed, I went to look out the window at the backyard.

Most of the houses in our small suburb had good-sized lots, but Angus's was a corner lot, so it was especially large. The view of the neighbors to one side and behind was obscured by thick maple trees, and I saw a flagstone path leading off through the unmown lawn to a plastic tool shed in one corner. A pair of gardening gloves sat abandoned on the porch rail, and I felt a tightening in my throat.

"Anything?" I asked, sounding more impatient than I had intended.

"Nothing. Maybe he only worked on it on the computer and didn't print it out." Newton sighed. "I'm afraid hacking into a computer is beyond my skills. Maybe we could come back with Isaac or Caleb . . . ?"

"We are not getting our sons involved in computer hacking," I said sharply.

Newton opened his mouth, stopped, and closed it again. Again.

"What?" I said suspiciously. "Are you implying they are already involved?"

"No, no," Newton said casually. "I didn't say anything."

"You looked it."

"It's just that they're teenagers, and I figure most teenagers know their way around a computer better than I do."

I thought a moment. "Angus was a teacher. He's used to working with paper, red pen in hand. I can't believe he wouldn't print it off."

"*I* certainly prefer working with paper," Newton said.

I tried to picture how Angus would have acted. He'd been so excited about this new edition coming out. Would he have sat at this cluttered, uncomfortable desk in this empty room in a hard chair to proofread his book online one last time before submitting it to his publisher? Not likely. I personally would have preferred to curl up in a cozy armchair with a printed manuscript. He would have savored the experience, the joy of a new publication coming out, the tingle of anticipation as his long labor of love came to its culmination . . .

"Where are you going?" Newton called as I headed down the hall.

I found Angus's bedroom at the front of the house and paused in the doorway. The room was tidy compared to the rest of the house, the twin bed depressingly narrow but neatly made with a plain blue quilt, a bathrobe hanging on the bedpost. A bedside table held a garish lamp and a collection of books. There was an armchair near the window with a book lying face down on its seat and a wilting potted plant on the floor beside it. I went into the adjoining bathroom, found a cup, and watered the plant. Then I went to the bedside table and moved aside several books and an empty water glass to reveal the thick sheaf of paper lying beneath them. Red ink curled here and there over it like Virginia Creeper, and a couple of yellow sticky notes drifted loose as I lifted it. I retrieved them and turned to Newton, who stood in the doorway.

"Found it."

Chapter Three

THE NEXT DAY, I HAD an appointment with my cardiologist. I had had some concerns with my heart over the past few months, so my family doctor had referred me to Dr. Post, who, as fortune would have it, had an office so close to our home I could walk there in just ten minutes. I took Angus's manuscript with me to read in the waiting room. I went over it with excruciating care, starting from the beginning. Angus said he'd simply added a new chapter, but I wanted to make sure I understood the original story thoroughly to better contrast with and highlight the added changes.

The plot was as I'd remembered. In April 1905, a Northern Pacific Railway train carrying the payroll of hundreds of railroad employees was five miles outside of Tacoma, Washington, when it slowed to make a turn. Three masked men jumped aboard the train, accosted the guard standing at the front car door, forced their way inside, and held the guard at gunpoint until he unlocked the safe. The gunmen took the two leather satchels containing the payroll from the safe and leapt off the train, taking the guard's gun with them. However, the guard, whose name was Walter Fleming, had a second gun locked in a cabinet in the same train car. He managed to get off a few shots and hit one of the men. Fleming then alerted the engineer, Harvard Frys, who made haste to reach the next station, where he and the guard reported the incident.

Police immediately went to the area where the men had jumped off the train and found the body of a masked man but no sign of the satchels or the other gunmen. The deceased had been shot twice, once in the hip and once in the back of the head. He was never identified. The money, stated to be just over a million dollars, was never recovered. Walter Fleming maintained that he had shot the man only once. Police conjectured that the man had been shot first in the hip by Fleming and then was finished off with a shot to the head by one of his colleagues after the train had fled the scene.

This last bit puzzled me. Surely the men had a car or horses hidden nearby. The theft had been well thought out and executed, and surely they would have anticipated needing some mode of escape. They wouldn't have chosen to escape by jogging across the open countryside. Why didn't they simply scoop up the injured man, pop him in the waiting conveyance, and take him with them? Why wait until the train was gone, then come back and shoot their accomplice in the head? Was it so they only had to share the loot between the two remaining partners? It seemed awfully cold-blooded to me, even for robbers.

The squinting was giving me a headache, and I found it in me to wish Angus had been more direct in his phone call. If he wanted me to know something, why not simply *say* it?

I was called into the examination room at that point and spent the next hour getting prodded and questioned and hooked up to various machines. I felt a bit like Dr. Frankenstein's monster, hooked up to what looked suspiciously like jumper cables. The lab technician looked Isaac's age, and she was wearing a Hello Kitty wristband. It did not inspire confidence.

After the testing, the cardiologist informed me that I had a heart arrhythmia (sinus tachycardia and premature ventricular beats, to be precise). There was no physical problem with my heart, and it was probably the result of exhaustion or stress. ("Oh really?" I felt like muttering.) I was to avoid caffeine—not much of a problem for a Mormon who was used to going without coffee and tea anyway—decongestants, sudden loud noises or adrenalin rushes—there went the bungee-jumping plans—and dark chocolate.

"Hold it! Wait a minute!" I said, holding up a hand. "No dark chocolate? Are you crazy?"

"Chocolate has caffeine in it," Dr. Post said apologetically. "Some dark kinds have even more than coffee does. But if you avoid those and try to get more sleep, you shouldn't have any problems with your heart. It's not an uncommon condition. If you experience dizziness while exercising, stop and call me immediately. Otherwise, I'll see you next year."

"That's it? There's nothing else to do?"

Dr. Post put a hand on my arm. "It's just something to be aware of, Annie. Other than those few avoidances, there really isn't anything else to do. Just listen to what your heart is telling you, and if its message seems to change, come see me. Okay?"

I left the office feeling depressed. Sudden noises I might be able to avoid. I'd have to warn Newton not to ever throw me a surprise party. The kids would have to be told no jumping out from behind furniture or sneaking up to pop balloons behind me. I rarely used decongestants anyway. But no *chocolate*? What was the point of living?

"Oh well, at least I'll lose weight." I sighed, then squinted at my watch. I had the morning free, Isaac was watching Andrew, and I felt in no hurry to get home. I needed a pick-me-up. This on top of my worries about Angus was too much. So I veered east instead of west and walked along Carter Road to my favorite restaurant, a French place called Tastes Like Crêpe that specialized in light lunches and desserts. It had been ages since Newton and I had come here. I would treat myself, just this once.

Indulge my impulse, I thought with a wry smile.

There were few patrons, and I got a table by the window overlooking the road. I ordered thin golden ravioli filled with butternut squash and goat cheese, and arugula and sautéed wild mushrooms, blessed with truffle oil and a sweep of pecorino. It was so good I wanted to weep into my plate. I wanted to kiss the chef's feet and bathe them with my tears. *That* good. I instantly felt better. What was a little heart trouble? I could handle that. I took another bite of goat cheese. I could handle anything.

As I ate, I read the rest of Angus's manuscript. The added chapter didn't address the moral issue. Rather, it described how the unsolved mystery had niggled at Angus for a number of years. It seemed such a straightforward crime, and yet it had gone unsolved for a hundred years. Finally, he'd had a breakthrough. The new chapter recounted how Angus had been in the archives in Seattle, Washington, looking at old newspapers for a separate research project, when he'd stumbled across a gossip rag from 1905 called *The Monthly West Coast Gazette*. In December 1905, a columnist wrote about a newcomer named Mr. Harvey Frieze, who had recently bought a very expensive home in Seattle. Mr. Frieze was now apparently living in comfortable retirement on a sizeable income, the source of which was unaccounted for. The columnist speculated on this fact because Mr. Frieze seemed to be quite young to be retired. The columnist had attempted to find out where Mr. Frieze was from and what manner of work he had been engaged in prior to retiring, but Mr. Frieze had refused to speak to him, and no one else seemed to know.

What puzzled the columnist had illuminated the puzzle in Angus's brain. Harvey Frieze was a very similar name to Harvard Frys, the name of the train engineer. Could he, in fact, have been the same man?

A little more digging produced a census of Seattle that gave Mr. Frieze's address as 49 Winchester Road. He had lived alone, and his occupation was listed simply as "retired." His birth date was given as September 12, 1865. Angus then looked up old railway employee records, which also gave Mr. Frys's birthdate as September 12, 1865.

At the time of the robbery, the guard and the engineer's picture had appeared in a Washington newspaper. The guard was a chunky man with short-cropped hair and a dangerous-looking squint, as if he were trying to look extra tough to distract people from remembering the fact that he had caved and opened the safe for the robbers. The more slender Frys was a solemn, mustachioed man with a Roman-beaked nose that looked too big for his face. A careful combing through further editions of *The Monthly West Coast Gazette* revealed a photo of Harvey Frieze, snapped at a town Fourth of July picnic in the summer of 1907. Though his head was turned slightly away, unaware of the photographer, and the mustache had been shaved, it was almost undeniably the same man. There was no mistaking that proud nose.

Angus ended the chapter with a paragraph that came very close to gloating: "It was Harvard Frys, all right. I was sure of it. The engineer had been an accomplice in the great train robbery, maybe even the mastermind behind the whole thing. He lived on his ill-gotten gains very comfortably until he died at the age of eighty-two in Seattle in the year 1947. The one-hundred-year mystery is solved."

"Well, sort of." I sighed. After all, Angus hadn't managed to identify the man's three accomplices who had boarded the train. For that matter, he also hadn't proven that Harvard Frys hadn't inherited the money from a rich maiden aunt back in the old country. Though I'd admit that the fact that he had changed his name was compelling.

But where did that leave me? The added chapter in Angus's book was interesting in and of itself, but what connection did it have with Angus's disappearance now? What had he meant for me to find "hidden in the new edition"? What did it have to do with the note he'd apparently found? Was he referring to the tidbit he'd found in the old newspaper? It all appeared quite straightforward, not hidden or enigmatic at all. I backed up and read the new chapter again, but nothing jumped out at me. Was he saying he was in Seattle? But then, why not just say so instead of being obscure about it? And if he *was* being held against his will, why waste his one precious opportunity to phone to discuss his research?

I wanted to do some thinking, so I headed south after lunch, walking through the wide sloping streets of beautifully restored heritage houses and spreading maple trees until I reached the lake. At this time of year, the beaches were generally empty of tourists, and I was pleased to see I had the long stretch of pale sand to myself. I took off my shoes and stockings and carried them as I walked, savoring the chill of the water that creamed up over the sand to splash my ankles. A fishing tug bobbed in place out on the gray-blue water, looking toylike in bright reds and blues. The welcome splotch of color cheered me.

Usually, walking on the beach alone cleared my mind and made the sometimes chaotic pieces of my life snap into perfect perspective. It was restorative and just another reason I felt blessed to live where I did. I had often come here seeking comfort or enlightenment or just plain solitude. Vast open watery vistas are conducive to communion with deity. But today I walked as far as the pier with its iconic lighthouse, and nothing new came to my mind, and my soul still felt jumbled. I was just as puzzled as ever, and the niggling worry about my heart condition hadn't eased. The beach hadn't worked its magic today.

So I wiped my feet dry with my socks, put my shoes back on, and took myself to the Arbor Restaurant beside the beach for an ice-cream cone. Just so the jaunt hadn't been a total waste, you understand.

That evening, I told Newton what the cardiologist had said and the precautions I had to take. My husband of twenty-three years shushed me gently, put his arm tenderly around my shoulders, looked deep into my eyes, and said, "*Boo!*"

I was still giggling when I went to bed. Thank goodness for Newton.

* * *

By Saturday morning, I had been over and over Angus's final chapter until I felt as if my eyeballs were on fire. As we made the two-hour drive to Brampton for our monthly visit with Newton's mother, I went over in my mind everything I'd studied. Could Winchester mean anything? 49? 1865? September 12? There was simply nothing to grab hold of. Nothing that smacked of a code or double meaning. What was it I was meant to find? I felt wretched I was no closer to figuring out what was going on. I was stumped, pure and simple.

"Maybe it isn't something so literal," Newton suggested when I'd finished whining—er, rather, explaining my lack of success to him. I had the manuscript, now worn and crumpled from my study of it, in my lap. "Maybe it's meant to be a metaphor or something."

"Like what?" I asked doubtfully.

"Oh, for example, this Frys fellow reinventing himself as Frieze. Maybe Angus was telling you he has gone off to find himself. Or try on another identity."

Even for a psychiatrist, this was a stretch. "Are you telling me Angus was putting his meal in the microwave one morning and suddenly decided, 'I think I'll go on walkabout and find myself' and left then and there? Just before school was to start?"

"Hmm. Well, no," Newton said uncomfortably. "Well, then, maybe it's the name itself. He went from Frys—which brings to mind sliced potatoes frying in hot fat—to Frieze, which brings to mind cold temperatures."

"So you're saying Angus went on walkabout to the Arctic."

Newton shot me a glare I concede I probably deserved.

"Let me see the blasted thing," he said and took the sheaf of papers from me. I yanked them back.

"Not while you're driving! Besides, we're almost there."

Janet Fisher lived in a tidy redbrick bungalow in a tidy housing development just off the freeway. When we pulled up, her fourth and current husband, Ed, waved at us from the open garage. He had installed a TV and armchair in the garage and spent most of his days there because Janet wouldn't venture into the dusty area. His last name was Raulston, but Janet still went by Fisher. As Newton nastily put it, if she changed names every time she got remarried, she'd spend a fortune getting her checks reprinted.

As the children trudged obediently into the basement to collect their Popsicles, Janet shook her head at Newton. "I swear, there are more of them every time you come to visit. What did you do, pick up a few strays along the way?"

"Well, now, there can never be too many little Fishers in the world, can there?" Newton replied serenely. "In fact, we're thinking of having a few more."

"Good grief, Newton, you aren't *serious*!" She gasped, looking from him to me. "Amy, he isn't serious, is he?"

"Of course not," I soothed her, gritting my teeth. Her inability to remember my name sometimes rankled even after twenty-three years. "He's only teasing you, Mother. Knock it off, Newt."

There is something in Newton that enjoys stirring up waves in peaceful waters, and I have not yet reasoned out precisely what causes it. Newton withholds his professional opinion.

True to form, the visit ended early when Andrew, running from Newton during a game of tag in the basement, slipped on the tile floor and banged heads with Maisie. Neither child was truly damaged, but Janet wasn't one to tolerate crying or other loud noises (how she had managed to raise a son who was a bagpiper, I have no idea). She whisked everyone out of the house as quickly as propriety would allow. None of the children looked overly disappointed.

"I could almost believe that happened on purpose," I said as the van spurted away from the curb.

Newton turned his handsome face toward me, brown eyes wide. "What are you suggesting, dear? That my mother premeditatedly polished the tile in order to cause the crash?"

"Hmm," I said.

"No, if she'd wanted us gone quickly, she wouldn't have been so subtle. So what shall we do with our unexpectedly free afternoon?"

"Mini golf!" "Pizza!" came the suggestions from the backseats.

"Apples," I said firmly.

* * *

Apple season in Ontario is a major event. I had three bushels waiting in the garage, and I'd been wondering how I would get to them. Worries or no, fruit won't wait. A free afternoon was a boon. When we got home, I had the kids change into grubbies and organized them into a sort of assembly line. Maisie and Ethan, being of energetic age, were in charge of shuttling the apples from the bushel baskets in the garage into the kitchen, carrying them a few at a time in mixing bowls (so if they dropped a bowl, only a few apples would get damaged). Scott and Jane peeled, using the crank peeler that attached to the table with a vice. Little Andrew's job was to catch the curling peels and put them in a bowl that would be emptied into the compost bin. As he caught them, I could hear him counting under his breath, "Twenty-seven, twenty-eight, twenty-nine, twenty-ten, twenty-eleven . . ."

Newton cored and sliced the peeled apples. Caleb shuttled empty jars up from the basement and washed them, and Isaac was in charge of packing the prepared apples into the jars once the jars were sterilized. My job was to keep a pot of cinnamon syrup boiling on the stove to pour over the apples and poke the air bubbles out with a wooden skewer. Science-minded Enoch was in charge of the actual processing of the jars, being the best at calculating water displacement.

The kids had been helping with this sort of thing for years, and we had it down to a well-oiled machine. It took surprisingly little time to process all of the apples, and by the evening, we had nearly sixty jars of premade apple pie filling on the shelves. This winter, I had only to dump a jar into a pie crust and bake it to have fresh, tangy apple pie that tasted of autumn. Somehow, it always tasted better when we worked on it as a family, as opposed to my doing it all myself. I thought again of the woman who'd written the article about indulging herself (and after all, what was more indulgent than apple pie?) and decided she was probably a lonely person.

After a quick late supper, I whipped up two hot pies for Mary Hessler and Donna James, the women I visit teach. Since our ward covered a sizeable area and they both lived fairly far away, I wouldn't deliver them to their houses but would meet up with them at church tomorrow. I'd never understood why they always seemed to make visiting teaching assignments based on who lived the farthest from the other. Then again, if it weren't for the assignment, I probably wouldn't have made the effort to get to know these two women because of the distance and would have missed out on the blessing of making two good friends. I have come to understand that most things that happen in life turn out to have good reasons behind them, if we just look for them.

I wondered if that was true of heart arrhythmias. Or missing friends.

* * *

There was no more word from Angus. His house had remained dark and silent, his car unmoved when we'd detoured past it on the way to church. He had been missing for over a week. I was beginning to fear the worst. But an idea had occurred to me during the night.

"Can we get a copy of my phone records from last week?" I asked Newton when I'd come in from waving the younger kids off at the bus stop Monday morning.

"I imagine so. Why?"

"I want to see if it gives the number of the phone Angus used to call me. Maybe we can call him back."

Newton's eyebrows shot up. "Why didn't we think of that sooner? I'll call the phone company this morning."

"I'm going to send Enoch over to mow Angus's lawn tonight," I added. "Much longer, and I'm going to have to break into his house again to water his plant." I wished I had thought to locate a house key while we were there the first time.

"I think Angus has heavier things on his mind right now than a dead philodendron," Newton said, sobering.

I studied his face for a moment, so long and serious. It had grown more so with each passing day. Newton made friends easily but tended to lose them just as quickly. Angus was one of the few who had remained by his side over the years, and I could tell Newton was worried that perhaps Angus's disappearance was permanent.

"What if . . ." I began, then stopped, not sure how to word it. "I mean, I know it was a hundred years ago, but if Harvey Frieze had a grandson, or maybe a great-grandson—"

"Who didn't want word to get out how the family had acquired its fortune?" Newton finished for me. "I've thought of that scenario. Abduct Angus, hold him until he agrees to stop the publication of the book, and then trust that no one at the publishing company will blab? It's ridiculous. And no demands have been received at the publisher."

"That we know of."

"Easy enough to find out. We simply phone and ask if the new edition is still coming out as scheduled. Besides, how would this hypothetical descendant ever come to know about Angus's research in Washington over the past two months?"

I sighed. "I don't know what else to think, Newton. What else can we do?"

"We must have missed something. It's got to be there. I don't have any clients until noon today. I'm going back to the house."

"I'm sure the police have looked all through it by now," I said.

"They might have overlooked a clue."

"You can't go barging in and poking around. I mean, it may be a crime scene," I added with a guilty remembrance of our pawing through Angus's papers. His corrected manuscript was, after all, on Newton's nightstand at that moment.

"So?"

"So that nosy neighbor will see us and phone the cops."

"And?"

"And breaking into a house is illegal."

Newton quirked one eyebrow. "That didn't stop you the first time. Are you coming with me or not?"

"Let me get my purse."

* * *

We pried Isaac away from the Xbox to watch Andrew, and then Newton and I drove to Rasmussen Road in silence, each caught up in our own brooding thoughts. We parked in the driveway before the silent house, and Newton neatly let us in again. But when we stepped inside and closed the door behind us, I could instantly sense something was different. Newton sensed it too, and we exchanged looks before we stepped into the living room.

Someone had been there. The cushions were taken from the sofa and piled on the floor. The books and magazines had been spilled from the shelves without care, some of them with torn or bent covers, the sight of which made me cringe. The large framed landscape over the fireplace had been lifted down and set against the coffee table.

"I thought when the police searched a place, they were supposed to be careful and put things back," I muttered angrily.

"The police didn't do this," Newton said briefly. He turned and bolted up the stairs to the bedroom Angus was using as a study, and I followed right behind him. Newton came to an abrupt halt in the doorway, and I smacked into him. It was annoying to note he wasn't even breathing hard, whereas I . . . Well, eight pregnancies *will* add a few pounds to one's figure, and Victorian staircases are notoriously steep compared to modern ones. I was defensively wondering about the degree of difference in steepness when I peered around Newton, and the sight of the room derailed my thoughts.

All of the papers on the desk were scattered across the floor like an unseasonal snowfall. The computer itself looked funny—and then I realized the hard drive was gone. The monitor sat alone like Deep Thought on the desk. The bookshelves were now empty, all of the books swept onto the floor, flung so far across the room that I thought they must have been swept off with one mighty, angry gesture.

"Oh, Newton!" I breathed.

Newton stood with his hands clenching and unclenching as if he didn't know what to do with them. I spun and strode down the hallway to Angus's bedroom. Again, every surface had been swept clear. The quilt had been ripped aside and tossed on the floor. The mattress was crooked on the box springs as if someone had lifted it to look underneath.

"That's just cliché," Newton exploded when he saw it. "No one hides things under their mattress anymore. Whoever these people are, they're utterly devoid of imagination, or they've been reading too much thriller fiction."

I decided now was not the time to mention the $250 emergency money in a Ziploc baggie under my side of our mattress. I would relocate it when I got home.

"But what were they looking for?" I asked.

"Maybe the same thing we were earlier."

"The manuscript?"

"It stands to reason."

"We should phone the police."

"And explain our presence how?" Newton held up his lock picks and looked at me questioningly.

"But how did they get in?" I argued. "The same way we did?"

"Who else would have a key?"

"Not the nosy neighbor. Maybe he had one hidden outside in one of those obvious little fake rocks. Or maybe the construction guys who are building the office. He must have given them a key so they could access the house while he was in Washington."

"Good thought," he conceded. "Has the construction crew even been here this past week?"

Newton turned sharply on his heel and went down the stairs, and I scampered after him. I had a prickly feeling between my shoulder blades, as if the intruder were still there, furtively watching us, and I had no desire to remain alone upstairs. Newton strode through the kitchen to the family room and opened the nearest door. It was a closet. He shut it again and opened the other door in the opposite wall. This time it revealed a half-finished room clad in sheetrock on one wall and fluffy pink insulation showing between the exposed pine studs on the other three walls. A large, orange, plastic toolbox stood on the plywood floor, along with a tangle of extension cords and a glass jar of assorted screws. Other construction debris was accumulated in corners, and a fine dust coated everything.

I stood in the center of the room and turned slowly, breathing in the delicious scent of newly cut pine. It was a good-sized room, perhaps twelve by fourteen, jutting out from the family room like the afterthought it was. There were large windows in three walls of it and built-in bookshelves around the only finished wall. I pictured the room with such shelves around all three windows, task lighting, deep carpet, rich walnut furniture, and rows of books. It made my mouth water. While we were ripping out our warping kitchen counter, could we possibly add on such a scrumptious room to the back of our house? The new addition would give Newton a place to work without having to clutter up my dining table.

Newton looked up from where he stood, contemplating the overgrown backyard from the window. The unmown lawn. The work gloves left abandoned.

"The toolshed," he muttered. And then he was out of the room and through the back door off of the kitchen.

I hurried after him, heart pounding from more than exertion. What if Angus had gone into his toolshed for something and the door had swung shut and locked behind him? He'd been missing for so many days . . . What would we find?

But the shed door opened easily, and I saw immediately that the shed could never have held a person trapped against his will, especially one of Angus's size. One determined kick could have put out any of the flimsy plastic windows. The door and walls themselves would not have been impervious to a desperate man's pounding fist.

The interior of the shed held only the usual clutter of lawnmower, leaf blower, assorted tools, a stack of plastic flowerpots, and a wheeled barbecue. The sun coming in the cheap windows filtered through dust motes dancing in the air. I could smell the mustiness of damp particle board and perhaps mice. The gloom of the little room, the dashed hopes—all of it was too much for me. I felt tears slide down my cheeks, and I sniffed loudly to try to stop them.

"Now, Annie, my dear, don't fret yet," Newton murmured, putting his arms around me.

"When?" I snapped. "When shall I begin fretting, Newton? Tell me so I don't forget to write it down in my day planner. Shall I wait until they find his decomposed body in a ditch somewhere? Can I fret *then*?"

To his credit, Newton didn't give me the short-tempered reply I deserved. He only held me a moment longer, doing that unconscious swaying dance that parents do when holding small children. It helped. When he finally released me, I was dry-eyed and in command of myself once again.

"My apologies," I said. "I didn't mean to be short with you."

"We're both feeling a bit frayed at the edges," Newton said gently. "Let's lock up and go home."

We closed the shed and began walking back up the long yard toward the back door. There was mud and construction debris around the back of the house, where the new office had pushed itself out onto the lawn. The landscaping would have to be replaced around the base of the new addition . . .

I stopped short. "We've been stupid," I said.

Newton's expression clearly conveyed that any stupidity that may have occurred certainly hadn't come from *him*.

"Angus's call," I explained. "He wasn't saying the new *edition*. He was saying the new *addition*. The new office. I misunderstood."

Newton brightened immediately. He hurried inside, with me on his tail, and returned to the unfinished room. He turned in a slow circle, studying the pink insulation, the dusty floor, the new bookshelves, every detail. "So Angus wasn't calling to discuss his research at all. He was saying he found something in this room."

"A note," I added. "He said when he called that he'd found a note. But what note would he find hidden in a brand-new room?"

Ignoring the dust, we rooted through the boards and bits of leftovers and the box of tools as well as the recesses between the studs. Newton went so far as to paw through the fiberglass insulation with his bare hands, which seemed foolhardy to me. Nothing looked significant, and certainly nothing seemed valuable enough to provoke a criminal act. I stopped searching, dusted my hands on my trousers, and thought some more.

"In order to build this room onto the back of the house," I said, "they had to punch through the original Victorian wall to make the door."

"I'm following you," Newton said. "Angus found a note in the original wall, perhaps." He went to the door we had come through. The frame was up around the door, but the trim had not yet been attached to cover the gap between the doorframe and wall. Behind the insulation, I could see bare brick, presumably original to the house. I shifted the insulation batting to one side and felt carefully along the edges of each brick.

"What are you looking for?" Newton asked.

"A loose brick or a hidden compartment."

"Watch your fingers. That insulation has sharp filaments, I have learned to my chagrin. You won't find anything," Newton added.

"Why not?"

"First of all, just because Angus may have found something here doesn't mean he put it back here. Not if it was important or valuable. But he might have locked it up or hidden it somewhere else."

"Maybe," I admitted.

"And secondly, you're standing in the new room. The bricks you're touching would have been on the *outside* of the house. No one would loosen a brick and make a hidey-hole in the outside of the house. The weather would get into it. It has to be on the *inside* of the house."

I don't know why I hadn't thought of it myself. I can only blame it on the stress of the moment in general. Ordinarily, I would have been more swift to come to the same realization. I stepped outside the office into the family room and ran my hand over the wall. This area was painted sheetrock, with no cracks or seams in it.

"Nothing. No access to the brick wall."

"He might have had it repaired," Newton said.

"What if we're going at this all wrong? What if he didn't find the note in the new room? What if he was saying he found it somewhere else but *hid* it here? It was so hard to hear him. It could be the other way round."

Newton mused a moment, then nodded cheerfully. "I think you're right. It makes the most sense, I suppose, though personally, I wouldn't hide anything important anywhere around the bumbling Wendell and his workers. I would have put it in my desk or somewhere else safe."

"I agree. But Angus did say 'in the new addition.' If not found there, perhaps hidden there."

"But we haven't found anything." Newton sighed. "And whatever the importance of this hypothetical note is, I don't think he would have wanted the construction crew to just stumble across it."

"He also wouldn't want them to inadvertently build over the top of it and prevent him from ever seeing it again," I added.

We both stood looking carefully around the new office, trying to imagine the ideal hiding spot. Where could he hide something he could access again later (assuming he'd want to) without it being discovered by the builders?

Newton shuffled through the assorted tools on the floor and produced a screwdriver. Carefully, he took the plastic plate off of the light switch on the wall by the door. He peered inside and poked around with his finger but found nothing but the usual wires I assumed one would expect in such a place. Meanwhile, I once again sorted through the clutter left by the workers, more slowly this time, but turned up nothing.

I was trying to fit my fingers into the stiff leather pockets of an abandoned tool belt when Newton gave an "Aha!"

I turned to see him kneeling in the dust beside the heat register on the plywood floor. He had lifted the metal grate and reached down inside the vent, and now he lifted out a tiny metal box. It was the sort of magnetic box people hide extra house keys in, the size of a pink eraser with a top that slides aside. It had been stuck magnetically inside the heat duct.

"Accessible but not obvious," I said, going to peer over his shoulder. "And in no danger of being tiled over unless his contractor is exceptionally inept."

Newton slid the top aside with his thumb and extracted a piece of paper. He held it up carefully.

"*Voila*. A note."

"*The* note." I breathed.

"I assume."

He stood and unfolded it, and we bent over the scrap, heads together.

The paper was pale blue, the size of a small notepad, with *WP* printed at the top like a logo. The paper was covered with scratchy writing, the letters forming in a funny way that made the note hard to read no matter how I squinted. As best as I could tell, it said:

"*The story of The Black Donnellys is heard Away Down South. Follow the bee balm to the start at Peter Pan. Walk beside Thoreau, but if you cross Denver now, you've gone too far. Where the route forks by Thoreau, follow Paul Haggis past the canoe. Now you can cross Denver. It will be found under the pilgrim's feet in Massachusetts, the biggest of three.*" It was signed, "*Love, Dad.*"

"Word salad," I said blankly.

"Free association," Newton agreed. "But catchy."

"And apparently valuable enough to hide away. A fictional character, a nineteenth-century philosopher, a modern screenwriter, a major city . . . Any idea what it means?"

Newton has occasional moments of justifiable arrogance, but he can also be disarmingly candid about his own failings.

"None whatsoever," he said. "Completely flummoxed." He refolded the paper and stuck it back in the metal box, which he put in his pocket. "It has the ring of a riddle or a set of instructions of some kind. Like clues in a scavenger hunt. But amateurishly constructed, if so."

"It struck me that way too," I said, though I wasn't inclined to judge harshly whoever had written it. After all, it's not as if one can take a class on how to write proper scavenger-hunt clues. And it's not something an ordinary person practices often. I linked my arm through Newton's. "I think we've found what we're looking for," I said gently. "Let's go."

* * *

Back in the car (with Angus's house key, found in the same dish as his car key, tucked into my purse this time), I asked if I could examine the scrap of paper again. It remained as enigmatic as ever, and the handwriting no easier to decipher. I was fairly sure I had the words right though. The paper was stiff other than the creases in it from being folded. It could have been one year old or ten.

"If it is a set of instructions, like for a scavenger hunt," I reasoned, "then we won't be able to figure out the later clues until we've solved the first one: 'The story of the Black Donnellys is heard Away Down South.' Presumably the other clues work off of that one. Let's just focus on it for now."

"Agreed." Newton swung the car toward home to drop me off before he had to dash for work. "What are the Black Donnellys? Are they a geographic feature, like mountain peaks or river rapids?"

"I don't know. They sound vaguely familiar to me, but I can't put my finger on why. I'll Google them when I get home." I cranked open my window to let the cool morning air rush over my face, refreshing me after the stuffiness of the closed-up house.

"Away Down South obviously ends with 'In Dixie,'" Newton said, turning on the car's heater with a snap. "But does that mean we're to head for Georgia?"

"It didn't say to go there; it just said the story is heard there."

"We don't even know what this scavenger hunt leads to," Newton said. "We don't know what it is we're meant to find."

"I just want to find Angus," I said quietly, closing the car window again.

Newton tapped the paper with his forefinger. "Whatever this is, apparently it's important enough that someone has nabbed Angus because of it."

"That's conjecture. But it does fit with what he said in his phone call."

"We'll keep it as our working hypothesis."

"Newton, do you think they're holding him hostage just for this? If there was a way to get this to them, would they let him go free?"

"How can I say what they're thinking? If obtaining this paper was their objective, wouldn't they have simply gotten Angus to retrieve it for them?"

I thought about this. "Maybe he refused to cooperate."

"Then it really *must* be important. I wouldn't call Angus the bravest of men."

It surprised me to hear Newton say that. He never had a word of criticism to say about Angus. How did you judge someone's courage when day-to-day life didn't really demand demonstrations of it? (Though some might argue that facing a roomful of bored high school students on a daily basis required a great deal of bravery.) Now that I thought about it, the one trait life usually demanded of a person was sheer doggedness. Wasn't endurance in the face of relentless routine and uncertain outcome a kind of courage? Or perhaps a better term would be faith. I decided to jot this down to think about later when I had leisure to do so. I carry a small notebook with me almost everywhere to take notes throughout the day that later inform my evening journal writing.

"Maybe if we can find a way to get this paper to them, they'll let him go," I suggested when I'd returned my notebook to my purse.

"But if Angus himself isn't willing to give it to them, who are we to do it? It isn't ours. If he thinks it's too important to hand over, how can we contradict him? We don't even know what it is. But Angus apparently saw enough value in it to prompt him to hide it."

"Well, it's a moot point because we don't know who to give it to," I said. "We have to get those phone records."

Newton's voice dropped lower, and he shot me an uncomfortable glance. "Annie, Angus has been missing for a week and a half. If the abductors were going to make demands, they would have by now. We can't rule out the possibility that they simply . . . well, did him harm. To silence him because he knew too much."

I didn't like this thought or the one that inevitably followed it. I was, after all, holding the clues in my hand. Did *we* now know too much?

Chapter Four

NEWTON DROPPED ME OFF AT home and headed for his office, promising to call the phone company when he got there. When I went into the house, Isaac announced he had made arrangements to meet some friends at the Robot Café, pecked me on the cheek, and left. The café was a place on Main Street that offered—incongruously—guitar lessons, vintage candy, robots, and "everything inbetween." I had never really understood the place or its mandate, but it seemed popular with teens.

Andrew and I went over his reading game, and then I settled him in bed for his morning nap. I took advantage of the lull to study the mysterious note we'd found again.

"The story of The Black Donnellys is heard Away Down South. Follow the bee balm to the start at Peter Pan. Walk beside Thoreau, but if you cross Denver now, you've gone too far. Where the route forks by Thoreau, follow Paul Haggis past the canoe. Now you can cross Denver. It will be found under the pilgrim's feet in Massachusetts, the biggest of three. Love, Dad."

I went to search the Internet for the Black Donnellys.

They were easy to find. They turned out not to be mountain peaks or river rapids. They were people, apparently a family of Irish immigrants who settled in Ontario, Canada, in about 1845, not far—as it turned out—from where we lived. They were caught up in a local feud with other Irish neighbors and ran a stagecoach business that competed with a rival's business. Then the man who owned the land where the Donnellys were squatting tried to evict them and ended up murdered. The father of the Donnelly family was found guilty of the crime. Then, in 1880, five of the Donnelly family were massacred by a vigilante group. More than a hundred years later, a TV show and a rock band both borrowed the name.

I sat back in my chair and scrubbed my cheeks with my hands, staring at the computer monitor. If the word salad *was* a set of clues to a scavenger hunt, what were they leading to? What did a high school history teacher's disappearance have to do with a massacre in 1880? Had Angus stumbled across clues to the murders during his research? Was there a link between the two historical stories—the train robbery in 1905 and the murders in 1880—at both ends of the continent and in different countries? But both had happened so long ago! None of the players from either story was still alive.

I scrolled down the screen, reading about the museum established in Lucan, Ontario, where visitors could hear the story of the niece who had had the misfortune of visiting the Donnellys on the fateful day and got clubbed to death. There was also the tale of a young farmhand who escaped being murdered by hiding under a bed. There was John Donnelly, who was shot when he was mistaken for his brother William . . . there were so many details, so many names and themes caught up in this one story. How could I ever pick out the right detail that would move my search forward? What was the writer of the note intending for us to find?

Well, obviously, he didn't want us to find anything at all. That's why it was in cryptic code, so that only the initiated would understand. But who was the initiated? Who was meant to find the note? Or maybe no one had been meant to find it, and the writer had written it only for himself as a memory-jogger. Well, no, he wouldn't have signed it "Love, Dad," then, would he have? Obviously, the note was meant for someone's offspring.

I pulled chicken from the freezer to thaw for dinner and phoned the visiting teaching coordinator to report my statistics for September. As I loaded the dishwasher with the neglected breakfast dishes, I pondered over what I had learned. Maybe one couldn't decipher the note without knowing the end object of the search in the first place. Had Angus managed to figure it out? Or was he as clueless as I felt? Surely he must have understood something from it because he had recognized it as important and had hidden it away.

Andrew awoke all too soon from his nap and began pitching picture books overboard, so I devoted a few minutes to finding new entertainment for him in the form of nontoxic play dough. The stuff may not have been poisonous, but it was messy and often ended up in tiny red and blue crumbs strewn all over the table and floor. I'd once tried keeping Andrew in the bathtub while he played with it, but that had proven a sorry mistake. A two-hundred-dollar plumbing bill later and I figured out the best way to contain the mess was to strap Andrew into his old high chair and place the chair in the center of a plastic drop cloth in the garage (this was also the only acceptable arrangement for eating pudding or other especially messy items). I left the door connecting the garage to the laundry room open so I could hear him singing to himself and went back to my desk where I'd left the laptop running.

I reread the information on the Irish Donnelly family, then scrolled through various sites regarding the TV show and rock band. Was there something about them that was significant? If "Dad" was writing the note for a child, perhaps the TV show or band would have been more familiar to the child than the historical event.

I was about to turn off the computer when I thought of something else I wanted to research. I typed in "bee balm" and waited. After a moment, pictures of a pretty red flower appeared. The flower heads looked like Animal the Muppet, all shaggy and fly-away looking. Bee balm was an herb, I read, closely related to oregano and used as an antiseptic and a stimulant. It was also known as Bergamot.

This caught my attention. There was a Bergamot Road a few miles west of us, with a greenhouse where I bought the mulch for our backyard last summer. I brought up Mapquest and fiddled with it until I found the road. It wasn't long, just a curving thin line cutting through the river bottoms . . . through Dixie Township.

"Away Down South," I murmured. Surely this was too much to be a coincidence. Follow the bee balm . . . follow Bergamot Road . . . in Dixie. Was it really that simple? Was the code just a substitution, a related word taking the place of the key word? If so, the Black Donnellys might not refer to the whole story of the unfortunate Irish family, the TV show, *or* the band, but simply to one word that could substitute for it. I played with a few combinations, trying to pick out words from my reading that jumped out at me as important enough to warrant a cryptic message, but only one scenario made sense. Was the writer of the code trying to record something about a massacre?

I forgot all about lunch waiting to be made and Andrew's contained circle of destruction in the garage. For the next thirty minutes, I prowled the Internet looking for reports of a multiple murder in Dixie Township in the last twenty years but found nothing I thought fit the bill. I expanded the search to the surrounding area, but still nothing.

I scrubbed my hands through my hair, making it stand up like Billy Idol's bleached brush cut. If the note did in fact refer to Dixie Township, as I thought, it made sense to say Angus must have found the note here in the Port Dover area—not, say, in Seattle. So wasn't it safe to assume that it referred to a local event? If nothing else, I could reasonably assume that the writer of the note was probably someone from this area who had something to do with—or at least was familiar with—Bergamot Road.

If the mysterious writer of this note had meant to preserve the details of a murder—maybe just in case something happened to *him*—wouldn't he have just written it down plainly so the finder could understand it? And why wouldn't he have just gone to the police with the information in the first place and not written anything at all? And who would hint at a grisly murder and sign it "Love, Dad"? None of this made any sense.

Maybe if I went to Bergamot Road, the next step would become clear to me. And a visit to the Black Donnelly museum in Lucan might be in order as well. It wasn't more than a two-hour drive down Highway 24 from where we lived, though I'd never been there.

Andrew had grown tired of the play dough and was feeding bits of it to Chairman Meow and squashing the rest of it into his ears (Andrew's, not the cat's). I rescued Andrew from the high chair, gathered the clay into the plastic container so it wouldn't dry out (I'd long ago given up trying to separate the colors), and settled on the living room floor to play a game of Candyland with him. This lasted about five minutes, and then he drew the card with the Queen Frostine snowflake, and my fate was pretty much wrapped up.

"You won." I cheered, clapped for him, and gathered up the pieces. "What would you like to do next? Would you like to watch a movie?"

Ordinarily, I didn't like using electronics to subdue a toddler, but admittedly, electronics never failed to do the job, and the housework *had* been somewhat neglected of late.

"Car fan," he said, jumping to his feet and going to the cupboard where we kept the DVDs. "Car fan" was what he called helicopters, and I knew which cartoon he wanted to watch, the one with talking vehicles and some inane plot about saving a fire engine named Charlie from falling off a mountain. I plopped him in front of the TV and put the DVD in.

But while I made sandwiches for lunch and washed down the fridge and scrubbed the kitchen floor, my mind churned in a circular fashion.

Who had written the note Angus had found? Someone with a knowledge of the area, if my assumptions were correct. Where had Angus found the note? Who was it who had recently mentioned to me . . . ?

Then I had it. I tossed down my washrag and went to find the phone.

It took a little doing, but I finally got Constable Donetti on the phone. He remembered me and told me no progress had been made on the case. I told him I hadn't heard any more from Angus, nor had there been any word to any of his colleagues at the school. Newton had checked.

"You said something the other day," I told him. "When I told you Angus had bought the old Victorian house, you said you knew the place, and you called it something, but I don't recall what."

"The old Philpott place, you mean?"

"That was it. The former owners were named Philpott?"

"Yes. Warren Philpott. But he died about a year ago—well, I guess that's when your Mr. Puddicombe bought the place."

I thought about the WP logo at the top of the blue paper. Did it stand for Warren Philpott? I felt a tingle of excitement prick my scalp.

"Do you know if he had any children? Are any of the Philpott family still around anywhere?"

"I think his daughter—the one who must have sold the house to Mr. Puddicombe—is still living around here. She's married now though. Wendy something. I went to school with her. But I don't know her married name . . . Wait. Yes, I do. It's Wendy DeRuvo. She married an Italian guy from over in Carlisle. Yeah, that's it—DeRuvo. One of the neighbors might know how to reach her. Why the questions, Mrs. Fisher?"

"I don't know yet," I replied honestly, "but I'm trying to think of any angle that might tell me where Angus is or why someone would want to abduct him."

"We don't technically know it's an abduction," the Constable chided me gently. "Right now, it's still just a missing person's case. There's no evidence of foul play."

"Except that his car is in his driveway and his lunch is in the microwave. Except for the fact that Angus phoned me to say he was being held. Except for the fact that Angus never would have simply not shown up for the first day of school unless something were prohibiting him from getting there."

"How do you know what's in his microwave, Mrs. Fisher?"

I waved a hand he couldn't see, wiping away the irrelevant. "You need to treat this as an abduction," I said firmly.

"I asked—"

"He didn't just wander off."

"Yes, well, you keep me posted if you learn anything," Donetti said with what sounded distinctly like a sigh.

I wondered if the police had discovered yet that someone had ransacked Angus's house. But I couldn't ask, or he'd really know I'd been inside the place. "You too," I said.

He was chuckling when I hung up the phone.

* * *

Directory assistance found only one DeRuvo in Carlisle and no others in the immediate area. I phoned the Carlisle number, and a raspy-voiced elderly man answered.

I introduced myself and explained that I was trying to locate a Wendy DeRuvo.

"Yes, that's my son Tony's wife," the man said. "But they don't live here."

"I'd like to reach them if I could," I said. "Would you be able to give me their number, please?"

"Well, now, I don't know that they'd want me to do that," he hesitated.

"Quite right. You don't know me," I said. "What if I give you my number and you pass it on to them and ask Wendy to call me?"

"I suppose I could do that. They'd be at work now, but I can tell them tonight."

I thanked him and gave him my number. Then I fetched Andrew, and we walked down to the library to pick out some new children's books, then swung by Sally's Bakery on the way home and got some crusty Italian bread to go with our chicken dinner. It was an idyllic September afternoon, the air crisp and golden, and Andrew was in a sweet mood because he didn't have to compete with anyone for my attention. He was the only family member who liked it when school resumed in the fall.

Once everyone returned home, we ate dinner, cleared it away, and then the children scattered to toys, computer, homework, or piano practice. I cornered Newton in the kitchen and told him what I'd managed to puzzle out so far from the code. He listened to my conjectures with a thoughtful frown, and when I finished, he nodded.

"I think Bergamot Road and Dixie Township are reasonably sound assumptions," he agreed. "The WP likely refers to Warren Philpott, and I think it's safe to conclude he wrote the note. Maybe Angus discovered it while renovating the house. Is there a connection between the Philpott family and the Donnellys?"

"I don't know. But the note isn't necessarily about the Black Donnellys," I said. "If the note is using a simple substitution code, then I'm theorizing that the Black Donnellys are simply a code name for a different massacre, perhaps a more recent multiple murder somewhere around here. I looked online but didn't see any mention of such an event in this part of Ontario in the last two decades."

"Angus hid the note in the heat vent in the new office," Newton said. "Why? What made Angus think the note was important and not just gibberish?"

"It must have jumped out at him, either the wording itself or the way the note was found in the first place. Whatever the reason, he obviously took steps to preserve it. He may have thought it contained the clues to a hidden treasure, the same thing we thought at first until we learned what—or rather *who*—the Black Donnellys were. Of course, being a professor of Canadian history, Angus might have known immediately who the Black Donnellys were and figured out the intent of the note quicker than we did."

"If, in fact, we're correct about the intent of the note." Newton scrubbed his fingers through his hair. The effect on him was more Stan Laurel than Billy Idol. "Can we say for certain that the note is about a more recent murder or massacre? I mean, the simplest explanation is usually the correct one. *Could* it in fact be about the Black Donnellys?"

"Why encode the rest of the note and not the key topic the note is about?" I argued—er, reasoned calmly. I picked up a paper plate and fanned myself with it.

"But you said you found no mention of a multiple murder in this area."

"Maybe the timeframe I searched wasn't correct. Or maybe it's a murder no one has discovered yet."

"And if that information comes out, it might be harmful to someone now," Newton said, nodding.

"Which is all the more reason to think it's about a fairly recent event," I said. "It could have ramifications for someone now, so they took steps to make sure the information didn't come to light."

"You mean they murdered Warren Philpott to keep him from speaking? Not knowing he'd written the clues down in the note?" Newton looked startled.

My mind hadn't actually made that leap. "I was just thinking it was the motive for abducting Angus. But I suppose it could be linked to Philpott's death."

"You haven't satisfactorily explained how said murderer became aware of Angus's knowledge of the note."

"I know. I don't know." I frowned, befuddled.

"In any case, I think it makes sense that the note refers to some relatively recent event," Newton said. "If it were about a very old event, with the perpetrators long dead, I doubt someone would be so anxious about keeping it quiet now."

"True," I said. "It seems unlikely they would be so concerned about preserving the good reputation of someone generations after the event that they would resort to abduction and—well—perhaps worse. I mean, your great-great-grandfather was hanged as a horse thief, but you consider it an interesting story to tell dinner guests, not something to hide to save the family from disgrace."

A funny look crossed Newton's face, but he just shook his head.

"Can I drop you off at work tomorrow and keep the car?" I asked. "I want to go wander around Dixie Township."

Newton drew back, looking at me anxiously. "I don't believe that's a good idea."

"I promise I won't get out of the car or approach anyone with questions or otherwise stick my nose into any dangerous places," I said solemnly. "I'm not an utter fool, Newton. I just want to drive around a little and get the lay of the land."

* * *

The next morning went smoothly, according to the now-established routine. Everyone departed on time with backpacks, lunches, permission slips, and the requisite money to their various schools.

I pride myself in the seamless functioning of the household even on busy school mornings. Even when I'm more than a little distracted with other events.

Isaac, gloating that he was not in school, changed his tune a bit when I told him I expected him to drop off ten résumés that day before supper. He would be leaving for his mission in December (he'd recently received his call to Brazil, but it always took awhile to get a visa), but if he thought he was going to sit around playing video games all day between now and then while his siblings were in school, he was mistaken. He would need every penny he could scrape together by the time he left for the Missionary Training Center. Grumbling, he set down the controller and went off to print out the résumés.

After I'd cleaned up the kitchen from breakfast, I strapped Andrew into his car seat and headed for Dixie Township, dropping Newton off at his office on the way. Newton repeated his warnings, with which he had regaled me for an hour the previous evening, about venturing into any situation that looked the slightest bit shaky. I assured him once again—admittedly with some acerbity—that I would do nothing foolish or rash and drove off, leaving him standing in the parking lot.

Dixie Township lay in the river bottoms that snaked through the surrounding farmland roughly a twenty-minute drive northwest of Port Dover. The area was intermittently swampy and sparsely settled, autumn-brown fields interspersed with stands of dead trees up to their ankles in murky water. The only town nearby large enough to appear on the map was Carlisle, which was little more than a collection of old houses at a crossroads. One of them presumably belonged to Tony DeRuvo's father, who had apparently not passed on my message. No one had phoned me.

There wasn't much else to the hamlet, just a derelict gas station and a hamburger joint with a burnt-out sign. I'd never had much cause to drive out this way before, and I couldn't see why the place had become a settlement at all, unless people had first settled there because of the river. Even that looked humble and neglected though. No more than five feet across, it bubbled along between long-grassed banks looking totally insufficient to have ever supported a mill or shipping industry or anything that would explain the presence of the little town.

Bergamot was a two-lane country road with a borrow pit on each side and no shoulders. It followed along the meandering river for a way, passed the greenhouse I'd visited last summer, and then turned to form one of the crossroads at the center of Carlisle. I followed it through and out the other side, past fields of ripe corn and grain the color of Andrew's hair. Andrew cheered whenever we saw the occasional cow. The few houses I passed looked sleepy, with weeds in the gravel driveways and mailboxes leaning at crazy angles as if they were too tired to stand up. I wondered what it would be like to grow up as a child in such a tiny village. I couldn't imagine my kids surviving this far from town when they were so used to movie theaters and friends all within walking distance.

Granted, Port Dover wasn't huge, but in the summertime, it swelled with tourists coming to the lake, and there was always some kind of activity going on. There were art classes and concerts and pizza parties and dances on the beach. What did teenagers do for fun here? Where could they find summer jobs? How far away was the nearest school? I felt suddenly depressed and sorry for the hopelessness of the place.

And yet, maybe I was wrong. I spied some signs of cheerful industry here and there: bright laundry on a line, flapping smartly in the breeze; a zippy-looking, lemon-colored Vespa parked in a driveway; a child's blue, plastic wading pool standing in the sun next to a swing set.

The road entered a forest of thick pine trees and ran for a while, the trees standing like walls on each side of the road and blocking my view. But even here I spied inviting-looking trails wandering away from the road, into the forest at intervals, and I pictured kids playing explorers under the trees, having picnics in clearings, wading in the river. There were signs that children played here sometimes. A plywood playhouse huddled under a spreading tree, and someone had painted it an unlikely shade of pink and hoisted a pirate flag above it. I imagined playing there, far from a mother's watchful eye, and a sense of its magic touched me. Maybe life in the country had its advantages. I rolled my window down and breathed in the scent of pine and wet earth.

Then I was out the other side of the forest and approaching another tiny village of rundown farmhouses. There was a bent sign saying "Bowden Falls," and then Bergamot met Sundown Street and ended in a T intersection, and I knew I had left Dixie Township. There was a pizza parlor, a McDonalds, a video store, and another empty Shell gas station at the junction.

I turned and pulled the car around to head back the way I had come, deflated. I wasn't sure what I was looking for. How could I solve a puzzle when I had no idea of the pattern or picture it was to form? I drove home no wiser than I'd come.

When I got home, the phone was ringing, and I hurried to answer it. The caller introduced herself as Wendy DeRuvo.

"My father-in-law said you wanted to speak with me?"

"Yes! Thanks so much for calling back. I know this is out of the blue. But I wanted to ask—Just to be sure you're the right person, could you please tell me if your maiden name is Philpott?"

"Yes, it is," she said.

Bull's-eye.

"My friend Angus Puddicombe bought your old house on Rasmussen Road," I told her.

"Oh! Yes." Her voice became warmer. I detected a slight British accent when she spoke. "I remember Mr. Puddicombe."

"I understand you sold him the place after your father died?"

"Yes. He was planning to sell it anyway. Daddy had had a heart attack that spring and didn't feel he could keep the place up on his own. My mother died several years ago, you see, and I'd married and moved away by then. My husband and I live in Brantford. Daddy's house was too big to live in on his own. So he was getting it ready to put on the market when another heart attack took him."

A heart attack. Not murder, then.

"I'm sorry to hear that," I said, ashamed of my relief.

"Then again, Mr. Puddicombe thought it was just the right size to live in on *his* own. He had no family, as I recall. So I guess to each his own, eh? Our little apartment is just right for us, I'll tell you. So easy to keep up. Though we are planning to build a house on some land we own by Carlisle once the kids outgrow this place."

She seemed ready to settle in for a long chin-wag, so I jumped to the point. "I'll tell you why I'm calling. Angus disappeared almost two weeks ago," I told her. "We're not sure where he's gone or if foul play is involved."

"Oh dear! I'm sorry to hear that," she said. My linguistic training kicked in as I analyzed her voice. Her accent was definitely English, probably from the southeast of England, made more pronounced by her surprise. Not London, I didn't think. "I hope he's all right," she added.

"Thank you. I'm trying to explore every avenue and learn all I can in hopes of finding out where he's gone," I told her. And then I stopped because I didn't have a clue what questions to ask her now that I had her on the line.

"Certainly, I'm happy to help you any way I can," she said sincerely.

"A little while after he disappeared, I got a strange phone call from Angus. It was very staticky and hard to hear, but it sounded like he was saying he had found a note and now he was being held somewhere. Possibly abducted because of what he'd found."

"Really! What was in the note?"

"We're guessing he found the same thing we found when we searched the house," I said. "There was a small note, handwritten, tucked away. I'm wondering if it could have been written by your father and left behind when you sold the house. I'll read it to you, and you can tell me if you recognize it."

I read her the enigmatic note. When I'd finished, there was a pause, and then Wendy said cheerfully, "He was always one for games, Dad was. It sounds like another of his treasure hunts. But I don't remember that one."

"Your father used to devise treasure hunts?" I asked excitedly.

"Every occasion called for one—birthdays, Christmas, even to find my Easter basket. He always led me on terrific goose chases all over the neighborhood. Some got pretty elaborate. The hunt was always as fun as the actual gift at the end. Once he even had my friends and me end up out on a boat on Lake Erie. But as I said, the set of clues you just read doesn't ring a bell with me."

"You've never heard it before?"

"Never."

"We're assuming Angus found it somewhere in the house when he moved in."

"We sold the house furnished, but I thought we'd cleaned out his drawers and things pretty well before we sold the place. If Dad wrote it, he never gave it to me. You know, maybe he hadn't completed it yet. He hadn't done up a hunt for some years. I mean, I'm grown up and gone now. I think the last hunt we had was when I graduated from college. He bought me a necklace as a graduation gift, gold with a little diamond pendant. That one was hidden in my grandmother's knitting basket, as I recall. In London."

"London, England?" I gulped.

"London, Ontario. I don't know if the one you have really means anything or not. I suspect it didn't get finished, and that's why Dad didn't pass it on to me. I doubt it leads anywhere. I'm sorry. I wish I could be of more help."

"If I scan it and e-mail it to you, could you tell me if you can figure out the clues? You're used to the way your father wrote up treasure hunts. Maybe you'll understand what he was saying."

"I suppose so," she said, sounding amused. "If it's important to you."

"It might help us find Angus," I said, feeling a little cold at her tone.

"Oh. Yes, of course," she said quickly as if just remembering Angus.

"Besides," I added, "it *could* lead to something, a gift of some sort, don't you think? Maybe you weren't meant to find it until after his death."

"I can't think what it might be," she said. "I mean, his will laid out all of the gifts and bequests. But yes, I admit that does sound like Dad, having one last game."

"I'm sorry to ask, but do you think he would have had the health or energy to put together a really elaborate hunt right before he died? You said he'd had a first heart attack, and I presume he would have put together a final hunt when he—er—had an intimation that maybe time was running out. And it *did* run out before he had a chance to give you this last set of clues."

"He slowed down a lot after that first attack, but he was still well enough to carry out his daily tasks. He worked right up to the end," she said. "Why do you ask?"

"I just wanted to get a sense of whether we were dealing with a fairly straightforward hunt, with the prize hidden in the laundry basket in the basement, or a really elaborate hunt and the end prize will be on a church roof in Belize," I explained.

She laughed. "Dad's hunts were never simple, Mrs.—I've forgotten your name."

"Fisher. Annie Fisher."

"Mrs. Fisher. If Dad devised that hunt, the prize won't be in the house. But I've never known him to end up out of province. As I said, he may not have even hidden the prize, whatever it was. He may not have had time to finish it. It may lead to nothing."

"Still, it's worth looking into. It's all we have to go on at the moment." I wrote down her e-mail address and promised to send a copy of the note as soon as possible; then I thanked her for her time. As I was about to hang up, though, I thought of another question. "Did your father ever discuss the Donnelly family with you? The Black Donnellys?" I asked.

"Are they a family? No, I'm sorry. I don't know who they might be."

"It's also the name of a TV show and a rock band. Are you familiar with either of those?"

"No. It does sound like a puzzle."

"Well, thank you anyway. We're not even sure this note has anything to do with Angus's disappearance, but I thought it worth a try," I told her. "Please let me know if anything occurs to you." I was about the hang up again when another thought occurred to me. "Oh! Peter Pan."

"What?"

"Your name. Wendy. It's from the story of Peter Pan."

"My parents didn't name me after Wendy in the story—I was actually named after my father's aunt Gwendolyn. But yes, Peter Pan was one of my favorite stories growing up. Because of my name, of course. Daddy read it to me often when I was small. I even named my dog Nanna, though he was a male poodle." She paused. "I guess that isn't very useful."

"You never know what may become significant down the road," I said. "Thank you for speaking with me, Wendy."

"Good luck, and please let me know if you find him. I rather liked Mr. Puddicombe," she said. "It would be a shame if the house were empty again."

With some fiddling, I managed to scan the note and e-mail it to the address she had given me. If anyone could figure out the clues, she could.

* * *

I picked Newton up from work that evening, but Andrew was noisy and talkative in the backseat, there were errands to run on the way home, and then there was the rush to fix supper and listen to the children's accounts of their days, so I didn't really have time to speak to Newton about my day's events beyond reporting I'd contacted Warren Philpott's daughter, who had confirmed her father's penchant for treasure hunts. I had a Relief Society activity at the church and was running late, so I hurried off as the rest of the family was sitting down to supper. I would grab something to eat later.

Ordinarily, I enjoyed having a night out with women friends, and usually, the activities were educational or valuable service projects. For instance, one month we learned to change the oil in our cars, and one month we knitted chemo caps for the hospital's cancer ward. Tonight was Sister Wilson teaching a class on packing school lunches that would entice, nourish, and basically bribe kids into eating. She advocated drawing silly faces on their boiled eggs, curling ham into curly hair around a rice-ball head with asparagus, olive, and peanut facial features, and making omelet wraps with steamed broccoli and shrimp stuffing. I pictured my children opening their lunchboxes in front of their friends to find their food smiling up at them. They'd be laughed out of the cafeteria. Or they'd open their beat-up backpacks to find smashed rice and bits of egg stuck to their binders. Or they'd develop food poisoning from eating eggs and shrimp that had sat unrefrigerated for hours. Or they'd start a food fight with the cold broccoli.

We watched her fuss over a cow-shaped muffin with spots made of kelp for twenty minutes, and then the squirming woman next to me,

Sister Davis, raised her hand. "Sister Wilson, it's taken you thirty minutes to arrange one sack lunch," she said.

"Yes?" Sister Wilson blinked innocently. "Nutrition and creativity take time, dear. Aren't your children worth a little extra effort?"

"I have to pack three sack lunches every morning," the woman said hesitantly. "I would have to get up at four in the morning to fit it in."

I pondered this. Seven lunches (assuming Newton declined to have his rice ball coiffed with ham curls) would take three and a half hours. Gulp.

One of the other women started nodding like a bobblehead ornament in a car's rear window. "And I can't send peanut products to the grade school. There's an allergy alert."

"And don't you think the little plastic Bento box you're using is kind of expensive?" someone else piped up.

"They're only a few dollars," Sister Wilson protested, still smiling sweetly.

"But my Benji's lunch bag ends up on the school roof at least five times a school year," the woman explained. "That gets expensive after awhile."

"Personally, I don't think we should have to bribe our kids into eating. I mean, are they going to grow up into adults who expect their boiled eggs to smile at them all the time?" someone else asked.

"When I was in school, we got a lettuce sandwich and a dill pickle. Same thing every day, and we were expected to eat it. We never complained," another added.

"My Sarah keeps trading her lunch for Pokémon cards," another said.

Sister Wilson was starting to get red in the face. I shifted uncomfortably. "Rebellion in the ranks," I murmured.

The Relief Society president stood. At six foot one, Sister Pierce commanded attention merely by standing. The room fell silent. She eyed each of us individually with a sharp blue gaze. Finally, she spoke. "Sister Wilson is just giving us suggestions to improve nutrition and promote enjoyment," she said firmly. "I don't expect each of you to pack this elaborate a lunch every morning. In fact, it's probably better if your kids learn to pack their own lunches in the long run."

There were still some women who looked skeptical, glancing at each other with dissatisfaction and shaking their heads.

I hesitated, then put my hand up.

"Yes, Sister Fisher?" Sister Pierce nodded at me.

I wasn't sure I could put what I was thinking into words, but I felt I needed to try. "I think God has given everyone an inherent need for creativity," I said. "It's part of our spiritual makeup. God is a creator, and

He's given each of His children a little bit of that same yearning to create. A few of us might compose beautiful songs or knit amazing sweaters. Others might write technical manuals or bake perfect pie crusts. Some create welcoming environments in their homes or plant lovely gardens. Some design elaborate treasure hunts for children." I couldn't help throwing that last bit in. I could see the other women begin to nod.

"That's true. My mother-in-law made fantastic birthday cakes you wouldn't believe," Sister Davis, who had started it all, said eagerly.

"And some of us create a lot of noise with musical instruments," I added, and they laughed. They had all had occasion to hear our family band. I shot Sister Wilson a smile. The redness had left her face, replaced by a look of relief. She smiled back. "That inherent creativity will always find some way to show itself in our lives," I finished. "It can come out in any form, even in sack lunches. And even a humble sack lunch can show your kids that their happiness is important to you."

Sister Pierce looked over the room of now grinning women and then back at me. "Thank you, Sister Fisher."

* * *

When I got home, I could hear Newton's voice in the kitchen.

"Lentil soup does not constitute a noxious substance, and you can't report us to Children's Aid for serving it."

I went in and found Ethan sitting arms folded at the otherwise empty table, a lone bowl of soup grown cold before him. His face was flushed with stubbornness and anger. Newton stood over him, hands on hips, fuming. They both glared at me as I entered, clearly wanting me to resolve the deadlock they'd gotten into. I knew from the look on Newton's face that he was racking his brains for a way to resolve the confrontation with Ethan's dignity and autonomy intact but still with parental authority upheld.

I said nothing. Setting down my purse, I went to the fridge and drew out a slice of luncheon meat (anonymously pink and unidentifiable). I sliced it into curly strips and heaped them around the top edge of Ethan's bowl as hair. Then I cut two rounds of cheddar cheese for eyes, floated half a cherry tomato for a nose, and added a curved strip of bread crust for a mouth.

"There," I said, handing Ethan his spoon. "You don't like your soup, but it likes you. It's smiling, see?"

I waited. Sure enough, Ethan looked at it a moment, then laughed and ate it all up without further ado. I nodded my head at Newton as if to say, "There you go, then!" and left the kitchen. That article writer hadn't known a fig about happiness or self-fulfillment, I thought. Caring for other people *was* self-fulfillment, pure and simple. Having someone to care *for* was happiness.

* * *

Isaac was lying on the couch in the basement rec room, reading a Bones comic. I leaned over the back of the couch and smiled down at him sweetly until he finally sighed and lowered the book.

"Ten," he said. "The Quick Mart, Simply Foods, Giant Tiger, two theaters, two gas stations, the dollar store, Pizza Hut, and Pizza Bella. Pizza Bella didn't say they were hiring, but I left one anyway."

"Good boy," I said. "Be sure to call them next week to follow up." I went around to the other side of the couch and sat down. He obligingly pulled his feet out of the way to make room.

"I want to ask you something," I said. He eyed me warily. "It's nothing. I just wanted to ask you what you want to be when you grow up."

He frowned. "You know. I'm going to apply to a computer engineering program."

"I know. I just meant . . . well, is that what you want to *be*? A computer engineer?"

Isaac sat up straighter and snapped his head to toss his longish brown hair out of his eyes. (He would be cutting it short come December—I figured I wouldn't make a fuss over the length of it meanwhile.) "That's usually what it means when a person applies to the computer engineering program, yes," he said patiently.

"And what does your friend Todd want to be?"

"I don't know. He's working at Walmart this summer. I think he's goimg to the community college this fall to become an electrician."

"And what about Steve?"

"He got a job fixing cars at that place on Dunstell."

"And Paul?"

"He's cleaning pools for the summer. He says it's a good company. I think he might just stay with that." He snapped his head again, and I got another brief glimpse of eyeball. "Why all the questions, Mom?"

"I remember when you all were little. You got a big refrigerator box and covered it in tinfoil and pretended it was a rocket. You were all going to be astronauts when you grew up."

He chuckled, remembering. "Yeah, well."

"And there was the summer you watched *Backdraft* at Todd's place when his parents weren't home, and then you all decided you wanted to be firemen."

"Right."

"And Paul said for a while that he was thinking of being a brain surgeon."

"Just because he watched that documentary."

I sighed. "So what I'm asking, I guess, is at what point did you all give up those big dreams? When did you stop wanting to be astronauts and firemen and surgeons and settle for being grocery baggers and pool boys?"

Isaac put a large hand on my shoulder. "Been going through the baby books again, Mom?"

"No, I'm not being sentimental. It's a legitimate question," I said.

"Well, I can't speak for my friends," Isaac said with a little smile, "but I gave up on the astronaut idea when I hit grade nine math."

I thought a moment about what had happened at the church tonight, and then I said, "I just want you to know it's okay, whatever you choose. Whatever your friends choose. If they are happy being grocery baggers and electricians, that is just as fine as if they became astronauts and brain surgeons. All that matters is that they can support their families honorably and love what they do. Even if it's drawing faces on boiled eggs."

"O-o-okay," Isaac said, looking at me askance. "Uh . . . I appreciate that."

As I went back up the stairs, I heard him sigh.

"My parents are so weird."

Chapter Five

At two in the morning, I suddenly sat straight up in bed, wide awake. I had the distinct feeling I'd missed something obvious, something important.

"What?" Newton mumbled, half asleep on his side of the bed. He sleeps on his stomach with his face pressed into his pillow. I don't understand how he doesn't suffocate.

I pushed my covers off, feeling unbearably hot. "I was just thinking about Angus and that code. Are you awake enough to discuss it?"

There was a pause, a groan, and then Newton turned over and sat up, rubbing his whiskery jaw. "I am now," he said somewhat peevishly. "What else have you been thinking?" I had finally managed to brief him before bedtime about my drive that day and my conversation with Wendy.

"So far, if we're correct, the code has been a matter of substituting some words for others. Hence, Away Down South is Dixie Township."

"*Hence?*" He peered at the glowing digital clock. "It's two in the morning, and you use a word like *hence?*"

"And bee balm is Bergamot Road. Are you following me?"

He nodded, yawned enormously, and scrubbed his eyes with his palms.

"I'm positive Wendy substitutes for Peter Pan. I think Wendy Philpott DeRuvo is key to this somehow. We can assume the message was meant for her, but her father died before he could give it to her."

"Warren Philpott, you mean." Newton was never at his best when first woken up, especially in the middle of the night. He pulled the blankets up around his shoulders and shivered. "Is the window open?"

"Keep up with me, dear. But it's more than the fact that the note was meant for her. She's mentioned *in* the note. *She* is one of the clues."

"But she said the message meant nothing to her."

"Well, no, I was replaying the conversation in my head, and she only said she hadn't heard it before. But that doesn't mean she doesn't know what it means."

"And she said she'd let you know if she figures it out," Newton said. "We'll have to trust that she will. I mean, whatever the prize is at the end, it's obviously hers. We wouldn't claim it."

He crawled out of bed and shut the window.

"I am not interested in the prize, only in what it has to do with Angus's disappearance. But I'm overlooking something. I can feel it. My heart is trying to tell me something, and I don't know what it is. Maybe we need to find out more about What's-His-Bucket. Warren Philpott."

"Such as if he witnessed the Donnelly massacre in 1880?"

"I'm trying to take this seriously, Newton." I sniffed. "And we agreed that the note refers to a more recent murder or murders, not literally the Black Donnellys."

"You agreed to that," he said. "I withhold judgment until I have further information. For all we know, it refers literally to the Donnellys." He crawled back under the covers, yanking them up around his ears.

"Oh, honestly, Newton. What more could be revealed about the original Black Donnelly story than has already been revealed? The names of the vigilantes were known at the time. The young farmhand under the bed witnessed everything, and his account was published in contemporary newspapers. There's a museum all about it. I can't imagine what else could be discovered about the story that would alarm anyone living now."

"All right, I concede the point. It's about a different event, then, likely a similar one, ergo a more recent murder or murders."

"*Ergo?*" I shot him a teasing look, but the effect was lost in the dark. "At least it sounds like Philpott died of natural causes. One less murder to worry about. I feel like we need to know more about him though. The mind behind the note."

"Tell you what. On my way to work tomorrow—er—today, I'll stop at the library and look at old newspapers from last year. I'll see if I can find Warren Philpott's obituary."

"Good idea," I said. "And please see if you can get home before the kids get home from school. I want to take another drive along Bergamot. Maybe it will jog loose whatever I'm trying to find in my head."

* * *

Wednesday morning was cooler, with a distinct taste of autumn in the air. The maple trees were touched with just a hint of gold, and there was a smell that made me think of burning leaves, thick sweaters, and hot chocolate. I tried not to think about the fact that Angus had now been missing for two weeks. I tried not to think about hot chocolate. Drat Dr. Post anyway.

After slicking up the house, throwing in a load of laundry, starting a crockpot of pulled pork for supper, putting together my Relief Society lesson for the following Sunday, and hitting the bathroom, I bundled Andrew up and took him outside. Our morning walk down to the library, just the two of us, had turned into a regular habit now. I enjoyed the mother-son time, and Andrew ploughed through picture books insatiably the way Caleb ploughed through pizza. Sometimes he even slept with books in his arms like stuffed animals. With the progress he was showing in his reading game, he would be able to read simple books by himself by Christmas.

As we passed a bus stop, Andrew pointed to a pair of blue tennis shoes sitting on the sidewalk. I couldn't help shaking my head at them. How could someone forget a whole pair of shoes? I imagined the bus coming by and whisking the passenger away so quickly that they were yanked right out of their shoes. Why was it that you often found shoes on the road or in the gutters? Never hats or socks or shirts. Only shoes. We were a nation of forgetful, barefoot people.

After the library, we ended up at Baskin Robbins for vanilla frozen yogurt eaten from paper cups with diminutive pink spoons just the right size for Andrew's little fist. This reminded me that he would need mittens before the snow flew because he had lost his at the end of last winter. So when we finished eating, we swung by Giant Tiger to buy some. We found some Andrew liked, bright purple knit with a porcine motif on the cuffs. They were pricier than Walmart's, but I tended to avoid the big box stores whenever possible, partly out of principle and partly because once in, it was impossible to get out again without purchasing much more than one intended. Giant Tiger was Canadian-owned, so it felt patriotic to shop there. And Walmart was farther away anyway, requiring a car to get there. Even in the smaller store, I got distracted by a sale on stainless-steel water bottles and plastic Bento boxes, and by the time we dragged home with our purchases, it was almost lunch time.

As soon as I entered the house, I knew something was wrong. It was the same sort of feeling I'd felt when we'd entered Angus's house to find it topsy-turvy. I stiffened, stopping cold in the doorway, all senses on high alert. Beside me, Andrew immediately caught my tension and paused, frowning up at me.

I couldn't see anything amiss at first glance. Of course, with ten people living in the house, our house was topsy-turvy anyway. But there was something out of place, something messier than usual that I couldn't put my finger on. It wasn't until I'd kicked off my shoes, put our bags in the kitchen, and come back into the living room that I noticed the filing cabinet drawer was open.

We kept all of our important documents, bills, insurance papers and other such stuff in a two-drawer, wood filing cabinet beside the couch. Its top served as a table, holding a lamp and a set of rattan coasters. The only people who went into the filing cabinet were Newton and myself. The kids knew better than to touch it and had no interest in doing so. I knew for a fact that the drawer had been closed when Andrew and I had left for the library because I remembered vacuuming around it that morning.

Cautiously now, I looked around the rest of the floor but found nothing else I could say for certain had been disturbed. I went up the stairs and peeked into each bedroom along the hall, seeing nothing unexpected. Jane's hairbrush lay in the middle of her floor. Ethan had dumped Legos all over his bed. The usual. But when I reached the bedroom Newton and I shared, I froze, one hand lifted to push the door open. I had heard something inside. Biting my lower lip, I shoved the door open.

Something heavy and dark hurtled past me, bumping into my shoulder and shoving me back against the hall wall. I glimpsed broad shoulders and the sole of a boot and then the person was gone down the stairs. It took me a second too long to regain my balance, catch my breath, and, with a shriek, launch myself after him. I am not a petite woman, but I am fast on my feet, thanks to years of dodging Frisbees, sprinting after school buses with forgotten backpacks, and heading off runaway toddlers bent on rushing into traffic. But the intruder had too big a head start on me. Before I could reach the bottom of the stairs, I heard heavy running steps in the lower hall and then the front door smacking back against the wall as the person wrenched it open. Newton would have something to say about the damage done to the wall, I was sure.

Andrew stood, startled, in the center of the living room. The front door gaped open, and the yard beyond was empty. I ran out onto the driveway in my stockinged feet and looked up and down the road. There was a small white car parked in front of the neighbor's house, the driver's door just closing. Before I could reach it, it screeched away from the curb and vanished around the corner onto Bleasdale Road. I heard myself scream irrationally, "Stop!"

As if they would oblige.

I didn't give chase. Even if I'd had a car, by the time I could have retrieved my keys and strapped Andrew in, the white car would have been long gone. And would I really have wanted to take my little boy on a high-speed car chase anyway? The practical thing would be to call the police and let them do the chasing.

I bent over with my hands on my knees for a second, catching my breath, furious with myself for not seeing the license plate or make of the car. Had it been parked in the street when we'd come home? It must have been, but I hadn't noticed.

I straightened and tiptoed in my socks to avoid the gravel scattered on the driveway as I went back inside. A pain in the ball of my right foot told me I hadn't succeeded in avoiding it on my way out. I closed and locked the front door behind me. My heart was pounding, and for a moment, I felt I was going to be sick. So much for avoiding sudden surprises! I hurried past Andrew again and went back up to my bedroom.

The intruder hadn't had time to do a proper job of tossing the place. The mattress had been looked under and lay crooked on the box springs (thank goodness I'd already moved my baggie of money to the freezer), and the drawers of both bedside tables were open. Some of my papers and books lay on the floor. But other than these small disturbances, I couldn't immediately see anything missing or broken.

I retrieved my scriptures, which had unfortunately become part of the mess on the floor and, running my hand over the undamaged cover, placed them gently on the bed. There was a faint smell in the room, as if the intruder had maybe been a cigarette smoker. I stood with hands on hips, surveying everything, but I couldn't see that anything was unaccounted for, not even the jewelry in the wooden box on my dresser. Not your usual thief, then.

I went back downstairs and checked the back door for signs of forced entry. It was unlocked, and I stood trying to think if I'd walked out and left it unlocked inadvertently. Probably. I hadn't expected to be gone very long this morning when Andrew and I had first set out, and our neighborhood, with the summer tourists gone, was normally considered safe.

I went into the kitchen and lifted the phone. I noticed with detached interest that my fingers were shaking as I punched in Newton's number. Andrew was still standing rooted to the floor, staring at me, and I held out one arm to him to beckon him to my side as I held the phone with the other hand. He came over to lean against my leg.

"Are you okay, honey? Did that frighten you?" Just then Newton answered, and I turned quickly to the phone. "Newt, it's Annie. Andrew and I went out for a couple of hours this morning, and when we got back, there was someone in the house." I told him quickly what I'd seen.

"Male? Build? Age? Distinguishing features?" Newton didn't waste time on idle chat, nor did he insult me by fussing over whether I was all right. Obviously, I was all right, or I wouldn't be able to call.

"I got the sense it was a male, yes. A few inches taller than me, heavily built but a fast runner. All I glimpsed was broad shoulders, a black shirt and jeans, dark boots, like maybe hiking boots with a waffle sole. I got the impression he had dark hair, but I can't be sure, and I didn't see his face at all. And a smoker—he left the scent behind. A different brand than Angus smokes, I think. It smelled different."

"Don't touch anything. I'll be home in twenty minutes," Newton said. "Call the police and get them to dust for fingerprints. But . . . um . . . don't mention that the same guy tossed Angus's place."

"Officially, we don't know Angus's place was tossed. And we don't know that it *was* the same person." Andrew was pulling on my sleeve, and I caressed his golden head, shushing him.

"Annie, what are the odds? They were looking for something at Angus's house without success, and when they saw us go in and come out a couple of times, they figured we must have taken what they were searching for. And I'd bet my fuzzy slippers it's the paper with the coded message they were after." He paused, and then he said in a strangled voice, "They didn't get it, did they?"

"No, I have it here in my purse." It gave me the creeps to think we had been followed home.

"Good. Don't let it off your person. Call the police. I'll be there soon."

* * *

It wasn't Constable Donetti who responded to my report of the break-in but a slim, young officer named Stephens and his female partner Flaherty, who looked more like a high school cheerleader than a cop. Her blonde hair was pulled into a ponytail, and I saw the silver bands of a retainer around two of her top teeth. I didn't go into details with them, only told them my son and I had returned home to find a strange man in my room and that nothing appeared to be missing.

I was giving them a description of the man and the car, as best I could, when Newton walked in. He said nothing, only put his arm around my shoulders and listened as I spoke, and I felt myself lean into his comforting solidity. I felt immediately better, knowing he was there.

"I'm afraid that's all I can remember," I finished. "It happened so fast."

"You didn't get a look at his face?" Flaherty asked.

"Sorry, no."

"He had a mustache," Andrew piped up.

We all looked at him where he sat on the floor playing with two action figures. Spiderman was facing off against Scooby Doo.

"What was that, honey?" I asked gently.

"He had a bwown mustache," Andrew said.

"A big bushy mustache or a thin little mustache?" Flaherty coaxed.

"Fat," Andrew replied. "Like Mr. Potato Head."

The two officers looked at me, and I shrugged. "He ran past Andrew on his way to the door. I guess he got a better look at him than I did."

Flaherty wrote on her notepad and then knelt beside Andrew. In the friendly, squeaky voice adults tend to use with toddlers and puppies, she asked Andrew more about what the man had looked like. Andrew obliged in his lisping, broken English, and the officer managed to learn the man had blue eyes, was clean shaven other than the mustache, wore clompy brown boots with black laces, had black leather gloves on his hands, and had been perhaps just shorter than my six-foot-two husband.

"You have an observant little boy," Flaherty said with satisfaction as she stood and tucked away her notebook.

Andrew returned to his action figures with a little shrug, and I stood looking with new eyes at his bowed, curly head.

The examination of the bedroom and the filing cabinet took some time. I left the officers to it and went into the kitchen to check on the crockpot and pour myself some orange juice. I sat at the table and felt as if I'd run a mile. A long while later, I heard the front door close, and then Newton joined me in the kitchen.

"They're gone."

"Did you tell them about the note?"

"Yes. I told them everything we've been trying to figure out. Putting it into words, though, the whole assumption that it had anything to do with Angus's disappearance or our home invasion sounded pretty flimsy. I mean, how to explain Peter Pan and Thoreau?"

"How did you explain how you came by the note? Did you tell them we'd been in Angus's house?"

"I just said Angus had left the note where we would find it. They didn't press about that particular point, fortunately."

"Newton," I said, thinking hard. "Do you think it's a coincidence that the day after I tell Warren Philpott's daughter I found his note, someone tries to steal it from us?"

"Do you think she has something to do with it?" he asked, looking genuinely surprised. "I was thinking someone just saw us going into Angus's house and put two and two together."

"I don't know," I said. "I don't know what to think or who to trust."

"You read Wendy the note over the phone. You sent her a scanned image of it. She would realize we weren't trying to hide anything from her. Why go to the bother of trying to steal it?"

"True."

He brightened then and fetched his briefcase from the hall. He pulled a piece of paper from it and held it out to me.

"I did some research on my morning break. Warren Philpott's obituary."

The photocopy showed a picture of a square-faced, heavy man with Roosevelt's round glasses and a collar that looked too tight for his thick neck. The tribute was short.

"Warren Davies Philpott, respected financier, died August 2 of cardiac arrest. Born December 3, 1947, in Hailsham, Sussex, England, to Warren Pinter Philpott and Martha Mayes. Graduate of Dennington College, 1968. Immigrated to Canada in 1998. Head accountant and then chief executive officer of Lucan Investments for many years. Predeceased by his loving wife, Helen Marchant Philpott. Survived by his daughter, Wendy Philpott DeRuvo; son-in-law, Anthony DeRuvo; and grandson, Michael, of Brantford; and brother, Edward Philpott, of England. Warren will always be remembered for his energy, vision, and strong work ethic. He loved games and took joy in his family. Services will be held Saturday, August 6, at 10:00 at Greenlawn Memorial. In lieu of flowers, donations to the Heart and Stroke Foundation would be appreciated."

I shook my head. "How sad."

"It's always sad when someone dies. But it sounds as if he had a good life," Newton said.

"'He loved games and took joy in his family,'" I repeated. "That's a nice way to be remembered. I think I'd like to be remembered as someone who always did her best but never took herself too seriously." I grinned at him. "Newton, what do you want to be remembered for?"

"I'd like to be remembered as the man who won the lottery at the age of fifty and retired to the Bahamas," Newton muttered, returning the paper to his briefcase.

The other kids wanted to hear all about the break-in when they got home, and Andrew became a bit of a celebrity, with much pounding on the back and tousling of hair for the role he had played. I kept an observant eye on him through dinner, but other than a certain smugness, the excitement of the day hadn't seemed to affect him.

After supper, we threw the dishes into the dishwasher and crammed everyone into the van to head for band practice, which had resumed after a brief autumn break.

I must digress for a moment and state my philosophy of child-raising very clearly at this point. I am always leery when I hear of people whose children have followed in their footsteps and taken up the exact career or hobby of their parents. One always wonders if the child chose that career themselves or if the parent did.

I've worried about our children feeling pressured to become bagpipers because, of necessity, when the children were small, we dragged them with us to band practices and competitions at Highland Games. But I've never forced the instrument on them. Bagpipes, after all, are not an easy instrument. Beyond the technical difficulties, they are socially misunderstood. Let's be honest: a piper does not make for an easy marriage prospect, and I eventually want grandchildren.

Newton's stance is that children will ultimately be whatever they want to be, regardless of what their parents are or what opportunities are made available. Of course, Newton has been proven correct as each of our children has developed their own individual interests. However, as it has turned out, five of our eight developed a genuine love of the bagpipes (Caleb preferred Highland drumming). So on band nights, all ten of us squeeze into the van with instrument cases and music binders for an evening of family togetherness. Maisie and Andrew are too young to show much interest or to play, but they're also too young to stay home alone and, therefore, participate with the rest of us.

The longsuffering pipe major of our local band was Bob McEachern. I was not sure what his true feelings were when our ramshackle van pulled up in front of Legion Hall and the troops fell out. Though Isaac showed real promise as a competition soloist, the younger kids weren't the best of players. But since our family constituted 60 percent of the band, Bob kept his opinions to himself.

Tonight, we spent the first hour around the table, learning the music on the small practice chanters. The second hour was spent marching up and down the gymnasium with the full set of pipes. For the first hour, my mind kept busy with the new jig we were starting to learn. It was as we were transitioning from chanters to pipes that my brain got a moment to think, and I was suddenly struck dumb with realization. I dropped the music binder I had just been putting away, seized Newton's briefcase, and began madly pawing through it.

"What are you looking for?" Newton asked, a little irritated. He was as territorial about his briefcase as I was about my purse.

"That paper," I said. "The obituary of Warren Philpott. Is it still in here?"

"Yes." Newton nudged me aside and fished the piece of paper from a side pocket.

I snatched it up and reread it.

"Here!" I yelped.

"What?"

"See here. He was the CEO of Lucan Investments."

"Your point being? We have no money to invest," Newton said mildly.

The others were getting their pipes out and starting to make squawky noises as they warmed up. I leaned close to hiss in his ear. "Lucan is the name of the town where the Black Donnellys lived and died! You know, where the museum is. It's two hours from here."

Newton pulled the obituary back and stared at it. "Is that so? Do you think that's the word that substitutes for Black Donnellys, then? The story of Lucan Investments can be found in Dixie Township?"

"I don't think Philpott means just the story of how they were established or something," I said. The full band was going now, the sound ricocheting off the high ceiling, and I had to shout to be heard. "I bet there was some sort of scandal that happened there, and Warren Philpott wrote it all down in an exposé. But he didn't want it revealed until after his death, so he hid it. When he knew his health wasn't good, he wrote down clues for Wendy to find and follow so she would be led to the truth. But then she sold the house without finding the note. And Angus found it instead." I folded my arms with satisfaction. I had nothing to confirm my theory, but it felt right. In my heart, I knew I was on the right track.

Newton nodded. The sound was unbelievable now, and he was never one to like yelling. He grasped my elbow and towed me out into the hallway, where we could hear each other better. As we left the room, I saw several of the children watch us go, with raised eyebrows, bits of orange earplugs standing out of their ears. I was the one who insisted on the earplugs. The human ear can only take so many decibels.

"It sounds believable," Newton said when the door had closed on the racket. "Yes, it certainly would fit the clues we have so far. And maybe the person involved in the scandal got wind of Angus's find—"

"Or Angus even decoded the note and confronted the person himself. You know how he acts without thinking things through—"

"So he kidnapped Angus to keep him quiet about it," Newton said, nodding vigorously.

I felt a chill go up my arms, and I felt sick again. "But then, he couldn't let Angus go, Newton. If Angus knew the truth and it was that awful, the abductor would have to silence Angus for good."

Newton stared at me and nervously licked his lips. "Maybe he has."

"But then the abductor learned we have the note now and we might figure out the clues too. So he's trying to get it back before we do. He— He might want to silence us too. And, oh dear, Wendy has the note now as well. Have we put her in danger?"

Newton ran a hand down his jaw, a grim look on his face. "There's no way to know right now. The way I see it, we'll just have to hurry and solve the clues and find the truth," he declared. "If we expose the bad guy—for lack of a better term—before all the world, there won't be any point in silencing us then. Everyone will know. It'll be too late."

"Do you think your mother would take the kids for a few days?" I asked quietly.

Newton reared back, astounded. "*My* mother?" he said as if I'd just suggested his mother take up pitching for the Yankees. "Whatever for?"

"They might be in danger," I persisted. I could feel my heart slamming against my chest as if it were trying to keep time with Caleb's drumming in the gymnasium. "We've had one intruder already. He didn't get what he wanted. He may try again."

"Surely not. First of all, he still can't know for certain that we have the note. He's only guessing we do."

"Unless Wendy is in on this somehow."

"True. Secondly, after today's events, he'll know we're hyper vigilant now. And he'll probably be aware that the police are involved. The intruder will be more wary."

"But if he still wants the note . . ."

"If he's in league with Wendy DeRuvo, he can get a copy of it from her."

"He doesn't want it for himself," I argued. "He *knows* what it is about. That's why he wants to prevent *us* from having it and solving the clues."

"He'll be more cautious now that we're on the alert."

"I still worry about the kids—going to and from school, the bus . . ."

Newton shifted uncomfortably. "We can't live in fear, Annie. The kids still have to go to school."

"I know. But there's always a chance . . ."

"To be on the safe side, I'll drop them off in the mornings, and we'll tell them to use the buddy system on the way home."

"That doesn't help Enoch. He's the only one in junior high," I said. "He won't have a buddy. And how are you going to tell Caleb and Scott they have to walk home with each other? It isn't cool to walk home with your brother when you're in high school."

"They'll do it if we ask them to. In fact, they could walk over to the junior high and pick up Enoch on their way. It isn't far off the route. Then the younger ones can meet and all go to the bus together."

"I suppose," I said anxiously.

"It's time to tell the children what's going on, for their own safety. We'll hold a family council on it tonight after practice," Newton said firmly and nodded.

As he went back into the gym, a burst of sound surrounding him as he opened the door, I saw his face relax into one of his rare smiles. Newton was always at his best when there was a plan to be made or action to be taken. I, on the other hand, still felt only worry. I couldn't concentrate on the music the rest of the evening, and even Maisie noticed my mistakes and shook her head at me. Bob McEachern just rolled his eyes and wisely said nothing.

* * *

The church urges families to have regular family councils to keep in touch with each other. It's a time to coordinate schedules, set family goals, and work through any challenges or disagreements together. But holding a family council at our house is harder than it used to be when the kids were younger. Getting that many bodies into a room and attentive all at once is an exhausting feat. For that reason, our family councils have usually ended up tacked on to family night. So when Newton announced on the way home that we would have an ad hoc family council before bedtime (and on a Wednesday!), the kids knew it was serious. And they weren't slow to put two and two together.

"Is this about the break-in today?" Ethan demanded.

"We'll talk about it when we get home. Eight thirty, around the dining table," Newton said firmly.

We were all congregated five minutes before the appointed hour. Newton, as always, was in charge.

I suspect he enjoys these types of family meetings, when he gets to speak without interruption. (His rules of order are stringent. I am surprised he doesn't actually take minutes.)

"As you all know, someone broke into the house today. As far as we can tell, nothing was taken and no one—thankfully—was hurt. And thanks to Andrew, the police have a pretty good description of the person."

Everyone clapped for Andrew. I wondered if perhaps all the attention was going to his head. He looked a bit *too* pleased with himself. Were we witnessing the birth of an attention-seeking egomaniac? I would have to consult with Newton later on the matter.

"We believe the intruder was after this." Newton produced the now-wrinkled encoded paper with a flourish. The children stared blankly at it.

"Your mother and I found it in Angus's house," Newton said, smoothly omitting the fact that we were lock-picking intruders ourselves. "Angus Puddicombe has been missing for two weeks now."

This was news to them. I felt the collective intake of breath. The younger ones didn't look overly concerned, but the older boys all exchanged worried glances.

"We suspect his disappearance has something to do with what's written on this paper," Newton continued. "And after today's events, we feel, in all likelihood, that our assumption is verified."

Some of the younger ones looked mystified. Isaac leaned over and interpreted in a whisper, "Mom and Dad think they're right."

"What does the paper say?" Jane asked politely when Newton didn't move on. He was glaring at Isaac for breaking the family meeting rules, i.e. no whispering when Dad is speaking.

"We think it's some sort of code," I said, taking the paper from Newton and smoothing it on the table. It was starting to look rather ragged, and I felt protective of it, not only for its content but because it was the only tangible link we had to Angus. "We've figured out the first bit, we think, but we don't know about the rest." I read the note to them.

"What does it mean?" Enoch asked with a frown. "It's nonsense."

"We think you simply substitute some words for others. The Black Donnellys means Lucan Investment Corporation—never mind how," I added before Newton could launch into detail. "We think there must have been some sort of scandal, something illegal that happened at the company. The Englishman who used to own Angus's house, Warren Philpott, worked at Lucan Investments. We are theorizing that he wrote the details of the scandal and hid them somewhere. And then he left this note in his house, giving clues as to how to find what he'd written— maybe in case something happened to him. He might have feared for his life and didn't want the story to go untold if he was killed."

"That's a bit dramatic, isn't it?" Newton frowned.

"And did someone kill him?" Caleb asked.

"He died of natural causes," I said. "A heart attack, last year."

"That's when Angus bought his house," Jane added.

"And Angus found the note in the house," I said.

"And so did you," Isaac said helpfully.

"Yes."

"That is our working theory at the moment," Newton interjected. "We could be wrong."

"In any case, the truth about Lucan Investments is hidden somewhere in Dixie Township, somewhere near Bergamot Road. 'Away Down South' is clearly Dixie"—I shot Scott a look before he could reach for his beloved banjo and burst into song—"and 'bee balm' is a plant of the Bergamot family."

"Who are the Bergamots?" Ethan asked, muddled.

"Not a family of people," I explained. "A family of plants."

"Plants have families?" Ethan asked in astonishment.

"Are you referring to the genus or the species?" Enoch asked. (He was the science-minded one of the group.)

"Bergamot doesn't sound Latin," Isaac mused.

"More French, I think," Caleb said.

"In the plant kingdom—" Enoch began to explain.

"Who's in charge of the plant kingdom? Queen Anne's Lace?" This from Jane.

"Order! Order!" Newton shouted, sounding like a fry cook.

"The actual classification of the herb itself does not matter," I said through gritted teeth. "The point is that the clues have led us to Bergamot Road in Dixie Township. That's about fifteen miles from here. But we don't know where the clues lead after that."

Newton tried to get the meeting back on topic. "We think Angus figured out these clues and someone got wind of it. They wanted to stop him from finding out the truth about Lucan Investments, so they abducted him. If we figure out these clues—"

"Someone will abduct us," Enoch said, nodding.

"They might lead us to the reason he was taken and maybe even lead us to Angus," Newton finished loudly.

"Well, then, what are we waiting for?" Isaac said simply. "Let's solve it."

Eight heads bent forward around the table, all trying to study the paper at once. I whipped it away before they could play tug-o'-war with it.

"I will make a copy for each of you," I said. "If you can figure any of it out, that would be great. But I'm more concerned that we all stay safe. *That's* what this meeting is about."

"So someone really *is* going to abduct us?" Jane asked, blue eyes wide.

"No. Well, I mean, they might try, that's true. Which is why, from this moment onward, we are on the buddy system."

The children groaned and exchanged looks.

Newton explained the plan: who would walk home with whom and under what circumstances it was permissible to be without one's buddy (this for Ethan, who worried that Maisie would have to go to the school restrooms with him). The children weren't thrilled but agreed to follow the precautions. Newton then surprised me by issuing each child a chrome whistle to be worn around their necks at all times (yes, even in the restroom), to be used for sounding an alarm should any stranger try to approach them. I envisioned eight whistles going off when the mailman tried to come to the door. But I was glad Newton had thought of it and glad he was taking my concerns seriously. And I wondered how he had produced eight whistles at a moment's notice.

The meeting adjourned at nine o'clock with a unanimous vote to finish off the evening with ice cream.

Chapter Six

THURSDAY MORNING, I WAS IN the bathroom when I heard a crash, followed by an ominous silence.

"What happened?" I hollered in a panic through the closed door. "Is everything all right?"

"It's fine," Ethan called back. "Just don't come out."

So I took my time. By the time I got downstairs, whatever the mess had been was cleaned up, except for some telltale flour caught in the corner between the linoleum and the baseboard. Ethan dusted his white hands on his pants and smiled innocently, while Jane slipped the broom casually back into its slot. The other children avoided looking at me directly.

No harm done, I told myself, making a mental note to hide the pudding cups in a separate cupboard from the baking supplies henceforth. At least they had cleaned up after themselves, which was all I expected anyway.

I went to the desk and sent off a brief e-mail to Wendy DeRuvo, the question of whose safety had been bothering me all night. We didn't know if she was involved in the break-in. But if she wasn't, she needed to be warned. I pondered over the wording for a while, trying to sound reasonable instead of overly paranoid, and finally settled on:

"Just a quick note to let you know our house was broken into the other night. We don't know if it had to do with your father's note we found, but I wanted to alert you in case it did. You may want to take some extra precautions until we figure this thing out. No luck in deciphering it yet, but I'll keep you posted. All the best, Annie Fisher."

It would have to do.

I pulled out a stack of recipe cards, on which I'd written copies of the clues from Angus's house, and gave a card to each child. I encouraged them to mull the code over during the day but advised that they not tell anyone else about it for now. Any ideas they came up with would be welcomed. The others headed off to school, but Isaac lingered at the breakfast table, reading his card with a thoughtful frown.

"Have you driven out to this Bergamot Road?" he asked me.

"Yes. I didn't see anything that jumped out at me," I said. "Just a few houses and a pine forest."

"Forest? If I were going to hide something, that would be where I'd choose," Isaac said. "Forests are full of hiding places."

"I know. But where to start? We can't tramp all over acres and acres of forest."

"Why not?"

"We don't even know what we're looking for. 'Follow the bee balm to the start at Peter Pan.' The start of what?"

"The hunt, I suppose," Isaac said.

I dumped some of the breakfast plates into the sink and turned to face him. "Warren Philpott had a daughter named Wendy, which ties into the Peter Pan story, but she doesn't live anywhere near there. She's in Brantford."

"Wendy? Peter Pan. Hmm, maybe." Isaac stood and carried the note away, still studying it. At the door, he turned and gave me a sweet smile. "We'll find whatever this leads to, Mom. And we'll find Angus. I know it."

"Thank you," I said gently. "But, Isaac, we need to be prepared in case . . . Well, two weeks is a long time to be missing. There's a chance something has . . . happened to him."

"Dead, you mean."

"I'm afraid there is that chance."

Isaac shook his head. "I don't think so, Mom. I've been praying for him since last night, and I just don't get the feeling that he's gone. I feel he'll be all right."

I watched my son go up the stairs to his room, and I felt a tightness in my throat that I couldn't swallow away. I had been flinging prayers heavenward all week, but true to form, I hadn't really taken the time to stop and listen. To *feel*. I paused and tried to sense what it was I was feeling. Calm assurance? Trust? Well, no. I had to admit I felt only worry and dread. I wondered if that meant I lacked faith or if I was just a fusspot by nature.

"You'd better be on walkabout in the Arctic, Angus," I muttered, going back to the dishes.

I spent the day putting together the handouts for my Relief Society lesson, finishing the washcloths I was knitting as a housewarming gift for a new sister who had just moved into the ward, setting bread dough to rise, and hemming Jane's old fall jacket to fit Maisie. I finished my article for the professional journal and e-mailed it to the editor. And then I set the supper table, even though it was Maisie's job this week. I was teaching Andrew how to play Sorry when the phone rang.

"Annie? It's Sister Thompson, the compassionate service leader in the ward."

"Ah, yes. How are—"

"Listen, Sister Elizabeth Humphrey is expecting her twins next week, and we're organizing who is going to take her meals while she's off her feet."

"Oh, I—"

"I figured you've probably got lots of time since you don't work," she went on in her chipper voice. "So I signed you up for next Wednesday evening's supper. Is that okay?"

"Actually, I have band practice on Wednesdays," I managed to cut in. "I'm often reduced to giving my own kids cheese sandwiches on those nights."

"Oh. Well, let's put you down for Thursday, then, all righty? Thanks so much. Oh, and Sister Humphrey says she doesn't eat dairy or wheat, and her husband doesn't like onions. Thanks!"

She hung up, and I set the receiver down with a sigh. I wasn't sure I knew how to cook anything that didn't require at least one of those three things. I'd have to think.

The buddy system worked smoothly, and we all met at home again at three thirty. Even Newton slipped away from work early to be on hand to see how it had gone.

"I felt stupid getting picked up by my big brothers," Enoch said. "Like I can't even cross the street by myself."

"It's just for a while, until we figure all this out," I reassured him.

"I've been reading this thing all day," Caleb said, pulling his folded recipe card out of his pocket. "But I can't think of anything useful. I do know who Paul Haggis is though. He wrote that TV show *Due South* about the Canadian Mountie in Chicago."

"There you go," I cheered. "*Due South*. Maybe that's a direction we have to go once we get to that point in the trail."

"Or to Chicago," Isaac added.

"I wouldn't think so," I said. "Not if he tells us the starting point is in Dixie Township. And I have reason to believe he wouldn't go out of province."

"You're right," Newton said, looking surprised. "These are literal, physical directions. Place names. Compass points, perhaps. It's directing us to an actual physical location."

I blinked at him. "What did you think it was leading us to?"

"Something theoretical," he said, spreading his hands. "A concept. Maybe even the true story about Lucan Investments hidden right there in the note. But if it's guiding us to a specific location on a map, that's different. I've been thinking too abstractly." He took Caleb's card and read it again. "Walk by Thoreau. *Walden Pond* is his most famous work. There's no place nearby that I know of called Walden. So I gather we're to walk beside a pond. Is there a pond by Bergamot Road?"

"Not that I recall."

"Could there have been one down a side road? Or hidden by trees?"

"If it was hidden, I wouldn't be able to say—" I began, but Isaac held up his hand.

"I can tell you," he said, and going to the laptop I kept on the desk in the kitchen, he signed in and punched in some words. Almost immediately, he was staring at a satellite picture of Dixie Township, Ontario.

"Where's Bergamot?" he asked as we all crowded around him.

I leaned over his shoulder and pointed to the wire-thin brown line winding across the screen.

"That should be it, I think."

Isaac scrolled along, adjusting the image to zoom closer. All I could see was the thick, dark green of forest, punctuated here and there by clear spots where houses stood along the road, but Enoch jabbed a finger at a dark spot I'd missed and said, "There!"

We looked thoughtfully at the pond, surrounded by trees, and I felt a shiver of excitement run up my spine.

"Could that be the pond the note refers to?" Newton asked.

I swept up my car keys. "Let's go see."

Of course, no one wanted to be left out of the hunt. We all piled into the van and headed for Dixie.

When we reached Bergamot Road, I slowed the van almost to a crawl. We studied the houses and trees as we passed, looking for any indication or glimpse of a body of water down one of the side roads. I could see nothing, no sign announcing a nearby park, no boat or canoe in a driveway. The closest thing to it was the child's plastic wading pool in the yard I'd passed before. How were we to tell where the pond lay behind all those trees?

"Keep your eyes peeled," Newton directed. "Your mother may have missed something her first time through . . ." He realized how this sounded and gave me an apologetic grimace, but I shook my head.

"Quite right. I'm the first to admit I might have missed something, especially considering I didn't know what I was looking for."

For once, there was no complaining about who got a window seat, no pinching or shoving. They all focused on the scenery passing slowly by the window.

"Before we get to the part about the pond, there's other bits," Isaac reminded us. "We can't expect to go directly to the pond, not if we're following the clues in order."

"True," I said. "There must be something else first that leads us to the pond."

"Read the note to us again," Jane suggested.

I fished it out of my purse.

"The story of The Black Donnellys is heard Away Down South. Follow the bee balm to the start at Peter Pan. Walk beside Thoreau, but if you cross Denver now, you've gone too far. Where the route forks by Thoreau, follow Paul Haggis past the canoe. Now you can cross Denver. It will be found under the pilgrim's feet in Massachusetts, the biggest of three. Love, Dad."

"We're following the bee balm. So next is Peter Pan," Newton murmured.

"We think Peter Pan has something to do with Wendy Philpott, the daughter of the man who wrote the note. Everyone, think carefully and remember what you see," I instructed.

When we passed the playhouse with the pirate flag, standing under the trees, Maisie gave a squeal of excitement.

"That looks fun to play in," she declared, sounding ready to jump out of the van. "Let's go!"

"It isn't ours," Ethan told her firmly. "You can't play in something that doesn't belong to you."

"I want to stop!"

"It's probably full of mice or snakes," Jane added dourly.

"Just to look," Maisie whined.

"We're in the middle of hunting for Angus," Ethan argued back. "We can't stop now."

"Actually I think we'd better," Isaac said suddenly.

I caught his brown eyes looking at me solemnly in the rearview mirror. I slowed the van even more. "Why?"

"Because Peter Pan was a British story, right? And didn't you say that Philpott guy was an Englishman?"

"Yes. What are you getting at?"

"In Britain, a child's playhouse is sometimes called a wendy house, isn't it? And there one was with a pirate flag on it."

Newton and I blinked at each other, and then I slammed on the brakes. I backed up carefully, and as soon as the van came to a stop at the side of the road, everyone piled out and hurried toward the little playhouse under the trees.

It looked ordinary enough, a simple square box built of painted plywood, about eight feet to a side. I peered through one rough-cut window and saw a child's plastic chair, a mildewy rag doll, and some cardboard boxes. A plastic teacup filled with dry leaves stood on one of the boxes that served as a table.

Enoch gave a shout from the other side of the hut.

"There's a trail leading off through the forest," he announced. "Follow Bergamot to the 'start at Peter Pan.' This has to be what it's referring to. The start of a trail."

"But Philpott couldn't have guaranteed this playhouse would always be here. Shouldn't it be a more permanent sort of reference point?" Caleb protested.

"He didn't intend his note to lie around unread forever," Isaac said. "He wrote it for his daughter, and he assumed she'd follow up on it after his death. The playhouse wouldn't disappear in that short a time."

"There's only one way to know if this is the right way or not," I said. I lifted Andrew onto my hip and took Maisie's hand. "Let's go."

The trail was a narrow dirt path littered with aged pine needles and overshadowed with ferns. It was damp from a recent rain, the air thick with humidity. Mosquitoes whined in the shade and rose in clouds as we passed in single file. Newton led the way, and I took up the rear to make sure we left no one behind. The kids automatically dropped their voices to whispers without prompting, tiptoeing along the path as if entering a hushed cathedral. I could feel the buzz of their excitement like electricity in the air.

The trees were thick on each side, and I could only see a few feet into the forest in each direction. The path curved and twisted, and before long, the silence of the trees muffled all sound from the road. I couldn't tell how far we'd come and no longer knew what direction I was facing. The effect was claustrophobic. I began to wish I hadn't worn my fifteen-minute boots (I can only wear them for fifteen minutes before they start to make my feet hurt). The pond hadn't looked that far from the road when we'd looked at it on Google Earth. I shifted Andrew on my hip and was about to call to Newton to take a rest stop when the line came to an abrupt halt. I peered ahead, trying to see Newton, and then everyone started forward again. We emerged into a clearing in the trees and gathered in a silent knot on the bank of a murky pond about twice the size of our community swimming pool. Its surface was festooned with algae and mosquitoes, and there was an unpleasant rotting smell. The edge of the water nearest us was in shadow from the surrounding trees, but at the far side, the late-afternoon sun turned the water a yellow gray.

"Walden it isn't," I murmured.

But Newton, looking pleased with himself, was pressing on.

"This has to be the right way," he said. "The clues are falling into place in perfect order. A pond right where we wanted one."

But in a matter of minutes, the conga line stopped again.

"Now what?" I asked.

The children sent a whisper down the line. "River."

A river in here? Surely not. I handed Andrew to Isaac and pushed my way past everyone on the narrow path, getting mud on my too-tight shoes and snagging on tree branches until I reached the front. I found Newton standing, looking bemused, at a narrow stream that bubbled quietly over golden-mossed rocks. Hardly what I would term a river.

"It's not very wide. We can jump it," I said.

"No. Think of the note."

I tried to remember what came after Thoreau.

"If you cross Denver now, you've gone too far."

"I'm trying to think if this stream has any connection to Denver or Colorado in some way," Newton said, hands on hips as he studied it. We all stood blinking at the trickling stream, trying to think.

"Not the city," fifteen-year-old Scott suddenly piped up behind me. "John Denver, the singer. He wrote a song called 'Ripplin' Waters.'"

I beamed at him. "I always knew those folk music lessons would come in handy."

"We've gone too far, then. Did anyone see a path branching off farther back?" Newton asked.

"By the pond," Isaac called from the back of the line. "You kept following straight along this path, but there was one that turned off to the right just as we left the pond."

"Would right be south, by any chance?" I asked.

Newton hesitated, hating to admit he couldn't tell what direction we were going.

I didn't wait for his answer. "About face!" I called to the children. "Back to the pond. Follow Isaac."

Sure enough, five minutes later, now decidedly muddier and noisier, we were back at the pond, and the trail was branching off both to the left and to the right. I looked at our options and then peered at the sky, but I couldn't tell exactly where the sun was because of the trees. The sky was a sullen gray now anyway, the cloud cover moving in, the light gone from the surface of the pond, and I wondered how much time we had before dusk fell. I saw no footprints leading down either new path. At least it was easy to see which way we had come. We'd left a significant wake of our own.

"Try not to destroy the trail as you walk," I suggested, pointing to some snapped-off twigs. "We may not want—er—anyone to know we've been here." It occurred to me to wonder whose land we were trespassing on.

Isaac lifted his foot ruefully. "Size fourteens, Mom. Not much I can do."

"Caleb broke those branches off. I saw him," Jane said.

Caleb merely shrugged his rugby-player shoulders and grinned.

"We're not pointing fingers," Newton said.

"Any idea which way is due south?" I asked the group at large.

"In biology, they said lichen grows on the north side of trees," Enoch offered.

"Good thinking," I said. "I've heard that too."

We studied the trees closest to us, but the yellow-green film of lichen seemed to equally encompass the trunks on all sides.

"That's a useless bit of information," Jane pronounced.

"That way," Enoch said confidently, pointing to the trail that seemed the most overgrown and muddy to me.

"Anyone have any objections?" Newton asked.

The children all shook their heads or shrugged or, in Maisie's case, yawned loudly.

"All right, Enoch's turn to lead," I said.

We all fell back into step, jostling for positions, winding along the path in single file, ducking tree branches and slapping at mosquitoes. Jane tiptoed exaggeratedly, and Maisie laughed. Someone ahead of me started whistling "From the Halls of Montezuma," and Newton hushed him with a baleful glare.

"I don't think you children grasp the seriousness of this expedition," he scolded.

I hadn't really given much thought to what we might find at the end of the trail. It seemed to me that we were making a lot of noise and whatever—whoever—was ahead of us, we wouldn't have the element of surprise. If we ran into the *bad guy*, who was also trying to find whatever-it-was, the possibility was very likely that we could encounter violence. What were we leading our children into? I began to feel sick to my stomach. I also—inconveniently—needed a bathroom. "Newton," I said in subdued tones.

"Look!" someone up the line called.

"Newton," I said more urgently.

"The canoe!"

We came across a large log fallen across the path. The wood had rotted away over the years to form a half shell that looked, sure enough, much like a canoe. We scrambled over it and almost immediately struck another stream. Or perhaps it was the same stream doubled around. The ground was mossy and soft, but it was impossible to tell if there were any footprints because the children got to it before me.

"It's okay to cross Denver now," Newton said cheerfully, wading across the stream with no thought for his leather shoes. I took Andrew from Isaac and held him until Isaac was safely over, then tossed Andrew across into his brother's arms. Andrew let out a piercing shriek of delight, and I nearly fell into the water in my hurry to leap across and put my hand over his mouth.

"We really are being too noisy," I said to the group, but by this time, they were beyond shushing. Slamming happily through the underbrush, calling to each other, they could sense the end of the hunt. I decided it was too late for stealth and opted for speed. Holding my arm protectively in front of my face, I crashed after them through the trees and came up abruptly against a stone wall.

Or rather, the stone face of a large boulder taller than I was. It was plopped down smack in the middle of the trail. The children milled around it, poking and muttering.

"There are three of them," Enoch stated proudly, as if they were his personal discovery. I looked around and noted two other similar boulders, no trees growing between them so we were in a sort of clearing. A green-painted picnic table stood a few feet away, adding a cheery note to the gloom in the shade.

"We want the biggest of them," Ethan said.

"Pilgrim's feet," I murmured. "Massachusetts. Of course, Plymouth Rock."

"Hadn't you worked that part out?" Jane sighed impatiently. "That was the easiest clue."

"Well, er—"

"And you an American!" Isaac said, shaking his head.

They all began to chime in.

"That's the biggest boulder, there."

"We're supposed to look under it."

"We can't lift that."

"Maybe it rolls."

"No way. And it's muddy around here. You'd have seen if it had been rolled before."

"But this has to be the right place. All the clues fit," Enoch insisted.

"No sign of Angus," I said in disappointment.

Newton raised one eyebrow at me. "Were you expecting there to be?"

"Well, sort of," I admitted. "If whoever has him wants whatever it is the note refers to, and if Angus worked out what the note meant and knew how to find the whatever-it-is, it seems to me the kidnapper would bring him here—assuming this is the right place—to collect the . . . whatever-it-is," I finished lamely.

The children were all looking blankly at me.

I scowled. "That made sense to me," I said defensively.

"You think they coerced Angus into revealing what the note led to and then forced him to bring them here to find it?" Newton said helpfully.

"Yes."

"But even if that happened, it may have been two weeks ago."

"Easy enough to find out," Enoch said. "Look under the rock and see if the whatever-it-is is still here."

"But we can't roll it or lift it," Jane reminded him. "It's the size of a car."

"Warren Philpott was ailing and alone. He couldn't have rolled a rock this size by himself," Newton said. He squatted down on his heels to look carefully around the base of the rock. The ground was spongy and bare but for some weeds tufting out of it here and there. There was a flat rock about eighteen inches square butting up against the base of the boulder, and Newton gave it an experimental nudge. He looked up.

"Find me a strong stick or something I can pry it up with."

The boys fanned out into the trees and returned with a choice of four sturdy sticks. Newton selected one, wedged the tip under the lip of the smaller rock, and pushed down. The stick merely sank into the mud.

"I need leverage."

Enoch slid another stone under the stick. "Push against that, Dad."

Newton applied himself again. The flat rock hesitated, then popped out of the dirt with a sucking sound.

Everyone crowded around, heads craned forward to see, and I couldn't tell what was happening. I stepped back and waited.

"It's a hole," Newton announced. "There's something in it."

He rose to his feet and held up a dirty but unrusted metal box about twelve inches long and five inches wide. It reminded me of the cash box we used at the elementary school fall fair. A padlock neatly nipped the lid closed. The box and lock looked a bit worse for wear but still very much intact.

"We found the buried treasure!" Maisie cried and hugged Ethan with joy.

Caught off guard, Ethan gave a startled yelp and shoved her away. Maisie slipped in the mud and windmilled a moment before I caught her and kept her on her feet. She scowled and shoved Ethan back.

"Knock it off, both of you," I said firmly. I reached over their heads and took the box from Newton. It wasn't as heavy as I'd expected.

Newton's eyes met mine. "Whatever it is, I think it's safe to assume Angus never came here."

Whether this was a good thing or a bad thing, I didn't know. I only knew I wanted very much to get out of the mosquito-infested forest and back to the van. My feet were throbbing, and the need for a bathroom had risen to dire extremes.

"We could try exploring some of the other paths we didn't take," Caleb suggested, disappointed that the adventure was ended.

"Maybe there's a clue in the lockbox."

"Maybe—"

"Home," I said firmly and struck off back up the trail. The others fell in behind me.

We had been in the trees longer than I had realized. It was nearly dark by the time we reached the pond. For a moment, I scouted around, trying to find the trail we'd come in on. Since we'd forayed up the wrong path earlier and had subsequently returned to the pond, there were two trails bearing the marks of our stampede. I was on the verge of admitting I was lost when Enoch, bless his little eighth-grade scientist heart, noted that the footprints on one ran in only one direction, whereas the footprints on the other, where we had backtracked, ran in both directions. He struck out confidently down the single-trodden trail, and we all followed him unquestioningly. Within ten minutes, we were back at the road.

There was an audible sigh of relief as we left the buggy, overgrown trail, and the children scampered for the van. I had everyone take their muddy shoes off and drop them in the trunk space before getting in. In the light of the headlights, I did a quick inventory of scrapes and welts from the whipping tree branches, counted heads, and kissed a couple of scrapes. We were a sight to behold, but no one appeared to have suffered more than superficial injury.

Once in the car, the kids chatted excitedly about what might be in the lockbox. Suggestions ranged from diamonds and gold to another treasure map. Newton maintained, most logically, that it would hold the handwritten account of the secret evil deeds going on at Lucan Investments, perhaps signed in Warren Philpott's own blood (Enoch's embellishment). I sat with the box on my lap and felt as if I were holding a time bomb. With one hand, I softly touched the cold metal, the thick lock, the sharp corners. Would the contents help us understand why Angus was taken or—more importantly—who had taken him? And if Angus hadn't come to get the treasure, did that mean he hadn't worked out the meaning of the clues? Or was he holding out and refusing to cooperate with his kidnapper? Or did it mean he *couldn't* come?

My mind skittered away from this thought. He had to be all right. I refused to believe otherwise.

* * *

I'd forgotten the bread dough I'd set to rise that afternoon. It had abandoned its bowl and was crawling across the counter like a great white slug. But there was no time to deal with it. I threw plastic wrap over the whole thing and put it on a cookie sheet in the fridge. Then I hit the bathroom and washed mud from children's extremities while Newton found a bolt cutter in the garage. With much struggling and biting of tongue, he managed to break the padlock. He placed the box in the center of the kitchen table with some ceremony and carefully opened the lid. Everyone crowded close.

Not diamonds or gold. Not a bloodstained exposé.

"Waxed paper," Scott said flatly.

"No. Glassine envelopes. Stamps," Newton said.

For a moment, we all stared at them, and then Newton gingerly reached inside and lifted out the handful of small transparent sleeves. Carefully ensconced within each one was a postage stamp.

"Okay, this is weird," Ethan remarked. He'd been voting for gold.

I peered closer at the stamps. They appeared to be in perfect condition, uncanceled, with their perforated edges intact. Some had portraits of people I didn't recognize. One said "Cape of Good Hope" on it and "1853," which sounded old to me. The denominations weren't large, and they appeared to be from all different places, including Hawaii and Mauritius.

"Warren Philpott wrote that note to lead us to his stamp collection?" Caleb asked doubtfully.

"I don't know anything about stamps," I said. "But I assume these are very valuable ones." I held up one that was of a very pretty flower garden overshaded with trees. Blown up a million times bigger, it would have been something I'd hang on my wall. "We could get them appraised. Don't take them out of their packets."

"This one's only worth two cents," Ethan said, lifting the Mauritius one.

"That's its postage value," I said. "But its actual value if you sold it at an auction would be much higher, I think. Like with your baseball cards."

This he could understand. He set the sleeve down respectfully.

"Why didn't he just put them in a safety deposit box like any normal person?" Isaac asked reasonably.

"That's not as fun as a treasure hunt," Maisie said.

I suspected Wendy DeRuvo would have agreed with her.

"He wanted them to be untraceable," Scott suggested. "No one was meant to know they existed."

"So now what do we do?" Jane asked.

I had assumed, like Newton, that there would be a letter in the box explaining everything. I fought the feeling of deflation and sensed tears threatening again. "I was hoping there would be something, some clue, that would lead us to whoever took Angus," I said softly.

"Well, we know who took him," Scott pointed out. "It's just a matter of getting him back."

I blinked at him.

"Who took him?" Ethan demanded.

Scott shrugged. "It seems obvious. Who could be threatened by information coming to light about wrong-doing at Lucan Investments, except for someone who works or used to work at Lucan Investments?"

"Well, yes—" I said and stopped. Well. Yes. Of course.

"That's all well and good," Isaac said, "but we can't waltz into Lucan Investments and announce 'One of you did something wrong, but we don't know what, and we have no proof. Oh, and incidentally, are you hiding our friend Angus in the janitor's closet?'"

"Well, no," Scott agreed.

"Then how do we find Angus?" Jane asked quietly.

All eight sets of eyes turned to Newton and me. I saw Newton take a deep breath, something I noticed he did when he felt some strong emotion and didn't want it to come across in his voice.

"Family prayer," he announced. It was all he could think of, I knew, but I also thought it was the only possible response.

Eight sets of knees promptly hit the floor. Newton and I knelt with them, and Newton said a short but heartfelt prayer.

"We've done all we know how to do, Father," he pleaded. "We seem to be at a dead end. Guide us to know what to do next. Please let Angus come back to us safely."

We had hardly said amen when we heard the front door open and close, and Angus walked into the kitchen.

Maisie turned to Newton in exasperation. "Next time pray first, Daddy, so we don't have to march through all those mosquitoes," she said.

* * *

We were all frozen for a thunderstruck moment, and then we were all on our feet, flocking around Angus, everyone exclaiming and trying to touch him at once. Angus looked taken aback by our response. He looked like he hadn't shaved in days, and his clothes were rumpled, but otherwise, he looked in good health. I squeezed between bodies and stood on tiptoe to fling my arms around Angus's neck. I could smell pine.

"You're all right!" I said, pulling back to look up into his startled face. "We've been so worried."

"Apparently," he replied and grinned.

Newton pumped Angus's hand up and down and then abandoned that in favor of clapping him on the shoulder. "Where have you been?" he demanded.

"I've—we've—" He stopped, looking in some confusion at the children milling around him.

I clapped my hands. "It's past suppertime," I said. "Everyone go get in your pajamas. Then come down to the kitchen for sandwiches. You can see Angus then."

"But—"

"You can hear all about it then," I said firmly. "And not before. Off you go."

"Come on. They want us out of their hair for a minute," Isaac ordered his siblings.

They went, moaning and making it very clear they were going under protest. As soon as the last one had disappeared up the stairs, I turned to Angus. "Well?"

I was surprised to see Angus actually looking a bit nervous. He looked from me to Newton and moistened his lips. "I'm sorry you were worried about me," he said. "But I did tell you not to worry."

"What? When?"

"When I phoned last week," he said. "I told you I was all right."

"I could hear hardly a thing you said in that phone call," I told him. "It was all broken up with static, and then it went dead. I only heard enough to know that it was you and you were being held somewhere. We thought you'd been abducted."

Angus pinched his lips together. "Well, yes. I was. At first."

"You were?"

"Sort of."

I took hold of the front of his shirt, pulled him over to a chair at the table, and sat him firmly in it.

Newton leaned over him with a steely expression. "You've frightened my family to death for the last two weeks. We've put the police on alert. The school is frantic not knowing if they have to permanently replace you. My children will be thundering back down here in about ten seconds, and then conversation will be impossible. Explain yourself before they come down here."

Angus's mouth dropped open. "You called the police?"

"You disappeared. School started nine days ago. What were we to think? Of course we called the police."

"I—I wish you hadn't. I told you not to."

I put my fists on my hips. "Static. I heard no such thing."

"You did manage to find the note though. So you must have been able to hear me tell you where to look."

"I couldn't tell what you were saying. You said something about being held and finding a note. Then you said something was hidden, so we guessed you wanted us to find whatever it was. Which we did. We found the note at the house."

"You found it anyway? Without hearing me tell you where to look? How did you find it?"

Newton began to explain. "At first we thought you said 'in the new edition' and that you meant in your book. That distracted us a while. We thought you meant a note having to do with your train robbery research. Then we realized—"

"Not now, Newton. It's a long story and not pertinent at the moment," I interrupted. Ordinarily I try not to interrupt Newton, except in extreme emergencies, as it irritates him.

"I found that note while I was dusting the bedside table in my room, soon after I moved in. It was under the lamp." Angus saw my look and raised his chin somewhat defiantly. "I *do* dust once in a while, you know. But apparently, whoever cleaned up the place to sell it to me did not move the lamp aside when they dusted, so they missed it. The lamp has little stubby legs, so there's a space beneath it, and maybe the note got pushed under it by accident."

I pictured Warren Philpott, on his deathbed, sliding the note under the lamp for safe keeping, assured Wendy would find it. And then she didn't. The dangers of sloppy housekeeping.

"I didn't know what it was . . . at first. But I could tell it was important, so I kept it. I hid it."

"Yes, in the new addition," Newton piped up. "You see, we thought at first—"

"You were in the woods," I said suddenly, interrupting Newton once again. I had been studying Angus as he sat running his thin hand through his hair. It looked like it could do with a wash, and there was mud on the cuffs of his jeans. I saw a thin red scratch on the back of his right wrist. And it hit me. "Just now, when we were crashing around trying to follow that note. You were there."

"I—"

"Don't try to deny it. You smell like pine."

"I'm not denying it," he said. "Listen to me, both of you, will you?"

"We would if you were saying anything," Newton said irritably.

Angus cast a glance at the clock on the wall behind me. "I'm sorry I upset everyone. I told you—or at least, I tried to tell you—not to worry. I was abducted, yes, but a little while ago, I was let go."

"Why?"

"Things changed," Angus said evasively. Another glance at the clock. "Listen, I don't have much time right now. I can tell you all this later."

"Tell us now." Newton gave him the eyeball, and Angus subsided.

"After I got back to town, I checked at my house and couldn't find the note, so I came straight here to your house. I figured you'd have it—I did tell you to find it—" he added defensively, "and I wanted to have a look at it and refresh my memory of what it said. I had the Bergamot Road part figured out and thought it was maybe something to do with the trees, but I didn't know the rest of it."

"You wouldn't until you actually started following the trail," Newton said. "You see, in Britain they call—"

"Not now, Newton." I could hear children's feet on the stairs. "So you came here this evening and found we weren't home."

"Right," Angus said. "I waited a bit, but you didn't come back. I figured you were out at rugby practice or something. So I decided to drive past the forest on Bergamot Road just to see if I could figure out any more. I couldn't remember all the note said, but I recalled bits and pieces. And then I saw your van parked at the side of the road. I wandered around some of the trails, hoping to find you or at least to remember what the note had said, but I only succeeded in getting lost. I emerged from the woods and saw your van was gone. So I followed you back home."

I tried to recall if I'd seen Angus's car nearby when we'd reached the van. It had been dark, and I'd been focused on keeping mud off the seats. I hadn't noticed.

"But tell us what's going on," Newton said, flinging his arms out. "Why—"

"Not now, Newton. Angus has to meet someone. Don't you, Angus?"

Both men stared at me, mouths open. I picked up the lockbox and held it in front of Angus so he could see the packets of stamps inside.

"You keep looking at the clock. You say you don't have much time. I'm guessing you're supposed to meet someone—and I'm also guessing you have to give them what we found. Is it the person who abducted you? He only let you go so you could find this box for him. He didn't know what the note said or how to find it, but he knew you knew, or at least, he knew you had the note."

The children were milling around the kitchen now, dressed in their pajamas and hoping for food. I gave Newton and Angus a look to tell them not to say anything further for the moment. Then I slapped ham, bread, a head of lettuce, a jar of mayo, and a butter knife on a platter, gave the platter and a package of chocolate-covered graham crackers I'd been saving for school lunches to Isaac, and told him to take the kids into the family room to make sandwiches and eat.

"But we want to hear about Angus," Scott protested.

"In a minute. Later."

Usually the kids would have argued with this, but I guess something in my tone or look told them I was serious. Isaac held the sandwich makings and cookies above his head and turned the tide of children the other direction, threatening them with no supper if they didn't listen to him. The herd moved off toward the family room, and I turned back to Angus. He was looking, befuddled, at the stamps, stirring them around with one finger.

"This is what you found?"

"Yes."

"Just now? In the woods?"

"Yes, following the note you say you told us to find."

Angus shook his head. "He isn't going to like this."

"Who? The person you have to meet?"

He looked at me, and for the first time in my acquaintance with him, I saw Angus frown. His chin jutted out stubbornly, and his eyes narrowed slightly. "Yes."

"He was expecting something else, wasn't he? A written confession?"

"He told me the note would lead to a great deal of money."

"It has," Newton said. "We think these stamps are very valuable."

"Of course." Angus's face cleared. "You're right, of course. Philpott must have changed it into something more portable, more easily carried."

"And likely untraceable," Newton added.

"Who is this person?" I asked. "Who kidnapped you?"

Again his face closed over. "Never mind."

I glanced toward the kitchen window, but it faced toward the back, not the street. Who was waiting out there for Angus? And were they waiting in a small white car? Would they let him go once he handed over the treasure? Was he still in danger? A chill ran up my spine, and I snapped the box of stamps closed. Angus jerked his fingers back just in time.

"Listen," I told him urgently, lowering my voice. "You don't have to go out there and give this to him. You can stay here in the house, and we'll call the police. He won't dare come in here after you with so many witnesses in the house. The older boys can help."

Newton, thinking along the same lines, reached for the phone. But Angus jumped forward and caught his arm, pulling him around to face him. "Don't! Don't call!"

"But, Angus, this person can't hurt you if—"

"You don't understand. I'm not the one who will be hurt."

Newton carefully released his arm from Angus's grip, his eyes never leaving Angus's face. "But someone is going to be hurt," Newton said slowly.

"If I don't do exactly as I was told. If you call the police." Angus moistened his lips and looked desperately from Newton to me. "You don't understand. I'm not abducted at this point. I'm cooperating with him. I'm *helping* him."

I shook my head, befuddled. "Why are you helping this person find Warren Philpott's stamp collection?"

"I can't explain. There isn't time. The deadline is tonight. Please, just let me go, and I promise I'll explain it all later if I can. Please—it's the right thing to do. I have to take this, now."

I exchanged a long look with Newton, and he nodded once. I handed the box of stamps to Angus. He let out his breath in an explosion of relief, but before he could turn toward the door, I caught his arm. "Come back to us," I ordered.

Angus hesitated, then grinned crookedly and dropped a kiss on my forehead. He nodded at Newton, tucked the box under his arm, and hurried out. We both went wordlessly into the front room to look out the window. Angus jogged away down the sidewalk under the street lamps, climbed into his car parked near the corner, and was gone.

"Those stamps rightly belonged to Wendy DeRuvo," I muttered. "It wasn't our place to give them to anyone."

"Since when did we ever pay attention to what our place is?" Newton sighed.

"I don't know if we did the right thing," I said.

"Sometimes you have to deliberate the pros and cons of your actions," he replied, still gazing out the window. "Sometimes you carefully weigh the facts and reason out the best decision. And sometimes you just have to leap and hope for the best."

I thought about that a moment and knew he was right. Give in to impulse. Listen to what your heart was telling you.

"The kids are going to be furious that they didn't get to talk to him," I said.

"Ah. Yes." Newton visibly squared his shoulders and headed for the other room. "Leave it to me."

Sometimes Newton can be positively heroic.

I left him to it and went to deal with the bread dough.

Chapter Seven

WE DIDN'T HEAR FROM ANGUS the next morning. If that night had indeed been the "deadline," and if he had turned over the treasure as directed, then shouldn't he have been free to return to us? I had a very bad feeling about it all.

I went through the motions of the day with one ear cocked for the phone, and at noon, Newton drove over to Angus's house just to check. It was locked and deserted, and his car was not in the driveway.

"I know Angus said not to call the police," Newton said when he returned home. "But they're already involved. I think we should at least let them know of recent developments."

"I agree. If—" I had to stop to swallow. "If things had gone right last night, he'd have come back once he dropped off the treasure box. Something must have happened."

"I'll phone Donetti." He went into the back room off the laundry room, where he could use the extension in private, and I wandered into the kitchen at loose ends. Isaac was sitting at the computer.

"I'm looking up some of those stamps," he said. "But I can't recall what they all looked like."

"One was from Mauritius," I said, trying to help. "Two cents. Blue."

"Do you remember what year it was?" Isaac asked, typing madly.

"No."

"Because if it was an 1847 two-penny Post Office Blue, it would be worth 1.7 million dollars," Isaac said grimly.

I felt dizzy. "Are you *kidding*?"

"If it was in mint condition," he added. "I don't know how to judge that."

"For a *stamp*?" I couldn't fathom how something that small and frail could be worth so much. "What about the Hawaiian one? It said thirteen cents on it."

"Was it this one?" Isaac showed me a picture on the computer screen.

"Could be. I don't remember. It looks like it."

"If so, that one was worth two hundred thousand."

I shook my head. "And the Cape of Good Hope, 1853?"

"This one here is worth forty thousand. Of course, there's no way to know if they were in as good condition as these."

I felt the need to sit down and wondered if my heart was palpitating. "I can't imagine how much money was in that box we held."

"A lot," Isaac said. "Enough to kidnap for."

"Enough to kill for," I said.

I went to bed that night with another sick feeling in my stomach.

* * *

The following day was Saturday. The boys had a rugby game, the final one of the season. It felt traitorous to go carry on with a normal day while Angus was still unaccounted for, but as Newton said, we couldn't live in fear. Life had to go on. We didn't know where to begin looking for him. And worrying at home wasn't helping anything. We had done what we could for now, and we had to leave it in the hands of God and the police. I put the boys in the van and headed for the club where the game was to be held.

I admit the game distracted and cheered me considerably. I have always enjoyed watching rugby. It doesn't have many of the annoying traits that, say, American football has. The last five minutes of the game takes five minutes, not thirty-five. The ball seems always to be in play, with no irritating stops and penalties. One can see the faces and actions of the players better because they aren't hampered by such trivialities as helmets or padding. And if a player from the opposing team manages to get near the goal with the ball, the defending team can simply pick him up and carry him out of bounds. Or grip him by the shirt, swing him around, and hurl him out as if doing the hammer throw. Which is what Caleb was doing at the moment. I heard a rip of fabric as Caleb flung the opposing player around and then released him to go flying off into the weeds at the edge of the playing field. There was a smattering of cheers, and the coach clapped Caleb on the back before sending him back into the fray.

"I had my doubts about signing Jeremy up for this sport," the petite woman sitting beside me murmured. She clutched a thermos in one hand and her throat in the other. "It's his first season."

"Oh, yes? Which one is he?" I asked politely.

She indicated a boy in an almost spotless uniform from the opposing team, dancing gingerly in place while he waited for the action to sweep him up. He looked timid, and he had one of those punctured rubber caps on that made his hair stand up through it as if he were getting highlights at the hairdresser's.

His mother shook her head and gave a nervous laugh. "When they had us sign that waiver saying we understood he could lose an ear . . ." She looked at me for reassurance.

"I felt the same way two years ago when three of my boys started," I told her. "Not one of them has lost an ear. And it's been very good for their confidence and their physical condition."

"Which boys are yours?" she asked hopefully.

"That one there. He's seventeen." I pointed to where Caleb was now shoulder deep in a ruck like James Herriot delivering a calf. "And that one there with his mouth guard hanging out. He's thirteen." I pointed to Enoch. "And that one. He's fifteen." The mud and blood smeared all over Scott's freckled face highlighted his white ear-to-ear grin. As we watched, he popped in his mouth guard, lowered his head, and drove himself straight into another player's stomach. The other boy doubled over, flipped over Scott's shoulder, and landed on his back in the trampled grass. We could hear the impact up in the stands. There was another smattering of applause.

The woman shot me a horrified look, pressed the thermos to her chest, and hurriedly excused herself. I saw her making a beeline for the coach on the sidelines, no doubt to yank the unfortunate Jeremy from the game.

I hoped she wouldn't. I hadn't been lying; I really did think the sport had been good for my boys. And it was good for me too to get out of the house and vent some of my pent-up worry and frustration. The thought occurred to me that hard experiences—even pain sometimes—could be good for us. We could dwell on the discomfort and give up, or we could rise to the challenge and grow in confidence and perseverance. I wouldn't spare my children from every difficulty, even if I could, because I knew it was the way to make them stronger people. Just as I knew God wouldn't take away our every challenge for the same reason. I wondered if this whole thing with Angus was just such a situation. If so, what were we supposed to be learning? Patience? Trust? Faith? I reached for the notebook I always carried to jot the idea down for further contemplation.

We massacred the visiting team. I had a great time. I let myself scream—er, shout supportively—and when I could no longer remain in my seat for excitement, I went down to the sidelines to help hand out ice packs. When the score reached thirty-two to zero, the opposing coach sidled over to our coach and asked him to hold the boys back so his team wouldn't become too dispirited. I was close enough to hear our coach reply sadly, "I told our boys to stop scoring fifteen minutes ago."

When it was over, I packed my filthy children into the van and hauled them home by way of the Rexall IDA to pick up some more Polysporin. The boys were euphoric, and I loved listening to them rehash the highlights of the game and compare injuries. I doubted Jeremy was having as good a time on his ride home.

* * *

Usually, Saturday afternoons were a whirlwind, filled with music lessons, piping practice, art lessons, homework, grocery shopping, and house cleaning. In a household as large as ours, there was very little time to sit and relax, and I was used to the routine. But after the morning's excitement at the rugby game, I felt let down, as if all my energy had been used up and now I didn't have enthusiasm for anything else. The worries I had managed to set aside during the game returned in full force. The only thing I was learning from this, if anything, was endurance. Newton took care of the carpools while I fidgeted around the house, picking up laundry baskets and setting them down again, forgetting where I'd put the furniture polish, and generally accomplishing nothing. When Newton returned from the last run of the afternoon, I cornered him in the kitchen.

"I'm going crazy," I said. "What could have happened to Angus? Why isn't he here if it was as he said and he was voluntarily helping someone? We shouldn't have let him go alone."

"He said it would be all right."

"Did he? In those exact words?"

"Well, no."

"What if whoever it was wasn't happy to find the money had been turned into stamps? What if they thought Angus was trying to cheat them out of the treasure?"

"What do you want me to do?" Newton asked in frustration, splaying his arms wide. "What could we do that we haven't done?"

I didn't know what to answer. I dropped into a chair at the table and put my head in my hands. Newton hesitated, then put a comforting hand on my shoulder.

"Time for another family prayer?" he suggested lightly, trying to smile.

"It worked once," I said with a groan. "Like Maisie said, why didn't we try that first?"

Most of the children were home, and Newton gathered them into the family room to explain that we were going to pray for Angus again because he hadn't come back yet. The children all nodded, their faces solemn and worried. But just as we were getting to our knees, there was a knock on the door.

Maisie brightened. "Angus!" she cried, and she ran to open it, with all of us right behind her.

But the man standing on the steps wasn't Angus.

He was of average height, his hair chocolate brown, his eyes dark. He wore tan slacks and a black jacket and a startled expression when he saw the horde of us descending on him *en masse*. He took a step backward, teetered for one breathless second, and then regained his balance without tumbling down the front steps.

"Whoopsie!" I cried, snatching his arm to help. "Are you all right? Sorry about that. We didn't mean to stampede at you. We were expecting someone else."

"Angus?" the man asked.

Newton and I exchanged looks.

"Were you expecting Angus?" the man repeated. His tone was urgent, his face pulled into a frown. "I need to talk to you. I was expecting him too."

* * *

It was pointless trying to find a quiet spot in the house. We ended up leaving Isaac in charge and walking down to Gussie's Eatery two blocks over. Newton, the man, and I were soon ensconced at a table in a corner, with orange juice for us and coffee for him. There were no other customers (no one ever actually ate at Gussie's, and I had wondered sometimes if the eatery was actually a front for something else—drugs? stolen goods?—because, certainly, no one could possibly earn a living from the place), so we had the room to ourselves. Only then did the man talk.

"My name is Douglas McKinnon," he said and paused as if waiting for our reaction.

It took a second before the light went on. "I thought you looked familiar," I said. "I saw you on TV a few weeks ago." When Newton gave me a puzzled glance, I added, "Mr. McKinnon is running for Parliament."

Newton was too polite to actually recoil, but he came close to it. He considers all politicians only slightly less repulsive than advanced gangrene. He tried to smile at Mr. McKinnon but only managed a tight-lipped grimace, baring his formidable teeth.

McKinnon recoiled instead.

"Go on," I prompted gently. "You know Angus?"

The man shifted his gaze to me and nodded, looking relieved. "He has been helping me for the last couple of weeks," he said.

I couldn't help myself. Both of my hands shot out and locked onto his wrist, holding on as if I expected him to evaporate on the spot. "You!" I said. "You're the one!"

Gussie looked up from the counter, where she'd been idly turning the pages of a newspaper and fanning herself with a flyer. Newton reached over and pried my grasp loose.

"You don't need to restrain him. He approached *us*, remember? I'm sure Mr. McKinnon isn't going anywhere," Newton said firmly and cocked an eyebrow at McKinnon to make sure he got the point.

McKinnon squirmed. Gussie subsided once more into her newspaper.

"I've come to you for help," he said. "Angus came to your house night before last."

"Yes," Newton confirmed.

"He was going to deliver something to someone for me."

"The stamps," I said.

McKinnon's eyes widened. "You know . . ."

"We are the ones who found them," I said. "Did you expect us to leave the box alone and not look inside?"

"I didn't know it was going to be stamps," McKinnon said. "I was expecting a great deal of money."

"Stamps are more portable," I said. "I'm sure they were very valuable. In fact, from what we could find on the Internet, they're probably worth millions, collectively."

Newton ground his teeth so hard I could hear them popping. "Angus was going to deliver the box to someone for you," he prodded impatiently.

"Yes. But he didn't come back." He looked from Newton to me. "Has he contacted either of you at all?"

"No."

"And you think Angus has taken off with the treasure?" Newton made it sound more like a statement than a question.

McKinnon shook his head. "I don't know. I would hope not. He didn't seem the type . . . but I don't really know him."

"We do," I said firmly. "We've known him for years. And Angus is not a thief; I can promise you that."

"I want to believe that."

"You can. To whom was he delivering the stamps? Where was he going?" I demanded. "Is he in some kind of danger?"

"I'm afraid he might be," McKinnon said slowly, ignoring the first two questions. "You care about Angus, I can tell. He spoke very fondly of your family. I need your help."

"You kidnapped Angus and scared us all half to death," I said. "Very questionable behavior for someone hoping to have a successful political career, I might add. And now you want our help?"

"Angus apparently thought he was worth helping," Newton said. "And he told us he was no longer being held against his will."

"That's right," McKinnon said. "I admit that at first I—I guess you could say I coerced him into helping me. I didn't think he'd agree otherwise. But once Angus understood the situation, he offered to assist. He really seemed like a very generous fellow. I wanted to trust him. And," he added, looking at me, "I sincerely hope nothing has happened to him."

I was too upset to answer rationally, but Newton leaned forward and fixed McKinnon with a calm brown eye. "Perhaps if we knew the situation, Mr. McKinnon, we would also be inclined to assist you. But you must tell us everything with complete honesty if you expect our help."

McKinnon returned Newton's stare for a tense moment and then exhaled in a long, ragged breath. "All right, but you have to promise not to call the police."

"I can't promise any such thing," Newton replied. "In point of fact, we have already told the police all we know of the matter, including about the stamps."

The man's mouth fell open in dismay. "You can't! It will ruin everything."

"Angus seemed to be of the same opinion. My friend was abducted, my family has been frightened, and my home has been broken into. It is unreasonable not to expect me to call the police."

"I understand, and I'm sorry you have been impacted by all this. But I'm telling you, the police can't know about any of this."

"Tell me what you have to say," Newton said. "I will judge it on its own merits when I hear the tale. If I feel the police need to hear it, I will promise not to contact them without first informing you. That is my only concession."

I held my breath. Newton's tone was uncompromising. The man had no obligation to tell us anything, and I wouldn't have been surprised if he'd stood up and walked out. But he was more desperate than I'd supposed.

McKinnon chewed his lip, then nodded sharply. "All right. Angus went that night to deliver the box you found to a man. It was to be in exchange for my son."

"Ransom?" I squeaked. I saw Gussie glance up from her paper, and I lowered my voice. "Your son is being held for ransom?"

"Yes. Kenneth is ten years old. He was abducted almost three weeks ago. The price of his release was the money—or rather, I thought it was money we were looking for. I guess it was stamps instead. Angus was to help me find it and to act as the neutral middleman in the exchange on Thursday. But he didn't come back from the exchange. My son wasn't returned. And I haven't heard from the man since then. I have no idea what's gone wrong."

"I imagine it takes time to convert stamps back to money," I reasoned. "He'd have to have them discreetly appraised to make sure you weren't cheating him. He'd have to make sure they were sellable."

"But why keep Angus? The kidnapper already has my son. He wouldn't need Angus. It seems he would have sent Angus back to me with an explanation that he would need extra time to have the stamps evaluated, if so."

"Wait," Newton said, drawing a deep breath. "Let us summarize. Are we to understand that Angus was negotiating the return of your son in exchange for a treasure, the nature of which neither you nor the man who took your son understood? You expected money to be in that box. You weren't even sure where the box was hidden."

"Yes."

"But somehow you knew of its existence."

"Yes. Well, I strongly suspected it existed."

"And for some reason, you needed Angus to help you find it."

"Yes. He owns the house that was once owned by a man—"

"Warren Philpott. Yes, we know," I said impatiently.

"Oh. Well, I knew Warren Philpott. I knew he had left some money. It never surfaced after his death. No one made any noise about it. Certainly his heirs didn't find it in his bank account—the kind of money we're talking about would have sent tremors through the banking world, and I—I have connections in that arena, you see. I would have heard. And I am close to Warren's daughter. I'm sure she would have mentioned it to me if she'd inherited something on that scale. So I figured the money must still be somewhere in the house."

"The house now occupied by Angus Puddicombe."

"Yes."

"Why didn't you just knock on the door and ask Angus if he'd found anything of that description?" I asked. "Why did you kidnap him?"

"Well, I did ask. Things went a bit wrong, is all," McKinnon said. "I thought he'd put up a fight, want to keep the money for himself once he got wind of it. But he turned out to be a very reasonable guy, really. Like I said, once he knew why I needed it, he agreed to help me. He told me he hadn't found any hidden money, but he'd found a note shortly after he'd moved into the house. The note had clues on it that sounded like the clues to a treasure hunt. He hadn't followed up on it, but he had put it in a safe place because he felt it was important. He'd been planning to ask Warren's daughter about it but simply hadn't gotten around to it yet. When I told him about the money I was seeking, he thought maybe the note was something to do with that. It did sound like something Warren would do. He liked treasure hunts."

"You say you are close to Wendy?"

"Yes. Do you know her?"

"I know her name, and I've spoken to her once," I said.

"Wait. You say you were close to Philpott's daughter," Newton said. "Yet you wanted to find the money—which is rightfully hers—without her help or knowledge?"

"Er . . . yes."

"And Wendy wouldn't have understood why you needed it? She wouldn't have helped you?"

McKinnon spread his hands. "It would have taken a great deal of explanation about where her father had gotten the money, an explanation she would have found painful, and she would have wanted a lot of questions answered. I just didn't have the time or inclination to get into it. We're talking about a great deal of money. If she found out it existed . . . I don't know what she would have done. Maybe she would have helped me find it and given it to me to save my son. But maybe not. I didn't want to take that chance, and there wasn't really time to think it all through anyway."

Newton shook his head. "It doesn't add up. You're a prominent public figure running for federal Parliament. If your son was abducted, why wasn't it in the news? Why isn't the story spread all over the country?"

It was a good question. I admit I hadn't thought of it.

McKinnon turned a pasty white, and I knew the answer without having to guess.

"Because you're into something shady up to your eyeballs," I suggested. "That's why you don't want the police involved. That's why you kept the kidnapping of your own son under wraps and made sure the media didn't get wind of it. That's why you don't want Wendy asking where her father got the money from. It was something illegal, wasn't it, and you were involved?"

"Where did the money come from?" Newton asked.

McKinnon squirmed. "It doesn't matter."

"I'm guessing if the reason Kenneth was abducted comes out, so will the truth about what you've been up to." I shook my head. "Sounds pretty selfish to me, Mr. McKinnon, risking your son to protect your own reputation."

He flinched at that and grew silent. For a moment, we eyeballed each other, assessing each other. Gussie, at the counter, grew bored, slapped down her paper, and began spinning the rotating napkin holder on her counter.

Newton gave a sigh. "I think you'd better start at the beginning and divulge everything if we're going to be able to help you," he advised. "Even if it doesn't make you come out looking very good. You'll have to trust us."

When McKinnon still hesitated, I said sharply, "Do the right thing. This is the life of your son we're talking about."

McKinnon ran a hand over his jaw, and I could hear his day-old whiskers rasping. He looked suddenly haggard with grief and exhaustion. "All right. I need your help. I'll tell you. I just want Kenneth back."

Newton eyed him a moment, then raised a hand and caught Gussie's attention.

"We'll have burgers all around," he called to her. Catching my look, he said, "I think we're going to need some fortification before we hear what he's got to say."

"Still, it's a bit extreme, don't you think?" I asked nervously. After all, I had never seen anyone actually consume the food at this establishment.

Gussie sprang into action, clanging and clattering in the kitchen as if overjoyed to finally have someone to cook for.

The man across from us drew a deep breath. "I was the chief financial officer of Lucan Investments for twelve years," McKinnon said, looking down at the wet rings his glass had made on the tabletop.

"Ah." The picture was clearer already. "Warren Philpott was CEO," I said.

"Yes." He looked away out the window at the drizzle that had started coming down. It would be a wet slog home. "We were . . . creative with the bookkeeping."

"Embezzlement?" Newton asked grimly.

"Yes." He clasped his hands on the table to keep them from drumming nervously. "Warren had the idea first and—well, I went along with it. I shouldn't have."

"A significant sum, I gather, from the value of the stamps," I said.

"We made fake payouts to trumped-up companies. We skimmed off millions," McKinnon added grimly.

I distinctly heard the ding of a microwave, and a moment later, Gussie reappeared with our plates balanced precariously on her arm. The silverware didn't look any too clean, nor did Gussie's hands, but I had to admit the burgers looked and smelled better than I had feared, and the french fries actually looked appetizing despite the microwaving. I must have been hungrier than I'd realized. When she returned to her counter and newspaper, I took a tentative bite of my burger. Oversalted and undercooked. Ah well. I reached for the sticky ketchup bottle.

"How did you get away with it?" Newton's tone made me look up. There had been, perhaps, a touch of wistfulness in it. I told myself that he had asked out of academic interest and not because he sought a tutorial.

"We brought the auditor, Ted Vandenberg, into it so he'd keep quiet. The three of us got away with it for several years. It made us cocky, and we started skimming even greater sums," McKinnon said. "We had a deal not to flash it around, not to make any obviously expensive purchases, to keep it under the radar. The money went into a joint offshore account, and we invested it together. All three of us could keep tabs on it, monitor the spending and the earnings."

"That's trusting," Newton said.

"Checks and balances," McKinnon said wryly. "But then Warren died of a heart attack. We were busy coping with that, getting in a new CEO at Lucan, and we didn't take anything else. You could say operations were suspended after that."

"And no one caught on?"

"No. But after Warren died, Ted and I noticed a large portion of the money we'd skimmed was missing. We realized Warren must have been double-crossing us, skimming the skimmings, so to speak. I shouldn't have been surprised. I knew he was a thief, but I'd trusted him anyway. Ironic, I suppose."

"Honor among thieves," I said. I thought of the three train robbers Angus had researched, how two had killed the other in cold blood and left him behind.

"I suspect Warren had been planning to take the money and disappear somewhere," McKinnon said.

"Wendy did say Warren had been planning to sell the house and downsize. Maybe he was laying plans to vanish," I said.

"For months after his death, I kept my ear to the ground," McKinnon said. "I spent some sleepless nights, I'll tell you. But no other offshore accounts were found. No great unexplained sums in the bank. No investments. And I wondered if maybe he'd just sat on the money and not secured it in a bank account after all. I started envisioning a basement of mason jars filled with money—it sounds crazy, I know."

"And you didn't break into the house to try to find it?" I asked skeptically.

"I thought about it," he admitted. "But there wasn't a chance. Warren was hardly in the ground before Wendy started cleaning out the house and preparing to sell it. And I wasn't exactly trained in burglary. I didn't know what to do, and I didn't dare hire anyone to do it for me because I didn't know who I could trust. I about had a heart attack myself, I admit, picturing Wendy finding millions of unaccounted-for dollars as she was sorting through her father's old golf clubs and Christmas ornaments in the basement. It would have made the authorities ask questions about where it had come from. Someone would have taken a close look at Lucan's finances, and the whole thing might have been discovered. I had political ambitions. I couldn't let the story come out. But, of course, Wendy never found any such thing. I'm sure she would have mentioned it to me if she had."

"Because you two are so close," I added, baring my teeth.

"If the story had come out," Newton said reasonably, "you and Ted could have let Philpott take the blame for all of the irregularities."

"Except Ted was the supposed auditor. He would have noticed millions go missing. Since he said nothing about it over the years, the authorities would know he had something to do with it. And if Ted was nabbed for it, you can be sure he would have brought me down with him."

"Honor among thieves," I said again.

Newton gave me an annoyed look. "You're sure Ted himself wasn't the one skimming the skimmings and that he just blamed Warren for it?"

"He was as genuinely shocked and angry as I was when we discovered it. It had to be Warren."

"So you knew Philpott had the money, but you didn't know where, and you couldn't ask Wendy since you were planning to keep it if you found it."

"Correct. A sum like that couldn't have just vanished."

"But who was to say Warren hadn't just spent the money as he acquired it?" Newton asked. "Why did you think it was still somewhere in his possession?"

"There was nothing in his lifestyle to indicate he had. As I said, we had all been careful to spend our portions of the money wisely, in a slow trickle, with no sudden visibly extravagant purchases so that no suspicions would be aroused. Still, that kind of money couldn't be spent without *some* sort of trail being left. But we couldn't dig too obviously or draw attention to the missing money. You appreciate it was a delicate situation. And frankly, I had enough money for my needs and then some. There was no need to pursue it intensely. Time passed, nothing surfaced, and I began to relax."

"And then your son was abducted," I said flatly.

"Yes," McKinnon said miserably.

"Who has Kenneth?" I asked. "Is it Ted Vandenberg?"

"Yes. That's how I know Ted wasn't in on the double-crossing: he thinks *I* was. He thinks I was in on the swindle with Warren and that I know where the money is now." McKinnon poked at his untouched fries with his fork. "He has spent the last year since Warren's death prodding and threatening me, trying to make me give up the money Warren took. He didn't carry it too far. He knew he couldn't blackmail me because I could blackmail him right back. I know he's been watching me closely to make sure I haven't been spending extravagant sums. He was convinced the money was still somewhere to be found."

"But now he's taken Kenneth. If it's Ted, why has he resorted to kidnapping after all this time?" I asked.

"I don't know, but I have two guesses. First, I announced I was running for MP. Suddenly, I had a lot more at stake than Ted did. I would be a lot more vulnerable to pressure or blackmail because I suddenly had so much to lose. Second, I think maybe his circumstances have changed somehow, and he really needs the money now. The morning Kenneth disappeared, I got an anonymous letter in the mailbox saying I had until Thursday of this week to cough up ten million dollars, or I wouldn't see Kenneth again." He glanced at us then away. "I knew right away it was Ted. That's the same amount of money Warren stole from us."

I could hardly breathe at the thought of that much money. And that was just the skimming of the skimmings! I looked at Newton. He cleared his throat.

"Silly to bother sending it anonymously when it was obvious who had taken your son," Newton commented.

"It's not like you'd sign your name to a letter like that," McKinnon replied. "Not if the police could use it as evidence."

"And yet you couldn't go to the police because of your involvement in the original crime." Newton sighed.

"You understand my dilemma."

"But now here you are, telling all, and to strangers."

"Things have changed," McKinnon said quietly. "I gave Ted the money—or the stamps—and my son hasn't been returned. As your wife said, his life may be on the line."

"Then why tell us? Why not go to the police with your story?"

"Because there's still the hope that somehow he can pull himself out of this mess without having to jeopardize his career," I said disgustedly. "He knows we may not care about him and his political ambitions, but he knows we *do* care about Angus. And we'll help him because we want to help Angus."

"Assuming that anything he has told us is true," Newton said mildly.

"You have to believe me!" McKinnon leaned forward and thrust his fork at Newton. "I'm telling you the truth. I don't care if I go to jail at this point."

"Then you won't care if we accompany you to the police station to tell them what you just told us," Newton said reasonably.

McKinnon slumped back in his chair, scowling.

"I didn't think so," Newton said. "Tell me this, Mr. McKinnon. Why did you involve Angus in this in the first place?"

"The money never surfaced. Ted was sure it still existed. I couldn't think where else to look—if not for the money itself, then for clues to its whereabouts. All of Warren's furniture was left in the house when his daughter sold it. What if she'd missed it, hidden in a drawer or box somewhere? If Angus had found the money in the house while he'd been living there, I wanted it from him. And if not, I needed access to the house. There had to be something everyone had overlooked."

"So you just barged into the house and abducted him at gunpoint?" I snapped.

McKinnon stared at me. "I was upfront. I told him I represented the Philpott family and wanted to know if he'd found any money hidden in the house. Some was missing; I didn't say how much. Angus denied it. I asked his permission to look through the house, and he said no."

"And then?"

His ears turned a light pink. "I got angry and turned a bit . . . aggressive, I admit. I was upset about my son. I was desperate. In my irrational state of mind, I came to believe Angus had found the money and was just refusing to give it to me."

"But how did an argument turn into abduction?" Newton asked.

McKinnon wriggled uncomfortably in his seat. "I tried to shove past him into the house. I didn't mean to knock into him, but I did. He shoved me back, I hit him, and he said he was calling the police and so much for my political career. He'd recognized me, you see. I hadn't stopped to think he would. And I could see the whole thing collapsing around my ears. My son, my career, my reputation . . ." He rubbed a hand through his hair and turned doleful eyes on me. "That's when the gun came out. I didn't stop to think. I was scared and angry. I didn't think it through. I forced him out to my car and drove to a hotel in the outskirts of Toronto and held him there. I was determined to keep him there until he coughed up the money."

"Ten million? Angus?" I laughed. "Believe me, he doesn't have it."

"Well, of course I came to understand that eventually."

"And you've been at the hotel for the last two weeks?" Newton asked.

"Well, no. We were there a few days, maybe a week, and I started to realize what I'd done. I felt so frightened and stupid. I broke down and told him I was sorry, that I hadn't been thinking clearly. I was too worried about my son. When Angus learned Kenneth had been kidnapped, he became very kind toward me. He offered to help. Of course, I didn't believe he'd help me. And I didn't trust him with the whole story. I just said Warren had hidden ten million in the house, and I needed to find it, or I'd lose my son, and I couldn't go to the police about it because it would endanger him. I eventually moved Angus from the hotel to my house because I was afraid I'd been seen coming and going from the hotel and recognized."

"I don't imagine that would be good for the career either," I said narrowly. "People would think you were up to another kind of mischief. What did your wife say about this stranger you brought home at gunpoint?"

"My wife died six years ago. A brain aneurism."

"Oh." This brought me up short. "Sorry."

"What then?" Newton asked.

"I was getting desperate," McKinnon went on. "Thursday was the deadline to get the money. Last Tuesday Angus said again that he'd help me find the money. And then, for the first time, he told me about the note he'd found that sounded like clues to a treasure hunt. Like I told you before, we had no way of being sure, but it sounded like it might be something to do with the missing money. Angus wanted me to let him go so he could go home to retrieve the note. I didn't trust him at first. I made him tell me where to look, and I went to his house. But—"

"The note wasn't there," Newton said, nodding. "Because we had it by then. We found it on Monday."

"Yes, I saw you tore the house apart looking for it," McKinnon said, frowning.

"We didn't do that. Someone else had already tossed the place when we went in. We found where Angus had hidden the note. The intruder had missed it."

"Then that was likely Ted, looking for the money himself. But how did you know there was even a note? How did you come to be mixed up in this in the first place?" McKinnon asked, sounding genuinely perplexed.

"Angus told us about it," I said. He had, more or less. "He phoned us a week ago Wednesday."

McKinnon shook his head. "He couldn't have. He was with me then. I mean, I had him . . . um . . ."

"Tied up. Yes. He must have gotten ahold of your phone somehow," Newton said. "Annie received a very staticky and hurried message from him, and she got just enough information to find the note eventually."

McKinnon swallowed hard. "He called you on my phone? I—I didn't know. I must have left it within reach." He wiped his palm across his forehead. "Angus had my phone, and he didn't call the police when he had the chance?"

"As you say, he's a kind person," I said. "I'm sure he doesn't hold any of this against you. When he heard your story, he understood your predicament and just wanted to help you and your son. He must have understood that notifying the police would endanger Kenneth."

"The anonymous letter said if I called the police, I'd never see Kenneth again." He paused, thinking. "A week ago Wednesday, you say? Yes, that was the day I told him about my son and what was going on. And he phoned you and told you to look for the note."

"I assume he wanted us to find the money," Newton said. "I think once we'd found it, he would have arranged to have us give it to you. He really was trying to help you, even though you didn't trust him. You might have saved a lot of time and grief for all of us if you *had* trusted him."

McKinnon squirmed again. "When I didn't find the note on Tuesday and I found the house so ripped apart, I went back and told Angus. He said he thought he knew who might have it and told me about you. It took him a couple of days to convince me to trust him and let him go free. Eventually I did; the deadline was looming that night, and I was at the end of my rope. I had to trust him. That evening he called to tell me you had found the stamps and given them to him. I had been expecting cash, but when he told me about the stamps, I figured that was what I'd been looking for."

"Then what?"

"I phoned the number given in the letter and left the message that I had what the kidnapper wanted. I got a call three minutes later with directions to the drop-off point. Angus took the money while I waited for him at his house. But Angus never came back."

"Why didn't you drop off the ransom yourself?" Newton asked.

"I was afraid it might be a set-up or something. I—I was still afraid of being exposed somehow. I didn't want my face at the scene, you understand, in case it all went wrong. If the media had been alerted, or if I was being secretly filmed, it would just give him more to blackmail me with later. I was a coward, pure and simple. If I had been the only option, of course I would have gone. But Angus was in it now too, and I decided not to risk it if I didn't have to. I figured Ted wouldn't care who brought the money so long as he got it. But I guess I misjudged it or something because Angus and Kenneth didn't come back."

Newton looked skeptical. I knew if one of his children had been kidnapped, he wouldn't have sent an intermediary to the drop-off. He would have been there himself, guns blazing (figuratively).

McKinnon set his elbows on the table and laid his forehead in his hands. "I trust Angus; I know he went to the drop-off. He wouldn't skip town with the stamps . . . Would he?"

"Of course not!" I barked. "How could you even think such a thing?"

"But I don't know where he is or where Kenneth is or if I'll ever get my son back."

"It seems to me," Newton said, "if I suspected Ted What's-His-Name of kidnapping, I'd go directly to him about it."

"Believe me, I've tried. I tried to track Vandenberg down. He's not at home, and he hasn't been to work for the past three weeks. No one seems to know where he is. *Three weeks.* That's how long my son has been missing."

Newton tossed down his napkin and stood, reaching for his wallet. His plate was clean, whereas McKinnon and I had only nibbled at our food.

"I'm not sure about every detail of your story, Mr. McKinnon," Newton said, "but I'm inclined to believe the generalities. Angus is clearly on your side, and I will trust his judgment."

McKinnon blinked up at him.

Newton rolled his eyes. "I'm telling you we will help you, Mr. McKinnon. For Angus's sake and for Kenneth's. Not for yours," he added darkly.

I knew this whole episode had only reinforced Newton's opinion of politicians. I sighed, pushed back my chair, and followed Newton from the restaurant.

* * *

On Sunday, I admit I paid little attention in church. I went through the motions of singing and herding children and shaking hands, but my thoughts were far away. There was something not right about McKinnon's story, but I couldn't put my finger on it. Why would an otherwise presumably rational and intelligent man freak out and abduct a stranger? Whatever the provocation or circumstance, most people wouldn't resort to such a move, and the fact that McKinnon had gone to the house with a gun in his pocket told me he anticipated having to take some sort of aggressive action and was prepared for it. That alone made me distrust him.

I looked down at Andrew's head, where it lay on my lap. He was once again accompanying me to Sunday School and had fallen asleep on top of me. I stroked his golden curls and imagined what I would do if someone took one of my children. I would be capable of drawing a gun, storming a stranger's house, whatever it took to get my child back. No, I couldn't judge McKinnon too harshly. I had never been in his shoes. A chill went down my spine at the thought of any danger threatening my—

I sat up straight, and the chill shot up my back and out the top of my head. I was surprised no fireworks burst from my skull. I swept up Andrew and my church bag, threw both over my shoulder, and hurried from the room as unobtrusively as possible.

Newton was a ward clerk, and I thought I would have to wade into the office to find him, but to my relief, he was already out in the hallway, on his knees, comforting Maisie, who was in tears.

"What happened?" I asked as I hurried toward them.

Newton gave me a look. "There was a substitute teacher in Primary today that Maisie didn't know, and Maisie was feeling a little lost, weren't you, sweetie? But she's ready to go back to class now."

I put a hand briefly on Maisie's head but couldn't leave it there long without endangering my grip on Andrew, who continued to sleep on my shoulder.

"Thank you for handling it, dear. Newton, I had a thought."

Newton, about to take Maisie back to her classroom, heard my tense tone and turned back toward me.

"What is it, Annie?"

"The man who broke into our house. Whoever he was, he knew about the note Angus found. He was looking for it at our house."

"Well, that's the hypothesis. He might have thought we'd found the actual money and brought it home with us."

"I don't think so. Ten million dollars would take up some space, even if it were in large-denomination bills. If he was watching us, he'd have noticed that we left Angus's house without any visible boxes or briefcases. And he looked in the filing cabinet—where you'd expect us to put paper; there wouldn't be room for a bundle of money."

"True. The hypothesis of a note stands."

"But we've forgotten to ask the most important question, Newton. How did he know about it? How did he know the note existed? McKinnon says he didn't know about it until Angus told him just last Tuesday. And Wednesday we got burgled."

"Do you think McKinnon was the one who broke into our house when he couldn't find the note at Angus's? How would he have known to look at our house? He didn't even know we existed at the time."

"I'm sure the intruder wasn't McKinnon. Wrong build, wrong eye color. But I'm wondering if McKinnon passed the info about the note's existence along to Ted Vandenberg. Ted was likely the one who tossed Angus's place. He was the one who saw us coming and going from Angus's house, and he was the one who put two and two together and suspected our movements had something to do with the affair. So he broke into our house."

Newton blinked at me. "Are you suggesting McKinnon and Vandenberg are in cahoots in this whole thing to get the missing money?"

"I don't know. But McKinnon gave you his cell phone number last night," I said. "Call and ask him nonchalantly if Ted Vandenberg has a Mr. Potato Head mustache."

* * *

I don't even recall teaching my Relief Society lesson. I've taught for years and have always joked that with the right visual aids, I could teach in my sleep, and I'm pretty sure I proved the point. I moved in a complete fog, and as soon as the class was over, I dashed for the door without waiting to speak to the women who came forward to comment on the lesson. I hoped they wouldn't think me too rude. Then again, they were probably used to my having to dash out of class to deal with one thing or another involving my children. (Boys are energetic creatures, after all, and when they find themselves short on entertainment, they tend to create their own. I still maintain it was the janitor's responsibility to have locked the attic access door last summer, and Ethan couldn't be held entirely to blame for the damage to the Primary room ceiling. The hole hadn't been extensive anyway).

When we got home from church, Newton disappeared into the back room to make the call. I changed Andrew into play clothes and set about slapping lunch on the table. I got Jane to make toasted cheese sandwiches, and I was in the middle of heating tomato soup (I refuse to get too culinary on the Sabbath. It is a day of rest. Though I would consider adding some ham curls and a face to each bowl to fancy it up a bit) when Newton came back into the kitchen, looking thoughtful. I turned off the stove and followed him into the backyard, where we could speak in relative privacy. Chairman Meow followed us and twined around our ankles as we sat on the porch swing. There was a chill wind blowing leaves about the yard, and Newton huddled in his suit coat. I unbuttoned the top button of my blouse and held my hair off the back of my neck to allow the wind to cool me down. Delicious.

"Well?"

Newton scratched his head. "McKinnon swears he never told anybody else about the note, certainly not Ted—who does have a bushy brown mustache, by the way. When I suggested the image of Mr. Potato Head, he was amused."

"So my hunch was right. Vandenberg was our intruder."

"Which means Vandenberg is in town or nearby. Or at least he was on Wednesday."

"Which means Kenneth might be being held somewhere in town too."

Newton sighed. "It's a big town. He could be anywhere."

I leaned over and put my chin in my hands and my elbows on my knees, thinking.

"It still doesn't answer the question, then. If McKinnon is telling the truth, and he wasn't the one who told Vandenberg about the existence of the note, how did Vandenberg learn about it?"

"The only other person you've told about the note is Wendy DeRuvo."

I considered this a moment, a sinking feeling in my chest. "You think she's in cahoots with Vandenberg?"

"It's one explanation, yes."

I watched the leaves swirl around the yard and against the fence, where they stopped, trapped. "Well, I don't know that *cahoots* is the correct word," I said. "If she was close to one of her father's partners, maybe she was close to the other one too. Maybe she simply told him, 'Hey, a strange thing happened today. I got a call from this lady who found the clues to Dad's last treasure hunt.' It might be as innocent as that. She may or may not know about the embezzlement and the vast sum of money involved, but Ted Vandenberg certainly does. He logically might draw the conclusion that the treasure was the missing money. Wendy may not know about the kidnapping and all the rest of it."

"True."

I could understand Wendy wanting to find the last treasure her father had left for her. I didn't want to think that there may have been anything more to it than that. Warren Philpott's obituary had mentioned Wendy's son, Michael. Could a mother be involved in the kidnapping of another person's child? I hated to think so, but the world was often a more evil place than I gave it credit for. I recalled her cheerful, friendly voice, that lovely English accent. I didn't want her to be involved. I liked her, even in that brief interchange.

The phone rang in the house, and I paused, waiting. Eight children in the house, and do you think a single one of them would answer it? It continued to ring. I sighed and climbed to my feet, but then the ringing stopped. I sat down again. Ethan poked his head out the back door.

"There you are. What are you doing out here?" he asked.

"Talking," Newton said.

"Sister Henry is on the phone. She says to ask you if she can have your recipe for Cashew Chicken."

"Is she still on the phone?"

"Yes."

"Can you read it to her, please? It's on a card in the recipe box." (My recipe box is a Rubbermaid container the size of a legal file drawer.)

As he turned to go back inside, I added, "It's filed under G."

He accepted this and continued on his way. Newton frowned at me. "*G?*"

"For Gertrude Hiscock. It was Gertie's recipe originally." I leaned back in the curve of Newton's arm and looked up at the branches of the maple tree, starting to show bare against the pale sky.

"That's something we didn't think of," I said.

"What?"

"Well, Gertie made that chicken recipe once for a Relief Society dinner. I asked her for a copy, and she shared it with me. Now Sister Henry has asked for it, and I've passed it on to her."

"And this is relevant to our discussion how?" Newton asked, lips quirking.

"If a friend asks for something, you share it," I said simply. "Wendy had a copy of the note with the clues. If she viewed Ted Vandenberg as enough of a friend to tell him about it in the first place, she probably would have let him see the clues. He might have asked to see them and offered to help her figure them out."

"I see where you're going. Why would he break into our house the next day to get our copy if he could get one from Wendy?"

"Maybe in order to keep us from finding the treasure first?"

"Vandenberg just wanted the money found. Who cares who found it? He could always take it from us if we found it first. I mean, someone who can kidnap a child and do a little breaking and entering wouldn't balk at theft."

I stood up and began to pace back and forth, as I have often found that walking aids the thought process. The cat left off chasing leaves and paced after me. "Then he didn't want the note to keep us from figuring it out. He wanted it for himself so he could find the money. He didn't have his own copy. She didn't share it with him. Therefore, he was not in cahoots with Wendy. Maybe we're wrong, and they're not even friends."

"In which case, she wouldn't have told him about the note in the first place." Newton reminded me.

I considered this and liked it. "I don't know if it's true, but it makes me *feel* better."

"So we still don't know how Vandenberg knew we had the note or were even involved."

"No. Now what?"

"I don't know," Newton said sadly. "I don't know where it leaves us."

I went over the facts again in my head, and only one possible lead came to mind. "The stamps."

"What about them?"

"Presumably Angus delivered them to Ted."

"Agreed. Or at least set out to do so."

"Ted was expecting cash. He'll now have to get the stamps appraised and turned into cash."

"A reasonable prediction."

"Where does one go to do such things?"

Newton pondered this a moment. "A philatelist's shop, I should think. A dealer in stamps. A collector."

"Someone qualified to appraise them and perhaps wealthy enough to buy them."

Newton shook his head. "In Port Dover? Not likely. I don't know of anyone like that."

"And probably Ted doesn't either. He wasn't expecting stamps, I'm sure. He'll be just as at sea as we are. So what will he do? He'll look up the nearest stamp dealer he can find."

Newton rose without speaking and went into the house. I followed him with Chairman Meow running close behind. Newton went to the laptop in the kitchen and booted it up. In a moment, he had Googled a list of stamp shops and collectors in southwestern Ontario.

"The first one to come up is R. Maresch, but he's in Toronto at Steeles and Yonge. Quite far away."

"Is there anyone closer?"

"Here's a site for the Canadian Stamp Dealers Association," Newton murmured, typing away. "I'll look on their membership directory."

"I had no idea there was such a thing," I said.

"Here. As I suspected, there are none in Port Dover. There's a place in Tillsonburg. It looks like the closest. And here's one—no, two—in Port Colborne."

"Those would be the most likely places he'd turn to," I said. "They're the closest. He's going to be in a hurry to change the stamps into cash and make sure they're worth what he thinks they're worth."

"And then what will he do, once he has the money?" Newton said, looking up sharply from the laptop. His forehead was lined with worry. "Surely he knows McKinnon knows he has Kenneth. He may not be worried about McKinnon telling the police; he can blackmail McKinnon because of his past involvement in the embezzlement. But he won't be able to just let Kenneth go and resume his normal life. Don't forget he also has Angus. Angus can finger him."

I felt a chill run down my arms and went abruptly to the window to look out at the graying evening. "He'll have to leave town, live on the run," I said.

"He'll have to silence Angus," Newton whispered.

I whirled around to face him. "Does he know McKinnon came to us and confided everything? Is he going to silence us too? He obviously knows we're involved."

Newton slapped the laptop shut and came to put his arms around me. I clung to him, regaining my composure with some difficulty.

Newton cleared his throat.

"Right. Here's what we do. It's the only way to save Angus. We have to tell the police about the embezzlement. It would be better if we could convince McKinnon to go to the police himself and start raising a ruckus in the media. We have to make sure a million people know about Ted Vandenberg so there's no point in his silencing anyone. It will be too late to cover up anything, so his motive to kill Angus or Kenneth or us will be dissipated."

"But Douglas McKinnon said not to. The letter said Kenneth would be in danger if we told—"

"He's already in danger, Annie. I only hope we haven't dithered too long and it's too late. Once Ted Vandenberg has his money, he'll want to clean up any witnesses and get back to his life. We don't have any time to lose. And we need to find out where Ted is and fast."

"You're right, of course. But it still frightens me."

"I'll phone Officer Donetti. You start phoning those stamp shops to see if anyone has brought in any highly valuable stamps to—" He looked at the closed laptop. "Oh."

"It's all right; I'll Google it again," I said. I gave him a little nudge. "Go make your phone call."

* * *

We'd forgotten it was Sunday evening, and the shops were all closed. Our attempt to track down Ted by that route would have to be delayed until morning. The policeman Newton spoke to—Donetti being off duty—made reassuring noises and said someone would look into the matter in the morning.

Newton was outraged. "We're talking about the life of a little boy and a history teacher," he snapped. "You need to locate Ted Vandenberg now, tonight. I only hope it isn't too late. I should have realized the implications right away. He's had the stamps since Thursday night. That will have given him Friday and Saturday to turn them into cash. Now, I don't think he could have accomplished that big of a sale in that short of a time. I mean, stamp shops don't typically keep that kind of money on hand in the till, I shouldn't think."

The officer must have made some sort of skeptical remark because I saw Newton's face flush red, and his voice switched to the supercilious tone he reserved for addressing particularly stubborn or rude people. I wouldn't have been surprised to hear him order the officer to "act forthwith, chop chop!"

"Vandenberg hasn't been home for three weeks. Surely that's enough to convince you he has Kenneth McKinnon." His words chipped out like stone fragments hit with a hammer. There was another buzz as the policeman answered.

"I realize Douglas McKinnon has not reported his son missing," Newton snapped. "I've told you there's a reasonable explanation for that. He doesn't want his involvement in the embezzlement exposed. Listen, I do not have time to go into the full matter right now. You need to put out a notice, an APB or whatever they call it, on Ted Vandenberg. I will come into the station right now and give a full statement if you like, and I will do my best to convince McKinnon to come forward, but it will take some time. Please be taking action while—"

There was an audible click. Newton glared at the phone in his hand in fury. "They think I'm a crackpot," he said.

No one was going to take him seriously unless McKinnon corroborated, that was obvious. If the police called McKinnon and he said, "Ridiculous. My son is in bed where he belongs," we wouldn't be able to get them to do anything.

"Call McKinnon and tell him we're down to the wire, life or death, and it's time to come clean. The police will have to do something if *he* makes the report." I realized how that sounded and tried hastily to correct it. "Not that *you* aren't important too, dear, but he is the embezzler, and he is possibly a future MP and the father of the child . . ."

"I comprehend your intent and do not fault your expression of it," Newton replied, hunting out his wallet. "I concur. If we can get McKinnon to make a clean breast of it, the police will leap into action."

He dug out McKinnon's number from his wallet and made the call while I anxiously hovered nearby. The children were all busy elsewhere, and I thanked heaven for small mercies. Inquisitive prodding would not be helpful at this point.

McKinnon apparently—after some reluctance—understood Newton's sense of urgency. It was only a matter of time before the stamps were turned into cash and Vandenberg started cleaning up his trail. I was certain McKinnon wasn't happy with the prospect, but he agreed to meet Newton at the police station.

"You've made a wise choice," Newton told him right before he hung up. He looked grimly at me. "Not that he had much choice. He should have done it sooner. If something has happened to Kenneth or Angus, I feel I will be partially to blame for not insisting sooner that he talk to the police."

I stretched up on tiptoe and kissed his cheek. "Go," I said. There would be time for talk of recrimination and comfort later.

"I'll be back as soon as I can. Er—keep the doors locked."

And he was gone.

Chapter Eight

THE EVENING WAS INTERMINABLE. I tried to fill the time by working on the knitted shawl I was making for Mary Hessler's birthday next month, but I kept dropping stitches and losing count and eventually had to stop before I ruined the whole thing. I made more peanut butter cookies (for the missionary luncheon on Saturday this time) and played Word on the Street with some of the kids. The game involved coming up with words at high speeds using particular letters. I don't think I could have remembered the name of my own mother at that point, and Maisie accused me of letting her win.

Finally, bedtime neared, and I was gratefully sucked into the engulfing routine of pajamas, toothbrushes, scriptures, prayers, songs, and kisses. Then just Isaac, Caleb, and I were left awake. I had filled both boys in on what was happening and expressed the utter helplessness I felt at not being able to contact the stamp stores until Monday morning.

Isaac thought a moment, then went to the laptop and booted it up. "What were the names of the three shops you're trying to reach?"

I told him, and he typed and searched. I watched over his shoulder. "Good grief, what size font is that? Two-point?"

"Eleven," he said dryly.

"Well, enlarge it a bit. Not all of us have the eyesight of a red-tailed hawk, you know."

He searched a moment longer and then wrote down three names and handed the paper to me.

"The proprietors of the shops," he said. "We can check for a listing for their names and call them at home."

Hope sprang up in my chest, and I pulled up a chair beside him. "Why didn't I think of that? How did you find this? Never mind, let's just see if we can find their home numbers."

The Tillsonburg shop owner's name was Archibald Glendenning, an uncommon name. We found one listing in Tillsonburg, and I dialed the number with shaking fingers. I glanced at the clock as the phone on the other end began to ring. Ten thirty on a Sunday night. Oh well, it was an emergency.

I tried to explain this state of emergency to the gruff voice that answered on the third ring. "I'm sorry to bother you at home, and I wouldn't if it weren't for a very important reason," I said. "I need to find out if someone came into your shop on Friday or Saturday with a number of extremely valuable stamps, looking to get them appraised or sell them."

"What stamps?" the voice barked.

"I don't know the exact type of stamps," I said. "One of them might have been a Mauritius Two-Penny Post Office Blue."

This got his attention. "What year?" he asked.

"I don't recall. I don't remember the details. But they all would have been unusual and rare. The gentleman had a big brown mustache."

"Look, no one has been into my shop with anything like that in months, if ever, and even if they had, I certainly wouldn't tell you. What business is it of yours? Are the stamps stolen or something?"

"Yes, actually," I said. "They belong to a woman named Wendy DeRuvo, but this gentleman with the mustache is trying to sell them without her knowledge." For all I knew, it could be true. We didn't *think* they were in cahoots.

"I don't deal in stolen merchandise," the man said snappily.

"No, of course not. I didn't mean to imply you did. Quite the opposite. I'm letting you know to keep an eye out."

He made unhappy noises under his breath, and I knew it was time to end the call.

"If anything like that happens, if someone comes in trying to sell a very valuable stamp or multiple stamps, could you please let me know?" I gave him my number, thanked him, and hung up.

"Well, that didn't go very well," I said.

Meanwhile, Isaac the Wunderkind had looked up the home number of the second name, Samuel O'Leary, proprietor of the Port Colborne Philatery Shoppe. But even though I let the phone ring several times, there was no answer.

"Drat. Who's number three?" I asked.

"Phil Johnson. Unfortunately, a common name," Isaac said. "There are three listings in Port Colborne for that name and another one in Dunnville. Any of them could be him."

"I'll just have to ask." I sighed.

The woman who answered the first call said her husband was out and who was I anyway, calling at this hour? She sounded suspicious of this female voice on her line, asking for her husband late at night.

I tried to reassure her. "I am trying to locate the owner of the High Street Stamp Shop in Port Colborne," I explained.

"Well, Phil isn't him," she said. "He's a driver for Ezee Rental Cars."

"Thank you. Sorry for disturbing you," I said and hung up.

Person number two turned out to be the owner, but he too said no one had come into his store wanting anything unusually valuable appraised.

"Believe me, I'd remember if someone had," he said. "Business has been awfully slow since that other shop opened up on Davenport."

I thanked him and once again left my number for him to call if Ted Vandenberg did contact him.

I set the phone down and looked glumly at the boys, who had been listening. "No luck. I'll wait until morning and try Samuel O'Leary again. If it's not him, we'll have to look further afield. Maybe we're wrong. Maybe Vandenberg wanted to go to a shop far from town so word never got back to anyone here about his selling an expensive collection. He wouldn't want anyone wondering where it had come from."

"Do you want us to wait up with you until Dad comes home?" Isaac offered.

"No, no. He might be all night," I said. I kissed them both on the forehead. "You have school tomorrow, Caleb. Head for bed. I'll bring you up to date in the morning if anything develops."

As it turned out, Newton didn't come home until two in the morning. He looked sad and drained.

"There's nothing they can do," he said as he slid into bed beside me.

I had been lying wide awake, staring uselessly at the ceiling in the dark.

"What do you mean, nothing they can do?" I said. "Didn't McKinnon tell them?"

"He made a full confession," Newton said, slipping an arm around me. "I was proud of him. He didn't try to justify or excuse himself at all. But the fact is, even though they agree Vandenberg is probably guilty, there's nothing to go on. He's not at home, he hasn't been at work, and no one knows how to contact him. No one knows if he has family around or where he'd hide out. It's a needle in a haystack. They can't very well start going door to door looking for him. They are going to go to the media though.

They saw the wisdom in that. They'll put out a whatever-it's-called—an Amber Alert."

"Our only hope in finding him is to get a lead from the stamp dealer," I said. "And that's a needle in a haystack too." I told him about my lack of success and my theory that Vandenberg might not use a dealer close to home but might try to find one farther away.

Newton sighed. "You may be right. Stamps! What a stupid thing to invest in."

"But virtually untraceable," I said.

"And why didn't he put them in a safety deposit box like anyone else?" he grumbled. "I really had been expecting an exposé to be in that box. A confession. Not stamps. I mean, it just shows that Warren Philpott wasn't trying to make things right before he died. He was grabbing what he could while he still had time."

"Sort of dampens your view of the goodness of human nature, doesn't it?" I patted his hand. "I'd rather think he had regrets and was trying to set things right before he died too, but I'm afraid it didn't happen that way. I fear he simply snatched what he could from the joint account . . . though I suppose maybe it was out of some desire to see that Wendy was provided for after his death."

"Perhaps." Newton was silent a moment, and I thought he'd fallen asleep, but then he murmured, "But why under a rock in the middle of a forest? Who would think to hide something there?"

"Maybe he thought no one would disturb it there. It wouldn't show up on any paperwork anywhere. Wendy wouldn't have to let anyone know she'd found the stamps once she did find them."

"But wasn't he afraid something would happen to them? Someone would stumble across them? Or water would get in and ruin them?"

"They were well sealed against the weather," I said. "And if anyone was going to stumble across them, it would have been Wendy or her husband anyway."

"What makes you say so?"

"I have been thinking about it, and I suspect the DeRuvos own that bit of land we were traipsing around on."

Newton sat up, and I felt him staring at me in the dark. "How did you devise that hypothesis?"

"I remember Wendy telling me they owned a building lot somewhere by Carlisle and were planning to build a house one day. Carlisle is about a three-minute drive down the road from the forest. I suspect Warren Philpott hid the stamps on his daughter's property. I mean, it would be more secure than leaving it on a boat in Lake Erie or—or a church roof in Belize." I started to giggle and tried to suppress it, very much afraid it was hysteria.

Newton lay down again and put his arm gently around my shoulders. "There was one other thing I haven't told you," he said after a moment. Something in his tone made me tense up, and I squirmed around to face him.

"What is it?"

"The police found Angus's car abandoned down by the pier earlier this evening," he said. "The word came in while I was at the station."

I considered this a moment. "The pier. That's where the drop-off was?"

"We can presume."

"No blood in the car?" I forced myself to ask.

"No."

I nodded. "Then it doesn't tell us anything we didn't already know."

"You are taking the news remarkably well," he said.

"If anything, it's good news. It will prompt the police to take all of this more seriously."

Newton dropped a kiss on my forehead. "Right you are," he said. "It's best to find the positive in it."

I got up to open the window a crack. Newton sighed and pulled the covers up around his ears. "Good night, dear," he said.

* * *

The next morning I zipped through breakfast preparations and then left the kids eating while I went into the family room to phone the Philatery Shoppe. A male voice answered, sounding younger than I'd expected. Somehow, stamps seemed like an old man's hobby, but I suppose that was a hastily and incorrectly formed assumption.

I introduced myself and explained my mission. To my joy, the man immediately responded, "Yes. Sure."

"Yes? Someone with a big mustache came into your shop with some valuable stamps?" I gripped the phone and sent Newton a wide-eyed look. He bent and put his ear close to the receiver so he could hear.

"Yeah, on Friday afternoon. I wouldn't forget those; they were fantastic specimens."

He started to launch into a detailed description of what the stamps were, but I interrupted as politely as I could. "I'm sorry, but time is of the essence. I need to locate this man. I don't have time to explain, but it's a matter of life and death."

"Oh?" He sounded intrigued.

"Can you please tell me his name and contact information? I know you're probably not allowed to give that out, but as I said, it's an emergency. If I need to get the police to get a warrant, I can, but it will just waste time we don't have."

"Police? Why? Were these stamps stolen?"

"Yes. But that's not the point. I would really, really appreciate it if you—"

"Hey, I understand, and I would if I could, but I can't. I didn't find out his name or number."

I froze. "You didn't?"

"No. I researched and appraised the stamps for him—they were worth more money than my whole shop will ever see—and I told him about an auction he might want to enter them in. It's the only way he'll get that kind of money for them. And then he left."

"You—you didn't get his number," I repeated stiffly. All hopes sank into my fifteen-minute boots. Newton turned away and looked out the window at the blowing leaves.

"I'm sorry," the young man said sincerely. "But since I couldn't buy the stamps myself, I didn't see any reason to get his name or anything. I passed on the information, and he left. I was just thrilled I actually got to handle a Two-Penny Blue, you know?"

"Yes. Well, thank you anyway," I said. "I appreciate your help."

"Sorry," he said again. And then, as I was about to hang up, he added, "I do remember one thing about him, if it helps."

"What is that?"

"I made a jokey remark about his mustache. The dude had this huge mustache like a walrus, you know? I said something about it, I don't remember what, just 'cool 'stache' or something like that. And he joked back that it kept him warm in the winter when his wood stove went out. I laughed and said nobody heats their house with a wood stove anymore. Was he off the grid or something? And he said he had a cottage by the Grand River. He had to be careful not to chop his mustache off when he was chopping kindling."

I shook my head to clear it. "Oh. Uh. He didn't mention where this cottage was, did he? The Grand River is very long."

"No, he didn't. I'm sorry."

My hopes fell again. "Well, thank you. That might turn out to be helpful anyway; you never know."

"Good luck," he said and hung up.

I shook my head again at Newton. "Vandenberg has a cottage somewhere," I said. "On the Grand River."

"Nothing more specific than that?"

"No. But think about it. If Angus's car was found on the pier, and that *was* the drop-off point, Ted was coming to it by boat. The Grand River empties into Lake Erie just down the shoreline . . . how far?"

"About a two-hour drive away," Newton said. "A hundred kilometers, give or take."

"Call McKinnon and ask him if he knows of a cottage Vandenberg might own somewhere near the mouth of the Grand River."

"Why the mouth?"

"Because if he had to travel too far up the river, it would be easier and quicker to come to Port Dover by car. Why go the long way around by boat? Ask McKinnon."

"Um, McKinnon is in court at the moment," Newton said. "I don't know if I can reach him."

"Court?"

"He's being arraigned this morning."

I stopped, surprised. And then I was surprised at my surprise. What had I expected? That they'd let McKinnon admit to embezzling millions of dollars and then send him home scot free?

"I'll try him a little later and find out what happened." Newton picked up his briefcase and looked at it gloomily. "I can't go to work today. How can I?"

"Work!" I shouted. "Newton, that's it."

He jerked, startled. "What's it?"

"Call Lucan Investments and talk to Ted Vandenberg's coworkers. See if anyone knows where his cottage is. Surely he's mentioned it to someone. People chat about that kind of thing with coworkers."

"But Ted doesn't work for Lucan."

"What? Sure he does."

"No. Remember, McKinnon said he was just the auditor. He likely works for a different firm, and Lucan is just one of his clients."

"Well, then, call Lucan and ask them which auditing firm they use," I (admittedly) snapped.

Newton set down his briefcase again and went to look up the number.

"Mom!" It was Maisie in the doorway. "I can't find my shoes. Ethan hid them, and I can't find them."

"I'll help you." I took her hand, and we went in search of Ethan, who denied any knowledge of the shoes. They were eventually located under Maisie's pajamas on the closet floor. Then we had to go through the whole I'm-sorry-for-falsely-accusing-you-and-I-will-not-act-on-a-theory-without-evidence-again routine. Ethan graciously forgave his sister.

I looked at the clock. "Ten minutes until the bus!" I hollered—informed the troops. "Jane, did you feed the cat? Scott, it's your turn to empty the litter box. Everyone remember we're still on the buddy system!"

As everyone began to mobilize, gathering backpacks and jackets, Newton came into the kitchen with a broad smile on his face. I froze with Maisie's hairbrush in one hand and Meow's water dish in the other, and seeing Newton's expression, the children froze too.

"What did you find out?" I demanded.

"He works for Harris Williams," he said, referring to a well-known firm based in London, Ontario. "I called them, and they didn't want to give me any information, but I finally found a chatty receptionist who was willing to ask around for me. She confirmed Ted hasn't been to the office in about three weeks, but she said he often works from home. I acted like I was a concerned relative who couldn't contact him at home and wondered if he'd gone to the cottage, but I didn't have the number. She didn't have it either and wouldn't have given it to me if she did. But she did unwittingly confirm he had a cottage."

"But then—"

"But then I got hold of McKinnon. He's been let out on his own recognizance due to the circumstances. He didn't know of any cottage, but he did remember Ted had a bumper sticker on his car for Lynd Island Point."

Lynd Island was in the Grand River, and Lynd Island Point was a little town spread along the shore opposite the island, not far from the mouth where the river emptied into Lake Erie. I cheered. "That has to be it. And it's only two hours away. I bet that's where he's keeping Kenneth." *And maybe Angus?* my mind added hopefully. I wouldn't let myself consider the vast stretch of empty lake between here and there, where an inconvenient witness could be slipped overboard. Would Ted keep him as an additional hostage or consider him superfluous?

"There are cottages all along the shore as well as in the town itself. It's a large area," Newton said. "The police can't very well traipse along knocking on every cottage. Ted will get wind of it and disappear long before they get to his door. *If* we even have the right area."

"Tell the police to set up a road block at each end of town," Isaac said. "There's only one road running through there, isn't there? He's got to come or go on that road."

"Unless he uses the theoretical boat." Newton looked pleased that his son assumed he could command the local law enforcement agency. "Many cottagers do. If he gets into the Grand River, he'll be out on Lake Erie in open water and will be difficult to apprehend. He could end up anywhere. We have to consider our approach carefully."

"*Our* approach?" I asked.

"Certainly," Newton said. "We're not going to leave it entirely up to the police, are we? They'll just get entangled in jurisdictional arguments between the Port Dover Police, the Lynd Island local force, and the Provincial Police. Or he'll get out onto the lake and the RCMP or Provincial Marine Unit or whoever patrols the lake will have to get involved. It'll be a bureaucratic mess. If he makes it across the lake, it will wind up in the Americans' hands, and then think of the paperwork! Meanwhile, Ted will get away, and we'll never get Kenneth or Angus back."

"But—"

"I'm in!" Isaac said.

"Me too," Caleb said.

"If you're going, so am I," Enoch piped up.

"Me too! You can't leave us home!" Scott said.

"Hold it!" I held up my hands. "School. The bus will be here any minute. And you're all going to be on it."

"I'm not," Isaac said reasonably.

"Me neither," Scott said. "Let's go bring Angus home."

I looked at Newton.

"It is a large area," he said reasonably. "More hands make for light work. With all of us, we could cover the area pretty swiftly."

"Be realistic, Newton. What do we do if we locate Vandenberg?" I demanded. "Swoop in and tie him up with our shoelaces?"

"Of course not. Surely you know I wouldn't put our children in danger."

"What, then?"

"We'll just scope the place. Once we're sure where he is, we'll notify the appropriate authorities, whoever that is. And keep an eye on the cottage so he can't sneak away while they're coming. He won't even know we're there," Newton said. "There's no sense in sending the police in if we're not sure we're right. But we can save the police a lot of time if we locate him while they're busy sorting out jurisdictions."

"Please, Mom?" Caleb begged.

"Absolutely not," I said firmly. "It could be dangerous."

"It won't be. And we can leave the smaller ones here," Newton conceded.

"Mom, we love Angus too. We can't possibly concentrate in school while he's out there somewhere waiting for us to find him," Enoch said.

"No."

"But—"

"No."

"We won't do anything brash. We'll locate him and then fall back and let the police do the rest," Scott insisted.

"No."

"Give in to impulse," Newton said, grinning.

"Nice try."

"Listen to what your heart is telling you."

I stopped short. Dr. Post's voice? No.

My own.

Five minutes later, Maisie and Ethan were on the bus on their way to school, Andrew was playing next door with Cindy Johnson's toddler, and the rest of us were in the van on the way to Lynd Island Point.

In life, some concessions must be made. And Newton had a point; more hands did make lighter work. Though, in point of fact, I was just too exhausted and worn down to withstand the concerted efforts of six people *and* my heart's nagging. I wanted Angus home, whatever it took. If there was a chance this might help things along, what could I do but say yes? But I told myself that at the first sign of danger, we were out of there, Angus or no.

We had taken the precaution of leaving a message for Officer Donetti indicating our suspicions that Vandenberg owned a cottage near Lynd Island. Newton omitted the fact that we were planning to meander in that direction ourselves . . .

The traffic was light, and we made it to the little town by nine o'clock. The sun glinted brightly off the river and gilded with butter the leaves of the trees lining the banks. The Grand widened out here in a brown band, preparatory to entering the deep waters of Lake Erie, moving gently around the small island in its midst. Lynd Island, twenty-two acres in size, was thickly treed with birch and maple and blocked the view of the opposite shore of the river. The trees were ablaze with yellow and red and white and looked quite lovely.

There were a few ritzy cottages on the island ("cottage" being what the wealthy owners called them. I personally wouldn't refer to a three-million-dollar abode with six bedrooms and separate maid's quarters as a cottage), but most of the houses were spread along the shore of the mainland facing the island. These were humbler homes, some of them seasonal and some of them year-round. In another few weeks, autumn would be over and the watercraft would be withdrawn onto shore and stored away in sheds and boathouses for the winter. But now, the weather was still mild, and the shared jetties and docks along the shore were colorful with the small motorboats and canoes tethered to them. The watercraft bobbed gently on the smooth current. Newton was right; if Ted had a boat such as these, he could be on the water and gone in no time.

We parked the van at a picnic area on a side road and walked down to the water. I took note of the public washroom standing under a group of pine trees (it never hurts to know where the nearest one is—the habits of a mother of eight die hard). Newton took a deep, appreciative breath of the cool, damp air coming off the river and looked around with his hands on his hips. "All right, let's be methodical about this," he said. "There are—what would you say?—maybe forty houses along the river itself? And another hundred or so farther back along the side streets, not on the water itself."

"I'd say closer to a hundred and twenty," Isaac said. "Assuming Ted's cottage is in the town of Lynd Island Point itself and not outside the town limits. Or on Lynd Island."

"He wanted to avoid ostentatious spending, so I doubt he'd live on the island itself," Newton said.

"Let's work on that assumption and start with the town," I agreed. "Otherwise, this whole thing will become overwhelming."

Newton nodded sharply. "Right. That's a hundred sixty dwellings, roughly, and there are seven of us. Twenty-three houses each, more or less."

"I'm not sure I like the idea of splitting us up," I said in protest. "It would be safer to work in pairs."

"I suppose, but it will take longer that way," Newton said slowly.

"And what do you propose we do, march along knocking on doors? You said if the police did that, it would scare Ted off before they could find him. If we do the same, it will have the same result. It's a pity we don't know what his car looks like."

Newton pointed to a large silver box at the side of the road. It was one of those multifamily mailboxes with a locked slot for each home.

"Right. Let's start with that. Are there names on the mailboxes?"

We all crowded around to look. Some of the boxes had labels with surnames; others simply had numbers. A quick glance showed there were no labels for "Vandenberg."

"This is only one of several such mailboxes," Newton explained. "There will be one every so often for each group of houses. Boys, you spread out that way and cover the side streets. If you find a label for Vandenberg, come find us. Don't do anything else. We'll cover the ones along the river and meet you at the far end of the main road, by the boardwalk."

I watched them go with some trepidation, but I decided if the four of them stuck together, they would be all right. Newton, Jane, and I walked along the river until we reached the next group mailbox, trying to look nonchalant. Again, there was nothing indicating the name Vandenberg.

It took us twenty minutes to locate and check the rest of the boxes along the river—with no success. The town ended in a boardwalk with a few little shops and restaurants, some of them closed for the season. The boys rejoined us as we stood beside a small bakery overlooking the water. There were a few patrons sipping coffee and eating breakfast wraps at the blue plastic tables set out on the sidewalk. The place apparently specialized in wraps and flatbreads; the painted sign on the bakery read "No Bun Intended." The lovely smell of frying bacon wafted out onto the sidewalk as someone opened the door. I heard five male stomachs rumble simultaneously.

"All right, all right." I sighed. "Let's get something to eat and rethink this plan. Obviously checking mailboxes isn't working. We should have brought McKinnon with us. Maybe he could identify Ted's car. Every car here has a Lynd Island Point bumper sticker."

We pushed open the glass door and shuffled in. I was the last to enter, and as I let my eyes adjust to the softer light after the sunlight's glint on the river, I peered around for a table large enough to hold all of us. The tables inside were also blue plastic, most of them designed to hold two or four people. Perhaps they'd let us slide two together.

I turned to speak to Newton and froze. At a table by the window, sitting by himself, was a broad-shouldered man with dark hair and a bushy mustache. He was eating a bagel and reading a newspaper. He was facing us but hadn't yet looked up and seen us. I jabbed Newton in the ribs—er, I drew Newton's attention to the figure.

"Is that . . . ? Do you think . . . ?"

"Possibly. It is unfortunate we don't have Andrew here to identify him," Newton whispered, turning his back to the man at the window. "Don't look at him directly. He will recognize your face. Boys, put the hoods of your sweatshirts up."

"Would he recognize them, do you think?" I asked in a hiss.

"If he's been watching our house, maybe. Boys, Jane, turn around quietly and walk back outside."

"But we—"

"Now."

They caught his tone and instantly obeyed. We shuffled back outside and around the corner of the building, where the children clustered together excitedly.

"Was that him?"

"Did he see us?"

"Are you sure?"

Newton had pulled a cell phone from his pocket. He didn't own one himself, and I saw it was the pay-as-you-go one Isaac had gotten for his birthday. Newton shushed the children and jerked his head at Isaac.

"Wander around to the side of the building and watch to make sure he doesn't leave. If you see him come out, let us know. Don't let him see your face."

Between Isaac's hoodie and his long hair, I didn't think there was much danger of that happening, but it was right to take precautions anyway.

Isaac slipped away. Newton stepped farther into the parking lot so as not to let his voice carry and began speaking rapidly into the phone. When he rejoined us, his face was tight with annoyance.

"Donetti says it will take half an hour or more for him to liaise with the local police and get someone down here. He had some—uh—choice things to say about our being here 'interfering with his investigation.' His words, not mine. I never cease to be amazed by the incompetence of the—"

"Now, Newton," I said hastily, not wishing to be derogatory toward the law enforcement authorities in front of the children. "It's our fault for not giving him fair warning before we came. If we had told him we intended to flush Vandenberg out of hiding in the first place, he—"

"Wouldn't have let us come," Scott finished for me, nodding.

"We weren't intending to do anything of the sort," Newton said grumpily. "We were attempting to locate his cottage, not the man himself."

"Isn't that just our rotten luck?" Caleb snickered.

"We should have realized the odds were high of running into him in a town this small," I said. "What do we do now?"

"Don't let Vandenberg out of our sight," Newton said. "If he leaves the shop, we'll follow him at a discreet distance. Don't engage him in any way. Stay out of his line of sight. But don't lose track of him—he might lead us back to his cottage."

We waited in the parking lot for what seemed half an hour but was probably only about ten minutes. The smell of the frying bacon teased our noses, and Jane began to hop from one foot to the other and whimper with impatience. I hushed her, not wanting to attract attention from passersby. I wasn't all that sorry that we had been blocked from indulging in a second breakfast, truth be told, though I knew the kids (and Newton) were disappointed. It's not like we needed the extra calories or bacon fat. I did try to maintain a modicum of restraint when it came to food, though I wasn't the type to diet fastidiously. I had never tried Weight Watchers or Jenny Craig or one of those other programs. To my mind, if people wanted to lose weight that seriously, it would make more sense and be much cheaper to just hire an eight-year-old to follow them around and slap their hand whenever they reached for the Nachos.

At last, Isaac came back around the corner of the building.

"He's standing up and throwing away his garbage," he reported. "I think he's leaving."

Newton tugged at Caleb's hoodie. "Don't let him see your faces, any of you. Try to blend in and look like ordinary scruffy teenagers cutting school."

"With their parents," Enoch said.

"And their little sister," Scott added.

Newton ignored them. "We'll let him get a hundred yards in front of us and then follow."

"What if he gets in a car?" Jane asked.

"Then we run like blazes back to the van and give chase," Newton said mildly. "There he goes."

We watched as the burly figure left the bakery and began walking south along the river bank. He wore a Maple Leafs sweatshirt and a baseball hat, and since there were few people about that morning, I didn't think we would lose sight of him. As we walked along a good distance behind, my heart thudded in my chest. I knew it was just from anxiety and excitement, but I hoped this little escapade wouldn't take too long. Prolonged tension couldn't be good for my heart arrhythmia.

I dragged my attention back to Vandenberg, who had stopped to tie his shoe, resting it awkwardly on the metal rail that separated the road from the river bank. Maybe he would lead us to wherever he was keeping Angus and Kenneth. He wouldn't want to leave them for long, as evidenced by the fact that he hadn't been to work in three weeks. I wondered if he had planned to take this long of a vacation or what he was telling his employers. Maybe he was working from his cottage and they didn't care if he never appeared at the office. How would it be to have a job like that?

I was musing on the types of employment that lend themselves to telecommuting and marveling at the advancement of technology that allowed such a possibility when Newton suddenly stopped dead. The rest of us piled up behind him on the sidewalk.

"He went into the bank," he said, turning his back toward Vandenberg again and thus shielding all of us from view should the man come back out onto the street and head toward us. I peered around him skeptically.

"Bank? In this small of a village? You're not serious."

"It's one of those little ATM kiosk places," Newton said. "Can anyone see him?"

"He's coming back out," Caleb said, tugging his hood farther over his face and attempting to look like any ordinary scruffy teenager cutting school. "It's okay; he's carrying on in the same direction."

We all resumed our surreptitious saunter.

For someone with two abductees waiting for him at home, Vandenberg didn't seem in all that much of a hurry to get back to his cottage. We followed along as he stopped at the minimart for a single bag of groceries, stopped again to read the notices posted on the community bulletin board, and chatted with an elderly man who was also reading the board. It struck me that Vandenberg was acting like a man who was supremely bored. I imagined it wasn't stimulating work, watching over two tied-up people.

At least, I hoped there were two. I hoped they were tied up and not drugged or something. One has to know what he is doing when using sedatives. They aren't to be trifled with.

And then Ted Vandenberg stopped beside a Volkswagen Jetta the color of lentil soup that was parked beside the last mailbox along the road and fished in his pocket for his keys. He opened the driver's door and got in.

I sucked in my breath and quickened my pace, shortening the distance between us. He was going to get away. He wasn't going home. Or home was farther away than we'd thought. And our van was a good three blocks away, by the picnic area. Even if we sprinted, we would never get back to the van in time to follow Ted wherever he was going.

"Drat!" Newton muttered. "Where's he going now?"

Ted had placed the grocery bag in the passenger seat and put the car into reverse. He turned to check over his shoulder for traffic. There was no time to lose. Heart condition or no, I had to do something. I dashed down the sidewalk and launched myself onto the hood of his car.

Ted jerked around with a startled, "Hey!" I lay spread-eagled on the car, gripping a windshield wiper in one hand and his side mirror in the other, and met his wide-eyed gaze through the windshield. His eyes were blue, and the mustache really did look like Mr. Potato Head at this close range. I sincerely hoped this *was* Ted and not some random look-alike stranger. I would have some explaining to do if it wasn't him. I could feel the hood of the car denting inward beneath me.

"Get off my car! Are you nuts?" he bellowed. Behind me, I heard Newton's mild voice say at the same time, "Really, my dear, do you think that's wise?"

"Get out of the car and give me your keys," I yelled.

I think it was at that moment he recognized me. His face went slack, and I felt a surge of triumph through my fear. It *was* him.

"Where is Angus?" I shouted through the glass. "You can't hide him forever."

Ted snapped his mouth shut and hit the gas. If I hadn't been clinging to the side mirror, I would have been left in the dirt. Ted backed rapidly into the road without looking for oncoming cars (luckily, the road was clear—or unluckily, if you look at it that way), and he threw the car into gear. I figured this was no time for dignity or false courage. I screeched.

He only got about ten feet down the road before he slammed on the brakes. I lost my grip and slid off the front of the car onto the asphalt, landing hard on my tailbone. I gasped, squeezed my eyes shut, and waited for him to gun the motor and run me over. But the car didn't move. I opened my eyes and looked up to see my children hanging onto the car, some on the hood where I had been, one on the roof. I painfully climbed to my feet and saw Jane holding the back bumper with feet planted. From the look on her face, I think she could have prevented the car from moving all by herself. Isaac had wrenched open the door before Vandenberg could lock it. Newton swiftly reached in to remove the keys from the ignition. All fell silent. Across the street, the elderly gentleman had stopped to watch us, his face blank with astonishment.

"You can't do that! Get these people off my car!" Ted shouted. He started to get out of the car, but Isaac placed one size-fourteen foot gently on Ted's chest and held him down against the seat.

"You're not going anywhere," he said, matching Newton's mild tone. "Where is Angus?"

"Who?"

"You know very well who," Newton said tightly. "Where are you holding him? And where is Kenneth McKinnon?"

"And where is Warren Philpott's stamp collection?" Scott added.

"I don't know what you're talking about," Ted shouted, but his face had gone a sickly color, and the bluster was starting to leave his voice.

I brushed the pebbles off that were embedded in my palms, straightened my clothing, and held a hand out to Enoch, where he perched on the roof, legs dangling down the side of the car.

"Shoelaces," I said.

Chapter Nine

IN THE END, THE SHOELACES hadn't been required. Ted blustered and roared about these insane people climbing all over his car, but he didn't try to get out. The police arrived sooner than expected (local, not provincial). Then there was a lot of talking and arguing.

Quite a crowd had gathered by that time, but no one, surprisingly, had interfered or seemed to question our actions too closely. They just stood around watching. That was Canadians for you—it took a lot to rile them. They probably figured we were shooting a movie. I was glad of their presence though. They may not have jumped into the fray of their own accord, but they would have willingly extended a hand if we'd asked for help. Not that we needed help, I thought smugly, looking around at my phalanx of scruffy teenagers, now slouching against the car and looking bored.

The officers had had the general outline of the story from Donetti and apparently didn't object to our having located and detained Vandenberg ourselves. Perhaps it wasn't the correct procedure, but it had at least been effective. I wondered how citizens' arrests worked and whether we had, in fact, effected one.

Vandenberg was shrilly proclaiming innocence of all wrongdoing. He'd been running a few errands, he asserted, and out of the blue, this mad woman had flung herself onto his car.

After a while, the kids and I got tired of standing around waiting while the police dealt with things. I left Newton to explain things and went to find a bathroom, and then I gave Isaac a fistful of money and had him take the kids back to the bakery for their delayed snack. The police were doing the talking now, in moderate tones, and I couldn't hear what they were saying to Vandenberg. I started to lose patience. I turned to the crowd of onlookers and saw that they were growing bored at the lack of gun play and were beginning to disperse.

"Sorry, wait, do any of you know where this man's cottage is?" I called to them.

But they were bystanders, probably many of them vacationers, and no one answered me. Even the elderly man Vandenberg had been chatting with shook his head, shrugged, and moved away.

When at last Newton rejoined me, he looked distinctly annoyed.

"They can't arrest him without a warrant or just cause."

"Just cause?" I said, nearly ready to burst. "What do they call kidnapping?"

"They have only our word against his. Right now, he's an upright citizen and you're the unstable woman who attacked his car."

I let this slide. "So they're going to let him go?"

"No. They're conferring with Donetti to see if they have anything to charge him with. The most they have is suspicion of embezzlement based on McKinnon's statement. But it's enough, anyway, to bring him in for questioning, at least. Eventually, they may be able to go over Lucan Investments' books and find evidence of the embezzlement. It will all take time, of course, though when Vandenberg learns that McKinnon turned himself in and told all, he may be willing to talk. He'll want to make a deal of some sort."

"But what about Kenneth and Angus?"

"We have no proof at all of kidnapping except McKinnon's belief that Ted is the one who took his son. And even McKinnon can't prove it. And Vandenberg knows it."

"Why don't they find out where his cottage is?" I said. "When they find Angus and Kenneth tied up in the closet, will that be proof enough for them?"

"He claims he doesn't own a cottage here. He was just passing through. And one of the officers told me there's no cottage registered in Vandenberg's name in this area. They checked."

"But I thought—"

"Maybe he's only renting. Then his name wouldn't appear on the records. We can only hope he'll decide to tell the police where he has hidden them."

"Why would he tell police? It would just incriminate him further," I said.

"Maybe they can convince him it's better to admit to kidnapping than to murder, which is what it will be if he leaves them hidden and uncared for while he's in jail for embezzlement."

His words turned my blood to ice.

"Would he do that?"

"Not if he's smart."

I had my doubts as to Vandenberg's intelligence, and I knew he had no compassion in him if he'd taken a child and held him for three weeks. I thought about how long the human body could go without water or food, especially a small child in an unheated cottage.

"I'm not waiting for him to make deals with the police," I said sharply. "And I'm not letting him use two lives as bartering chips. We need to find them, Newton. They have to be nearby, somewhere. He parked near this last set of mailboxes. I would draw the conclusion that he parked there to check his mail before walking down to the bakery for breakfast. Ergo—to use your word—his cottage is one of the cluster to which this particular group of mailboxes belongs."

"I agree. But how do we know which cottages are associated with it?" Newton waved an arm, encompassing the whole town and environs. "It's the last group. Some of the mailboxes could belong to cottages within walking distance, but theoretically, they could also belong to cottages spread throughout the woods, and the owners drive down to collect their mail—as Vandenberg did."

"True," I said, stomach sinking. "It's of no help, then, I guess."

"How else can we find them? We must think. It's like the needle in a haystack. Where does one begin to look?"

Newton glanced at Vandenberg, who was now sitting in the back of the police cruiser, arms folded and jaw set. He looked more bored than worried. The kids had returned from the bakery. An idea began to grow in the edges of my mind. It was time to go with my impulses.

I held out my hand. "Car keys."

Eyebrows raised, Newton handed me the keys to the Jetta.

"Not those. Our van."

He handed them over, and I turned and handed them to Isaac. "Go get the van and bring it here, will you please?"

He jogged away, and I stared off over the river while I waited. Vandenberg had driven into town to run his errands. His cottage had to be out of town, then, logically. Somewhere along the river bank farther to the south or back in the trees somewhere. Hopefully my plan would work, and the needle would make its whereabouts in the haystack known.

When Isaac pulled up in the van, I reached in the back trunk area and extracted his black pipe case, left there after the last band practice. Laying it on the sidewalk, I unlatched the lid and lifted it to expose the bagpipes nestled within.

"What's the point of playing the pipes if you can't make a disturbance once in a while?" I asked no one in particular. "Bagpipes are inherently good at making disturbances."

"I'm way ahead of you. Aren't you glad I left them in the car and didn't put them away when you told me to?" Isaac knelt and assembled the pipes quickly, then lifted them to his shoulder. He blew up the bag and tuned for a few minutes, and I saw the police officers look up in surprise from their work. The crowd that had dispersed began to reassemble in curiosity. Bagpipes are always guaranteed to draw a crowd.

Isaac started into a simple tune he knew was one of Angus's favorites, a six-eight march called "Pipe Major Bobbie." It was a good one to swing along to, and he strode down the sidewalk toward the edge of town along the road, heading south. The other children followed like the inhabitants of Hamblin. Newton looked at me with one eyebrow raised.

"If Angus hears it, he'll know we're here nearby. Maybe he'll find a way to let us know where he is. Anyway, this can't hurt, and it's good practice." I realized my backside was hurting, and I hobbled over to sit down on the curb, which didn't help much but at least took my weight off my feet. Newton spoke to the police briefly and then sat down beside me and put his hands on his drawn-up knees.

"You were quite heroic earlier," he said after a moment.

"You mean when I was being an unstable woman throwing herself on the hood of an upright citizen's car?"

"Yes. I thought it astonishingly quick thinking and selfless. Though perhaps a tad corny."

"Thank you. I didn't mean to be, but I couldn't think what else to do," I said. "It was a team effort, really."

"I think we do make a rather nice team," Newton said quietly, smiling at me.

The skirl of bagpipes sounds especially nice over open water. The music bounced along the shore and echoed through the trees for quite a while after Isaac and the children disappeared from view. I saw distant figures on Lynd Island come to the shoreline and raise their hands to shield their eyes, trying to locate the source of the music.

About fifteen minutes later, Isaac and the others came back into view.

Scott shook his head at my inquiring look. "No sign. But a nice lady came out of her house and gave Isaac five dollars for playing 'Flowers of Scotland," he reported. "Are my pipes in the van too?"

"No, I think everyone else took theirs in the house as they were instructed. Those are the only ones we have with us," I said.

"Pity. We could have covered more ground that way," he said. Though I suspect he was also thinking of the money he could have made.

"Except someone needs to listen for Angus's signal, and you can't do that if your ears are next to your drones," I said reasonably. "You won't hear him if you're standing too close to Isaac either."

"Fan out and search the town again," Newton said. "Each of you take a quarter. Take Jane with you; I don't want her off by herself. Listen for banging. Angus might not be able to yell if Vandenberg gagged him, but he might be able to pound on something."

"Good point."

Scott rejoined the others and relayed the message. They scattered in different directions, jogging off down side streets and cutting across lawns (I would have to have a word with them about that later), while Isaac continued down the street, past the bakery, heading out of town in the other direction. The police officers watched them go and then glanced at Newton and me, where we sat on the curb. I saw two of them look at each other and shake their heads. I considered the soreness of my nether regions and decided I was able to join the hunt. "If you will kindly assist me to my feet, we can join the children," I told Newton.

"Do you think you should? You took a rather hard jolt, my dear."

"I believe I've recovered."

"Heart okay?"

The concern on his face touched me. "It will be once we find Kenneth and Angus," I replied.

But at that moment we heard the sharp blast of a whistle somewhere behind the houses opposite us, and a minute later, Caleb came running down the street, waving his chrome whistle at us.

"It worked! Look! Look there!"

I craned to look over my shoulder, toward the south end of town. A column of black smoke was rising over the trees.

"That's not—It wasn't there before. Do you think that's a signal?" I asked, climbing to my feet. "How far away do you think that is?"

"I don't know if it's Angus or not, but either way, it looks like a cottage is on fire," Newton said, bouncing to his feet. He turned to call to the police officers, but I didn't wait for him. Caleb and I started running up the road toward the smoke.

It was farther away than I'd thought. My bruised backside began to throb, and my heart began to pound uncomfortably. After a few minutes, I slowed to a jog. Was that dizziness I felt? It was probably nothing, but I decided to take the precaution of calling my cardiologist when I got home. Though, if I were going to die of fibrillations, I supposed this was a more noble cause than dark chocolate. Caleb was moving ahead of me, and I called to him to wait for me.

Our van pulled up beside me, and Newton leaned over to open the door for me.

"Care for a ride? Or is this a new fitness regime?"

I gave him a sour look and hopped in. Caleb jogged back to us and threw himself into the backseat, and I saw Jane had joined us too. Isaac, Enoch, and Scott must still be out running around the town. I knew Newton would have something to say to Scott for not sticking with Jane as instructed, but there wasn't time to think about it now. In the rearview mirror, I saw one of the police cars turning around to follow us.

About a mile up the road, there was a dirt lane that turned west through the trees. The smoke seemed to be rising from that direction.

"There! Turn there!"

Newton bounced the van along the ruts, and I heard branches scrape our roof. To his credit, Newton didn't even wince. He spun the van up out of the woods and into a clearing, where a small wooden cabin stood. There was a porch with a pile of firewood stacked to one end of it and a barbecue grill on the other end. A gravel spot showed where a car was usually parked, but none was there now. Black smoke rose out of one window, forming a straight column in the still, windless air. I heard a soft crackling sound.

"Quick!" Newton was out of the van and running toward the cottage.

"Be careful!" I cried, but he was already up over the porch and pounding on the solid door.

"It's locked!" Newton picked up the propane canister from the barbecue, wrenched the hose free, and hurried down the stairs with it. "Get this well away from the fire or it will explode," he yelled, tossing it to Caleb. Caleb staggered under the unexpected weight and hurried it away into the trees at a safe distance.

Newton had returned to the cabin and, using his elbow, knocked the glass out of the window farthest from the smoke. As Jane, Caleb, and I joined him on the porch, we could hear faint sirens behind us somewhere along the road beyond the turning.

"Angus, are you in there?" I shouted. The smoke was thicker now, making my eyes sting.

"Jane, see if you can unlock the door," Newton said, hoisting our ten-year-old daughter into his arms and feeding her through the hole he'd made in the window. "Careful of the glass. And if you encounter flames or thick smoke, come back. Don't push through."

Jane shot him a look that clearly said she didn't have to be told and disappeared inside. I gripped Newton's arm, certain that if anything happened to Jane I'd throttle him then and there with my bare hands. But she was fine. Before I even had time to imagine the worst and get a good fright going, the cottage door opened, and we all pushed our way inside.

Even while I saw orange flames dancing through gray clouds of smoke in a doorway to my right, I registered a sofa strewn with a pillow and rumpled blanket that faced a big-screen television, and there were dirty dishes in the kitchen sink (moms can't help it; our eyes just automatically notice unmade beds and dirty dishes).

Then I saw Newton head through the doorway into the bedroom, heedless of the danger. I yelled, "Wait!" But he kept going.

I gripped Jane and Caleb by the arms and held them back as they fought to follow their father.

"They're chained to a post!" Newton's voice came back to us above the snap of the fire. "I need something to cut them free."

I pushed Caleb and Jane toward the front door, ordering them out, and then I hurried back toward Newton. I stopped in the bedroom door and saw two figures lying on the floor, one short, one long. Each of them was chained by one wrist to a stout wooden post that stood floor to ceiling. The thick smoke had filled the top half of the room, but where Angus and Kenneth lay, it was still fairly clear.

"Find something that will cut through these chains!" Newton shouted.

I turned back toward the kitchen and collided with a police officer who had come up behind me. I tried to squeeze past him, but he gripped my arm. He was trying to ask me something, but I didn't listen.

"There are two people chained up in there!" I told him, pulling free and trying to push past him. "We've got to cut the chains."

Thankfully, he didn't detain me. He went into the bedroom, and I did a frantic survey of the kitchen, finding nothing stronger than a carving knife and a can opener. I could hear Jane beginning to wail outside, and I went out onto the front porch, gulping in a lungful of fresh air. Caleb was holding Jane well back, his arms around her, both their faces strained with worry. Another police car was pulling up the narrow drive, lights flashing. Was there a fire department in this small of a town? How far away was the nearest station? I didn't wait for the new arrivals. When I'd regained my breath, I plunged back into the cottage.

Newton and the officer had given up trying to cut the chains, and now they were both kicking and shoving at the post with their feet, trying to snap it in half or force it loose. It was a weight-bearing column, however, and was thick and well placed. The young boy stretched out beside Angus was crying, his free hand futilely covering his head as if to shield himself from the flames. With his other hand, he struggled helplessly against the chain that held him. Every motherly instinct in me flared into high alert. But I resisted the urge to dash forward. I would only be in the men's way in the cramped space.

Suddenly, I remembered the woodpile on the far end of the porch. I ran back out the front door and quickly searched, hoping to find an axe, but all I could find was a small orange-handled hatchet leaning against the railing. I carried it back in and called to Newton.

"Will this help?"

"Thank you." Newton came to snatch it from me, ordered the police officer to stand back, then lifted the hatchet and swung hard at the post.

"If you cut that down, the roof might fall in," Angus said as my husband worked the blade free of the wood and stretched back for another try. I was glad to hear his voice. I'd thought at first glance that he was unconscious.

"The ceiling is the least of my worries right now," Newton replied, coughing, and swung.

The flames leapt and crackled, spreading along the ceiling and down the corners of the walls. The post didn't seem to be responding to Newton's efforts. It was dry oak that had stood there for years, not a fresh green tree he was felling. As the depressingly small chips and splinters flew, I heard the ceiling groan and knew it was taking too long.

"This is too dull!" Newton shouted.

"Let me try." The officer reached for the hatchet, and Newton stepped back reluctantly to make room.

"Lady, you've got to move!" Rough hands grabbed me around the waist and hauled me backward. I struggled to free myself, but the newly arrived officer was stronger than I was. He pulled me back out through the kitchen to the porch and then stood in front of me, barring me from doorway. "Move out onto the lawn," he ordered.

"You don't understand. There are two people back there, a little boy—"

"You need to stay out of this house," the officer ordered.

"They need help!"

"Then do what I say so I don't have to babysit you so I can go help them!" he barked back.

I knew I wasn't being any help, anyway. They weren't going to get through that post. The fire engine wasn't going to arrive in time. I stood helplessly on the lawn, feeling a wave of panic rising in my chest and throat. The post . . .

I had a sudden impulse and ran to the van, where it stood with doors still open. I rummaged in the trunk space, around the spare tire, searching.

"What are you looking for?" Caleb asked beside me.

"Rope. Or more chain. If we could hitch the car to the post and pull it—"

Behind me, there was a loud sighing sound, a screech of wood on wood, and then a *whump!* I spun around and stared in confusion at the cottage. It took me a moment to realize what was different.

"The roof fell in!" Caleb said frantically.

The section of roof over the bedroom had collapsed, bringing down part of one wall with it. Sparks flew up like fireworks and disappeared into the overhanging trees. In horror, I raced back toward the cottage. To my shame, I forgot all about Angus and Kenneth and the police officers. Only one thought was in my head: Newton was in there.

I could get into the kitchen, but the section of burning ceiling had fallen and was blocking the bedroom doorway, a wall of flames I couldn't get through. It was eerily quiet, only the crackling of the fire. And then a shrill cry of fear somewhere behind the flames. Kenneth.

I whirled and went back out and around to the side of the cottage, Caleb and Jane on my heels. I was vaguely aware of more people on the lawn, voices raised, and somewhere another siren growing louder and louder and then cutting off abruptly.

There was a window on the side of the cottage, partially open, smoke billowing out of it. The edges of it were wreathed in flame.

"The bedroom window!" Caleb shouted, instantly getting the same idea I had.

He ran back to the front porch and returned with a chunk of firewood. He used it to push the sash fully open. I pulled my sweater off and, with some effort, managed to smother the flames on the windowsill. Then, shielding my hands with the smoking sweater, I gripped the charred sill and hoisted myself up to thrust my head through the hole. Caleb and Jane each braced one of my feet, trying to lift.

The smoke was eye-stinging, and the burned wood seared my hands through the wool sweater, but I could see into the room. Only the portion of ceiling by the door had collapsed, the rubble awash in orange flame. Part of one outer wall had gone down too, but it was likewise alight, and there was no getting through it. The roof by the outside wall was still intact, and I could see five figures on the floor, curled inward in its shelter, hands over their heads—like that would help. Burning debris was scattered around them, but even as I opened my mouth to scream Newton's name, the figures began to uncurl and move. Newton climbed to his feet and groped toward the broken post, lifting the coils of chain off the stump. Then he was at the window, gripping my shoulders and forcing me back down to the ground. I fell awkwardly, and Newton's face disappeared above me. In an instant, he was back again, pushing a figure out the open window and dropping it down on top of me. I managed to catch Kenneth before he hit the ground.

"Here!" Caleb hauled himself through the window, and I watched in dismay as his feet disappeared over the sill. But before I could even climb to my feet, with Kenneth clinging to my neck, Caleb and Newton were back at the window, pushing another person through. It was like watching tigers leap through fiery hoops at the circus. One after another, the police officers fell out onto the ground, followed by a very filthy-looking Angus, then Caleb, and then Newton himself.

I dropped Kenneth unceremoniously into the arms of an officer and flung myself at my husband.

Newton wrapped his arms around me and lifted me off my feet. And then I realized it wasn't in a rapturous embrace. He was carrying me away from the cottage as the wall collapsed in a whoosh of sparks.

He set me down on the lawn at the front of the house and held me away from him, grinning down into my face. There was a bare patch in his hair, and his skin was reddened and starting to blister. One eyebrow was gone. Black smudges streaked his face. He was beautiful.

"That was a little close for comfort," he said and began to cough.

A paramedic appeared at my elbow. "Was there anyone else in there?" he asked urgently.

"No, no one. They all got out."

I looked back at the lawn, where Kenneth was stretched out on his back and Angus was sitting hunched beside him while various emergency personnel hurried around them. Caleb was bending over one of the police officers. Jane had completely forgotten her shyness and had attached herself around Angus's neck.

"Is everyone okay?" I asked Newton.

"Right as rain. We've all been very lucky. Though I think that policeman might have broken his arm when the ceiling came down. He—um—made an unpleasant sound when I picked him up." Newton sat down on the ground and stretched his legs out in front of him. "I feel a bit shaky."

I sat down beside him, with my arm around his back. And realized how painful my palms were. I examined them in the red-orange-blue light. A small blister, a little cut. Nothing, really, in the big scheme of things.

"Are you all right?" Jane was asking Angus anxiously. "Are you okay?"

Angus wheezed. He pulled himself into a sitting position, made more difficult because Jane continued to keep her arms around his neck. His face was dirty from the smoke, his hair was sticking out like a blowfish, and his shirt sleeve was singed. He pointed wildly at the cottage. "Stamps! On top of the fridge." He coughed.

Newton and I looked at each other. Then Newton leaped up and ran toward the house.

"Wait! You can't go in there!" A man, possibly a neighbor, intercepted him as he reached the porch. Before I could so much as blink, Newton— quiet, dignified psychiatrist and university professor who never liked to so much as raise his voice—straightened his right arm, not slowing his pace, and rammed the fellow in the chest like a quarterback. The man sat down hard. Newton leaped over him like Aries Merritt doing the high hurdles and disappeared into the kitchen. Several police officers let out a yell and started after him. But Newton was back out in less than ten seconds, holding the metal box we'd found in the woods. Angus nodded and sagged back to the ground.

I got up and went to join Newton, where he was helping the man on the porch to his feet and apologizing for his rough treatment. The man had been knocked breathless and couldn't respond for a minute, so in the breach, I turned to Angus and said, "I saw you lying on the floor and thought it was too late." I wiped at my tears. (The smoke really did make my eyes sting.)

"We were lying down to get under the smoke," Angus croaked. "We're not hurt." His voice was hoarse, but he shot me a smile that told me he really was all right.

"How did you—"

"I know you're always after me to stop smoking." Angus laughed. "And no doubt at some point I'll heed your warnings. But in this case, I'm really glad I still had my lighter on me."

Newton went to sit beside him. "Don't ever do that to me again," he said gruffly.

I moved over to Kenneth. A paramedic was bent over him, checking his vitals, but even though he looked a bit worse than Angus—his face and hands filthy, the tears making tracks in the dirt on his cheeks, his blond hair unwashed and spiky—I could see he was all right. I put my arms around him. His body trembled with adrenalin, but even through his tears, the grin he gave me was triumphant.

"He said you'd come."

"Yes, well, we were nearly too late," I said, shooting Angus a glare. My children have been heard to say that my glare could kill a horse at twenty paces. Angus flinched. "What were you thinking, setting the place on fire?" I demanded.

He sat up straight. "I knew we were too far from town for anyone to hear us shout. Believe me, we've been shouting for days." Angus reached over to give Kenneth a gentle nudge. "This little guy is a trooper." He turned to me. "When I heard the pipes, I knew you were here. But then the pipes started to fade into the distance again, and I was afraid you were leaving. So I made sure you could find us."

"Yes, well, don't you think your method was a little drastic?"

"I'd intended to keep it contained in the garbage can and just send smoke out the window," Angus said defensively. "But the flames shot up higher than I'd expected and caught the curtains. And then spread from there. I couldn't do anything about it, chained as I was. So we just waited for you to rescue us."

The excitement had dropped now, and I found my stomach was beginning to get queasy as understanding of the implications dawned.

"What if we hadn't come in time and you'd burnt to a crisp?"

Angus shrugged. "I knew you would. I just—I can't explain it. I just knew you would. We needed you, so you came."

I stared at him a long time, taking this in. He blinked and smiled at me, that slow lopsided smile I had been so afraid I'd never see again. And then someone was putting blankets around our shoulders and moving us out of the way so others could fight the fire, and I was unable to talk again for a while.

It was all over pretty quickly. The local volunteer fire department subdued the flames. The police took everyone's statements and began shooing the gathered onlookers away. The dirt road through the trees was clogged with cars, which the police were trying to get turned around and cleared out. Vandenberg still sat, now hunching his shoulders, in the back of the police car, looking strangely lonely without the officers fussing around him. Of all people, he probably had the most to gripe about, since, after all, it was his rental cabin that had burned, but no one paid him much attention. I almost felt sorry for him, until he turned his head and shot me a scowl I could physically feel. I turned my back on him and walked away with more confidence than I felt. My knees were unsteady, but I didn't let him see it.

Newton came over and put an arm around my shoulders, and Angus joined us a moment later, both of them forming tall pillars on each side of me. It felt nice to be between them, nice and safe. We stood looking at the ruined black shell that was the cabin.

"Tetotaciously exfluncticated," Newton pronounced solemnly.

"Made a right hash of it," Angus agreed, looking gloomily at the mess. "With my luck, Vandenberg will sue me for burning down his cabin."

"Just let him try," I said firmly.

"So I guess it's over," Angus said with a sigh. He held the box of stamps against his chest with one hand. With his spiked hair, all he needed was a torch uplifted in the other hand to make a rumpled Statue of Liberty.

"Yes." I gave Newton a hard nudge with my elbow. "So much for our staying well back and letting the police handle it all. Vandenberg would never know we were here, you said. No danger at all, you said."

"Admittedly, all did not go according to the scenario I'd envisioned," Newton said in a mellow tone. "It was impossible to anticipate every possible factor. But all's well that ends well."

I scowled. Clichés irritated me.

"How did you manage to find out we were in this town?" Angus asked.

"McKinnon told us he thought it was Vandenberg who was responsible for taking his son. It was just a matter of tracking Vandenberg down," Newton said with a shrug, as if it had been nothing.

"McKinnon turned himself in, by the way," I told Angus. "He told the police everything about his involvement in the embezzlement."

"I'm glad. He needed to do that, for the good of his own soul."

I nodded.

"You know, it's the classic story all over again," Angus added. "Just like in my book about the train robbery. It's the one in charge, the conductor, the CEO, who ends up being the bad guy. The one who should have known better. The one in whom the public placed trust."

"Somehow, that makes it harder to understand," Newton said. Which was something for a psychiatrist to admit.

"And there's another parallel," I said. "Three robbers who turned on each other in the end."

"True."

"Well, it's all sorted out now," I said with a sigh. I wondered if the bathroom in the cabin was still functional and if the firemen would let me near it.

"We'll catch you up on everything that's been happening," Newton said. "But I suppose now is not the time to go into detail. You'll need to go to the hospital to be checked out, and I'm sure you want to rest and eat and wash." As if he didn't require the same.

"Yes, I need to do that," Angus said, not moving. "But then I've got to get back home to make sure I still have a job."

"Of course they'll be glad to have you back at school." Newton shook his head. "Think of the stories with which you can entertain your students. It will add interest to the ordinarily dreary essay assignment, 'What I Did on My Summer Vacation.'"

"One question I have that's still bothering me," I piped up. "Vandenberg broke into our house looking for the note with the treasure hunt clues on it."

"He did?" Angus looked startled.

"How did he know about the note? Do you know if McKinnon told him?"

"No. I don't know what would have led Vandenberg to you at all."

"Then we can only assume he merely saw us coming and going from your house and surmised we were involved," I said.

Another thought, more urgent, occurred to me. I glanced to make sure we couldn't be overheard and lowered my voice. "What will happen to Kenneth McKinnon? His mother is dead, and his father is likely going to spend time in jail."

"There's probably a relative to look after him," Newton said.

"And if not, then *I'll* look after him," Angus added peacefully. "He really is quite a fantastic kid."

I smiled up at Angus. "Come to dinner tomorrow night? I'll invite a friend of mine I'd like you to meet."

Angus looked at me from the corner of his eye. "I just might do that," he answered and laughed.

A paramedic bustled Kenneth and Angus into an ambulance to be more thoroughly checked over. He wanted Newton to go too, but he refused, insisting there was nothing wrong with him. As the ambulance pulled away, Newton gave me a poke. "Let's go find the rest of the kids and go home."

As we walked back to the van, I looked up at the sky, hazy with dispersed smoke. I could still hear bagpipes far off in the distance, echoing among the trees, and the air was sharp with the smell of burnt pinewood, reminding me of long-ago campfires and s'mores. Smoke rolled in charcoal billows out over the river and wafted toward the lake. My palms still stung. But my heart had returned to a steady, comforting thump, and I was filled with a distinctly satisfied feeling, as of a job well done.

We soon reassembled everyone and told them what had happened and that Angus was safe. The rest of the kids were disgruntled at having missed the height of the excitement—it astonished me to realize the whole thing had taken less than twenty minutes start to finish while Isaac, Scott, and Enoch had been combing the north end of town—but they'd had a good breakfast, Isaac had earned five bucks, and Angus and Kenneth were found, so they were content. We drove home in high spirits to face the wrath of Donetti.

"Do you think they'll go light on McKinnon?" I asked as we pulled onto the highway. I shifted in my seat, painfully aware again of the damage I'd done to my backside. "Maybe not for the embezzlement but for kidnapping Angus initially? He had good cause, and Angus won't press charges. I mean, it was extenuating circumstances. Who wouldn't do drastic, crazy things to save their child?"

My husband looked fondly into the rearview mirror at the faces of our children in the backseats, from Caleb's smoke-smudged face to Isaac's hair flopping over his eyes. Newton opened his mouth, hesitated, closed it again, and smiled.

* * *

The rest of the day felt rather like a holiday, with the kids home from school on a weekday and the worry of the past two weeks lifted from my shoulders. The boys went out to play basketball on the driveway, and Newton, cream smeared on his burnt face, played blocks with Andrew in the family room. I threw together a potato salad, planning to grill burgers for supper, and Jane offered to make a carrot cake, one of the things she was practicing. I had long ago set out a list of core competencies every child had to acquire before being allowed to leave home, and basic baking was one of them.

"I'll give you some money, and you can run down to the store for cream cheese for the frosting," I told her, glad we didn't have to fret about the buddy system anymore.

"All right."

I rummaged in my purse for a five-dollar bill, and my fingers touched the rumpled paper with Warren Philpott's clues. Newton had told the officers about the note, but I still had the original. I wondered if they would want it for evidence in wrapping up the case.

I sent Jane off to the store and then carried the clue paper to the phone. I wasn't in a hurry to speak to Donetti because I knew he would have some unpleasant things to say about our brash behavior that morning, and did I really want to spoil the afternoon? I felt we could justify our actions, but what we had done, essentially (at least the way Donetti would see it), was that we had implied we didn't put any trust in the police's ability to find Vandenberg. We had taken it upon ourselves to do it, and we had foolishly put ourselves in danger. It had been sheer luck that Ted hadn't been armed. It all could have ended quite badly.

"But Angus is found and safe, and nobody got too hurt," I repeated to myself in a fierce whisper. "We had to do it."

Well, yes. But maybe we hadn't needed to do it in quite the way we had.

"We won't do it again," I promised the empty kitchen and somehow felt better for having made that promise. As if such events could ever possibly occur again in the future.

I turned back to my cooking, laughing at myself, and then another thought occurred to me. Wendy DeRuvo would want to know Angus had been located. I dug through my purse again for her phone number and dialed.

Her voice came through on the third ring.

"Wendy? It's Annie Fisher," I said.

"Oh! Mrs. Fisher! I've been trying to reach you. I misplaced your phone number, and you haven't answered your e-mails." Her pleasant English voice sounded slightly put out.

"Oh, sorry. I haven't checked my e-mails lately," I told her, stating the obvious. When had I last looked at them? I couldn't remember. Perhaps not since I'd warned her about our break-in. "Things have been busy. Were you calling about my e-mail to you? You don't need to worry about it anymore. I hope I didn't alarm you. The danger is past."

"Oh?"

"And if you solved the clues, you don't need to worry—we solved them too."

"Oh! You did? You said you'd keep me updated if you figured anything out."

"Sorry, I didn't think of it. As I said, things have been bustling lately."

"So where did the clues lead you? Did you find something?" I caught a note of tension in her voice and thought she wasn't as disinterested as she'd made out earlier.

"Yes, we found the treasure. And the good news is we found Angus Puddicombe. He's fine. It's a rather long story, but I'll write it all down and e-mail it to you. I have hardly had time to get my own brain wrapped around it yet," I said.

"I'm glad everything ended well, then."

"Yes. Couldn't have been better," I told her.

"So . . . we were right that the note was one of Dad's treasure hunts?"

"Yes. The clues led us to the woods on Bergamot Road. You know, if I'm not mistaken, they led us right to your property."

"My . . . ?"

"You said you own a building lot near Carlisle when I spoke to you earlier. Is your lot off Bergamot Road? A stand of trees with a trail leading through it past a pond to some boulders? Where there's a picnic table?"

"Yes, that sounds like our place. We had picnics there the last summer before Dad died. Fancy Daddy picking a spot on our own property. My, you figured that out in a hurry, didn't you?" She hesitated, then said, "If you have the treasure, I would have thought you'd have phoned me."

"Well, we don't have it at the moment."

"Oh. Where is it?"

"The police have it at the moment. You see—"

"Wait. You gave them to the police?" Her voice grew a little shrill.

"It was used as a ransom in a kidnapping. The police took it as evidence. It's all very complicated to explain, but I'm sure the police will—"

"You had no right to give anyone those stamps. They rightfully belong to me," Wendy said, and her voice reminded me of Maisie about to throw a temper tantrum.

I took a deep breath and modulated my own voice downward to try to soothe her. "It was to save Douglas McKinnon's son," I said gently. "He was the one being held for ransom."

There was a shocked silence for an instant. "Douglas's son? Kenneth? What are you talking about?" she snapped.

"Ted Vandenberg, the auditor for Lucan Investments, kidnapped Kenneth McKinnon and demanded his father hand over some money your father embezzled from the company," I said. "He thought Douglas had it or could find it. I'm sorry, this isn't the way you should be hearing this news, but your father stole a great deal of money—"

"That's not true! How dare you? My father wouldn't do such a thing!"

"Douglas McKinnon confirmed it. He told us himself." I figured it probably wasn't up to me to tell her about Douglas's own involvement in the embezzlement. No doubt she would learn it later, but it wasn't my place to break confidences.

"I don't believe it. And if Douglas's son had been kidnapped, he would have told me. We're friends."

"He didn't tell anyone. He—er—had his reasons."

"But he told *you*?"

"Yes, when it became clear that Angus was in trouble."

"And who was it you said had kidnapped Kenneth?"

"Ted Vandenberg. Auditor for Lucan Investments," I repeated.

"I've heard the name, but I don't know him," she said.

Surely she would know Ted could either confirm or deny her statement. I concluded that she really hadn't been the one to tell him about the note, and she wasn't involved in the kidnapping. So the other theory stood, I thought with relief. Ted had surmised our involvement from seeing us coming and going from Angus's house.

"It all ended happily anyway," I continued. "This morning Vandenberg was apprehended, and Kenneth and Angus were rescued, so sooner or later, the police will return the stamps to you . . ."

I stopped, what I had heard finally registering in my overworked brain.

"You know, Wendy, now that I think about it, I'm not sure they really could be considered your property anyway, since they were purchased with stolen money . . . but you knew all about them already, didn't you?"

"What? Of course I didn't."

"Yes, you did." I nearly throttled the receiver. "Just now when we were talking, I only called it treasure. You said we didn't have the right to give the stamps to anybody. There's no way you could know the treasure was stamps unless you . . ."

"I didn't say that." Her voice was uncertain.

"You did."

"You must have told me they were stamps."

"I didn't. You were the first to mention stamps." I paused, mind racing. "The story of the Black Donnellys," I said as the last piece clicked into place. "Stamps aren't a story. Money isn't a story. A confession would be a story. It *was* a signed confession your father buried in that box, wasn't it? Along with the ten million dollars."

Newton would be glad to hear it.

"I don't know what you're talking about." But her voice had gone a notch higher.

"Your father wrote down all that had happened, and he put it and the money he'd stolen from Vandenberg and McKinnon in the box and hid it at your picnic spot. He wrote down the clues so you would find it after he died."

"This is nonsense. I'm hanging up. I don't have to listen to this."

"Maybe he did give you the clues before he died, and the scribbled copy Angus found was the rough draft. Yes, I could see that," I said, thinking aloud now. "He jotted the clues down as he went through the woods to bury the box. It explains why the handwriting was so poor. When he got home, he did up a cleaner copy for you and left it where you would find it. But for some reason, he didn't get around to throwing out his rough copy. It ended up on his bedside table."

"It wasn't there. I cleaned his room myself after he died."

"It was under the lamp. Maybe he hid it there. Maybe it got shoved under it by accident. You really should dust better, Wendy, and not just go around the lamps."

"Ridiculous." She was fuming. "It doesn't matter who got what note. I'm telling you, there was no confession and no money. My father wasn't a thief."

"You may have destroyed the written confession, thinking you were safe, because you thought surely your father's coconspirators would never speak up about it or their roles in it. And you turned the money into those stamps, or at least part of the money, and returned them to the hiding place. After all, it was as good a hiding place as any, wasn't it?"

"This is all wild conjecture. You can't prove any of this," she said coldly.

"No, I can't, but Douglas McKinnon can corroborate. He knew about your father's embezzlement because he participated in it himself." So much for keeping confidences. I rolled my eyes.

"Good luck getting him to confess to that." She laughed coldly.

"He already has. He told the police everything they needed to know. And once Ted Vandenberg starts to plea bargain, it will all come out again."

There was silence on the other end of the phone.

"Why didn't you go retrieve the box when you found out we had a copy of the clues?" I asked. "If it had been me, I would have dashed out there and retrieved it from the hiding spot as soon as I knew someone else might find out about it."

"I did, two days after you called me, on Thursday night. It was the soonest I could get away on some pretext," she said bitterly. "It's not a quick dash from Brantford, remember?"

"But when you arrived, you found we'd already been there," I said quietly.

"You certainly were quick to figure out the note. Why do you think I've been trying to contact you?"

"You had to find a pretext . . ." I echoed thoughtfully. "Lucan Investments is going to want their money back, Wendy. I suspect your husband would agree with me, and that's why you're hiding the money from him. Were you afraid if you used a safety deposit box that your husband would find out? He doesn't know about the money, does he?"

Again, there was silence. I sighed. Obviously I would have to phone Officer Donetti this afternoon. The police would be interested to know what I had just learned. I wondered what the official charge against Wendy would be. Accepting stolen property? Not reporting a crime? Would purchasing the stamps with stolen money count as money laundering? I would let them sort it out.

I thought of various things I could say to Wendy, but there really wasn't anything more to add. She was running through the facts in her head and seeing the escape hatch growing increasingly smaller.

"I guess the last game is over," I said and gently hung up the phone.

When I turned around, Newton was standing in the doorway, Andrew in his arms. Both regarded me solemnly. Or, as solemnly as a man can look who has white goo spread all over his face.

"You heard?" I asked, feeling deflated.

"I heard your last few sentences and can deduce the rest," Newton said. He held out an arm, and I went to lean against him, one arm around him and one around Andrew.

I sighed. "It's disappointing. I wanted her to be an honest person."

"Her father was a crook. She grew up on stolen money," Newton said reasonably. "What would make you expect her to turn out to be honest herself?"

"Don't you think she had a choice? I mean, you're a psychiatrist, Newton," I said. "You don't think the way a person is raised determines everything about their character, do you?"

"Of course not. But as you say, she had a choice. If someone handed you ten million dollars no one else knew about and said you could have everything you ever wanted, would you be tempted to take it? Or would you turn it in and expose your father as a criminal?"

I looked around my cramped kitchen, with its peeling Formica, the mismatched chairs around the scuffed table. I looked at my little boy in his brothers' hand-me-downs, his golden curls standing out like a halo around his face. I listened to the *thud thud* of the basketball bouncing off the garage. "I already have everything I ever wanted," I said, laying my head on Newton's shoulder.

"Good," he said cheerfully and kissed my forehead with a smack. "Then I take it the renovations are off."

Brownies in a Mug

MIX IN A CERAMIC MUG:

¼ C. white flour
¼ C. sugar
2 Tbsp. cocoa
1 Tbsp. ground flax
A pinch of salt

ADD AND STIR WELL:

2 Tbsp. vegetable oil
3 Tbsp. water

Microwave on high for one minute and 40 seconds, uncovered. Cool slightly and eat with a spoon. You can top it with powdered sugar, ice cream, or whipped cream if you like. You could also try adding chopped nuts to the batter.

About the Author

KRISTEN GARNER MCKENDRY BEGAN WRITING in her teens, and her work has been published in both Canada and the US. She received a Mississauga Arts Council MARTY Award in Established Literary Arts in 2012, and her book *Garden Plot* was nominated in 2011 for a Whitney Award for excellence in LDS literature.

Kristen received a bachelor's degree in linguistics from Brigham Young University and has always been a voracious reader. She has a strong interest in urban agriculture and environmental issues. She enjoys playing the bagpipes, learning obscure languages, growing wheat in the backyard, and making cheese. A native of Utah and mother of three, she now resides with her family in Canada. As a linguist, Kristen is annoyed by English homonyms, and it was the contemplation of these that led to the idea for this book.

For more information on Kristen and her books, check out her website at www. kristenmckendry.webs.com, where you will also find a link to her blog, *My Daily Slog Blog*.